LOVE, LIES AND
Murder

SHILOH WALKER

ELLORA'S CAVE
ROMANTICA PUBLISHING

$\mathcal{W}$hat the critics are saying...

ಬಿ

Telling Tales

"All I have to say about **Telling Tales** is: hot, hot, hot! Any lover of erotica will be thoroughly pleased with the scorching intensity that Shiloh writes into her scenes, as well as with the realism of the plot." ~ *A Romance Review*

"This book is a great suspense novel; it keeps you on the edge of your seat wondering who the killer is. Of course half way through the book it does become obvious, but you still keep reading. [...] Shiloh Walker has created a story that is sure to keep you glued to your screen until the bitter end." ~ *The Romance Studio*

"Shiloh Walker's book **Telling Tales** is a suspense/thriller full of twists and turns. Just when you think you have it figured out, there is a new twist. [...] Fans will already know that this is an excellent book, but for those of you who have never read Shiloh's work, this is the book to read." ~ *Novel Spot Romance Reviews*

His Every Desire

"This book is exciting, emotional story with violence and sex, but also a tale about trust and love." ~ *Cupid's Library Reviews*

"His Every Desire is one of the most intense books I have read in a long time. Ms. Walker took it to the next level when she penned this one. Every physical and emotional struggle of the characters is written so eloquently you can see it happening as you read the page. I highly recommend this book. It is classic tale of what happens when good beats evil!!"
~ *ECataromance Reviews*

"**His Every Desire** is everything your romantic heart longs for: a strong, passionate bad boy hero who finds the love of his life just when he needs to; a bruised heroine who finds the strength to trust; and action a plenty." ~ *Erotic Escapades*

Five Angels and Recommended Read "*His Every Desire* is a gripping paranormal story that significantly intrigued my interest. [...] am delighted to confer!" ~ *Fallen Angel Review*

"Explosive passion and scary villains make Shiloh Walker's latest story a thrilling tale. [...] Shiloh Walker knows how to create razor edge tension, both sexual and situational, and His Every Desire is a great example of her unique writing talents. This tale is sure to win Ms. Walker many new fans!"
~ *The Romance Studio*

"This is an engrossing, one-night read." ~ *Just Erotic Romance Reviews*

"When you think an author, could not possible create something new and different, Ms. Walker steps up and slams this one home. Ms. Walker takes her erotic pen and flings it to the wind — scalding the pages with primal male sexual viciousness." ~ *Road to Romance*

An Ellora's Cave Romantica Publication

www.ellorascave.com

Love, Lies and Murder

ISBN 9781419956843
Edited by Pamela Campbell.
Cover art by Syneca.

This book printed in the U.S.A. by Jasmine-Jade Enterprises, LLC

Trade paperback Publication July 2007

Also by Shiloh Walker

❧

A Wish, A Kiss, A Dream *(anthology)*
Back From Hell
Coming In Last
Ellora's Cavemen: Legendary Tails II *(anthology)*
Ellora's Cavemen: Tales from the Temple IV *(anthology)*
Every Last Fantasy
Firewalkers: Dreamer
Good Girls Don't
Her Best Friend's Lover
Her Wildest Dreams
His Christmas Cara
Hot Spell *(anthology)*
Make Me Believe
Myth-behavin' *(anthology)*
Mythe: Mythe & Magick
Mythe 2: Vampire
Once Upon a Midnight Blue
One Night with You
Sage
Silk Scarves and Seduction
The Dragon's Warrior
The Dragon's Woman
The Hunters 1: Declan and Tori
The Hunters 2: Eli and Sarel
The Hunters 3: Byron and Kit
The Hunters 4: Jonathan and Lori
The Hunters 5: Ben and Shadoe
The Hunters 6: Rafe and Sheila
The Hunters 7: I'll Be Hunting You
Touch of Gypsy Fire
Voyeur
Whipped Cream and Handcuffs

About the Author

∞

Shiloh Walker has been writing since she was a kid. She fell in love with vampires with the book Bunnicula and has worked her way up to the more...ah...serious vampire stories. She loves reading and writing anything paranormal, anything fantasy, but most of all anything romantic. Once upon a time she worked as a nurse, but now she writes full time and lives with her family in the Midwest.

Shiloh welcomes comments from readers. You can find her website and email address on her author bio page at www.ellorascave.com.

Tell Us What You Think

We appreciate hearing reader opinions about our books. You can email us at Comments@EllorasCave.com.

LOVE, LIES AND MURDER

ဢ

TELLING TALES
~13~

&

HIS EVERY DESIRE
~133~

TELLING TALES

ﬦ

Trademarks Acknowledgement

℀

Prologue

ॐ

Made her fucking sick.

Absolutely sick…look at her.

She thought she was so damned special. Skinny, pale-faced, evil bitch.

Watching Darci Law walk down the street made her belly feel all tight and hot with disgust. Little slut. That was what she was, an attention-getting little slut.

Men looked at her, like the Sheriff was doing, thinking nobody noticed how he watched Darci's ass. And Darci…acting like she didn't know.

Everybody knew. She was a whore. They all knew it.

And she thought she was so damned special, with her surreal photographs. Everybody called them that…surreal. Extraordinary.

Bitch.

She should get what was coming to her.

A slow, mean smile curved over her lips as she watched Darci. Yes, she should definitely get what was coming…

Chapter One

ဆာ

Darci stood staring at the school board members in a state of shock.

"Ummm…excuse me, *what*?" she asked. She hadn't heard what she thought she had heard…had she?

Daniel Sommers leaned forward, crossing his hands in front of him. "So are you denying it?"

"Hell, yes, I'm denying it. Joe is *married*," she snapped, rising from her chair, walking over to the Superintendent's desk and slamming her hands on it.

"Yes. That is part of the problem. This is a small town, Darci. We can't have our schoolteachers carrying on with married men, or even carrying on indiscriminately with *un*married men. People talk and parents don't want an immoral woman teaching their first graders."

Darci fought the urge to grit her teeth. Instead, she just took a deep breath and said softly, "I am *not* immoral."

"So…you're telling me you haven't been promiscuous?" Cathy Travers asked, flushing and shifting her eyes aside as though she couldn't look at Darci while she asked.

Darci barely managed to stifle a hysterical laugh. This was so unreal. Damn it, she hadn't had sex in nearly two years, and she was getting dragged on the carpet…*for what*? Her voice shook as she said, "My sex life is *none* of your business. *None*. But I do *not* sleep with married men, and that's the bottom line."

The board members looked at each other and sighed. Daniel studied her thoughtfully, maybe she was just desperate but she thought she saw a shred of belief in his eyes. "Darci, I try not to put a lot of stock in rumors."

She watched as he slid his glasses off and rubbed the bridge of his nose. When he looked back up at her, it was with a slight smile and Darci felt her knees wobble with relief. "Let's just forget about this, okay?" he said softly.

* * * * *

Darci sat on the stool behind the counter at Becka's gallery, Dreams in the Mist, staring morosely at Becka. The woman, just a few years older than she, listened sympathetically as Darci repeated the incident with the school board.

"I just don't get it. Where did they get that story about me and Joe?" she said as she finally finished explaining what had happened.

Becka glanced away.

If she had just looked away, Darci might have thought she just didn't have an answer, but she bit her lip. Becka bit her lip when she was nervous.

Narrowing her eyes, Darci said, "What?"

Becka swung innocent eyes to Darci. "I didn't say anything."

"You bit your lip," Darci accused, coming off the stool. "You do that when you're nervous. What do you know?"

Becka forced a smile, shaking her head. "Nothing, baby. I promise. I'm just as shocked by this mess as you are." Her face crumpled as Darci just stood there, crossing her arms over her chest, tapping one sandaled foot impatiently.

"Oh, hell." Becka turned around and said, "It's Carrie. I had to go to Wal-Mart to get my daughter's prescription—she didn't know I was standing an aisle over. You know how her voice carries. I don't know who she was talking to, but she said she'd seen you and Joe go into the Golden Inn together Wednesday."

Darci's jaw dropped.

Now that was low. Carrie had pulled a lot of stunts, made a lot of innuendoes, but this...this was outright lying. "Damn it, I was at a *birthday* party Wednesday," she gritted out.

Her hands opened and closed into fists, her nails biting into her flesh.

"I know," Becka said, making soothing noises. "I knew it was bullshit, that's why I didn't say anything. It's just like all the other..."

"Other?" Darci asked as Becka's voice trailed off.

Becka's round face flushed and her dark brown eyes looked absolutely miserable. "Darci..."

"What others?"

Becka sighed, moving around Darci to take the stool she'd vacated. "Honey, she likes to tell tales. You know that. She can be very malicious to people she considers her enemy. And you...well, you didn't hate me the way she wanted you to."

Darci heard the regret in Becka's voice, even through her own anger. Sighing, she shoved a hand through her spiked, black cap of hair as she turned around, staring at Becka.

"There was no reason to hate you, Becka."

Becka scowled sourly. "Can't tell by me. Half of my old friends don't even talk to me anymore," she muttered, folding her hands together and tucking them between her knees.

"That's because they are stupid." Darci forced a smile. "We always knew that."

Becka didn't even try to smile back at her. Soberly, she studied Darci, sighing tiredly. She brushed the corkscrew curls back from her face and said quietly, "There are other stories. I guess I should have told you, but I...hell, I didn't want to see you hurt. Didn't want to see you angry."

Darci caught her lower lip between her teeth, shaking her head. "Oh, I'm not. I'm beyond angry. But it's not your fault, Becka. I know whose fault it is, and you can bet she's going to hear from me about it."

Darci turned to go, but Becka's voice stopped her. "Honey, there was something I was going to tell you. I just heard about it this morning...planned on telling you when you came in today. I hate making this worse for you."

A sick knot formed in her belly. Slowly, she turned back to Becka and asked, "What?"

"It's about Della. And...Max."

"Max?"

Becka licked her lips, reaching up to pat her pocket, then her hand fell away. "Keep forgetting that I quit smoking," she said with a slight twist of her lips. "Times like this, I wonder why."

Sighing, Becka met Darci's eyes squarely and said, "Della called earlier, looking for you. She's pissed. I couldn't make out most of it, but I think she thinks you've been fucking Max."

Just then, the phone on the counter jingled. Slowly, Darci reached out and picked it up, lifting it to her ear as she said by rote, "Dreams in the Mist, this is Darci."

Della's voice blasted in her ear and Darci just closed her eyes, slumping against the counter.

That was just perfect...

* * * * *

If ever a more pathetic, sad creature existed, Darci hadn't met her. Studying Carrie Forrest as she sat at her desk, Darci wondered why in the hell some people were just so damned unhappy with life. Carrie was one of those people who liked to play martyr. Somebody who liked to play a mother figure, liked to pretend that she was everything to everybody, and she was damned good at it.

She had even pulled Darci in for a little while.

Just for a while, though. Darci had started watching things, listening to people talk...to the stories Carrie told, comparing her stories to the people she was supposedly so worried about.

Just lies. Almost everything that came out of her mouth was lies.

The problem was that this last one could damage somebody's career, either Darci's or Joe's. Worse...it could wreck a marriage.

Generally, Darci didn't give a damn what anybody else thought. It wouldn't matter...if it weren't for Joe, and for her job.

She taught art at an *elementary school*...in the Bible Belt of America. The parents wouldn't tolerate the teacher of their kids being a tramp.

And Joe...he was a married man, a new daddy. They didn't need this.

All Darci wanted to do was to take her pictures and be left alone.

All some other people wanted to do was cause trouble.

And damn it, some people believed what they said.

Della believed it. Della actually believed Darci was going around fucking every man she could get her hands on, including Della's current man—one she was moon-eyed in love with. Max was the first man to come along in a long time who made Della want more than just a quick fuck.

Never mind the fact that Darci and Max didn't generally even like each other.

Hell, she believed the bullshit that Darci was at a hotel in the middle of the afternoon fucking somebody else's husband, believed she had fucked everybody she could…from the head of the city council to the boy who was delivering pizzas.

Darci knew, because Della had just finished shouting that garbage in her ear.

So far, Carrie hadn't even noticed that Darci was in the room.

Darci, smiling an evil smile, lifted her heavy purse high over her head and let it fall to the glass table. The purse clattered loudly, keys jangling, digital camera falling out, coins rolling and jingling merrily. Darci smiled angelically as Carrie jumped and shrieked, whirling around in her chair, her chubby face white and pasty with shock, her eyes wide behind her glasses.

"A little jumpy?" Darci asked in dulcet tones.

Carrie had one hand pressed to her chest, and she swallowed, glaring at Darci. For one second, malevolence flashed in her muddy brown eyes before she pasted a smile of false sympathy on her face and said, "My, you gave me such a start. You need to be more careful, tossing your things down. You know how easily startled I am. How are you doing, love?"

"Don't call me 'love,' Carrie. And you know damned good and well how I'm doing with the bullshit you started," Darci said coldly, flicking her short, spiked hair away from her face. "I'm surprised Kim didn't buzz you and tell you I was on my way up. Give you warning and all."

"I asked not to be disturbed," Carrie said, smiling her patented mother-earth smile. "I've been trying to…well. I'm trying to understand what is going on, why you would do what you've done."

"Cut the bullshit, Carrie. You and I know who started this, and why I was called into my boss's office today, and why I received a very nasty, angry phone call from Della Bennett," Darci said quietly, sitting down on the suede couch, crossing one leg over the other. "Why Joe is having to defend himself against a bunch of slanderous rumors that he was seen at a hotel…with me. Why Della thinks I spent the weekend fucking *her* man."

Darci saw the flicker in Carrie's eyes, watched the tiny smile on her face. But Carrie only arched her brows and shook her head, heaving that patented martyred sigh. "What are you doing, Darci? Why are you lying to yourself, to everybody, like this?" she asked mournfully. "Don't you understand how destructive this behavior is?"

But Darci could sense the crafty glee in her voice. Hear it there. And she knew. Any doubt she might have had that somebody else was behind this was gone. Gently, Darci said, "Maybe *you* don't understand how destructive this behavior is, Carrie. I don't take shit lying down. Never have, never will."

Darci stood up, running a hand through her short, spiked cap of black hair before focusing her green eyes on Carrie's face once more. A small, cold smile danced on her lips as she moved closer to the older woman.

"It's one thing when you try to make my life miserable, Carrie," she said, circling to lean her hip on Carrie's table, studying the work in progress there.

Carrie just sat there, glaring at Darci, her small mouth puckering in an ugly scowl.

"But it's another when you start messing with my job, when you start dragging my friends into it."

Carrie opened her mouth, sputtering, but Darci just slashed at the air with her hand and snapped, "Shut the fuck up. Got it? You totally fucked up this time. You fucked with my job. Bad enough you have to try to smear *my* name, but you had to go and smear the name of a good man and try to ruin his marriage. You've probably ruined friendships, but they can go to hell, because if they believe a word that comes out of *your* mouth, then they've got rocks for brains. But you hurt people this time. And not just me. That totally, *totally* pisses me off, and me pissed off is a very, very bad thing."

Carrie's face was florid now and her mouth opened and closed. Something not quite lucid passed through her dark, muddy eyes as her hand closed around a cutting tool and Darci narrowed her eyes. "Try it, babe. Just try it. I dare you."

Carrie's hand fell away, fisting in her lap as she stared at Darci, hatred lurking in her eyes.

"Why did you have to drag Joe into it?" Darci asked quietly. "Why him?"

Bitingly, Carrie said, "I didn't drag him into it. He did it himself. Maybe he should have thought of the consequences before he broke his wedding vows." She folded her hands primly in her lap and forced her mouth into that proper, mothering smile.

Darci rolled her eyes and muttered, "You'll be like that at St. Peter's gates, won't you? But Peter will know the truth. And so do I. So don't waste my time." Narrowing her eyes, she asked, "Is it a hobby? Do you enjoy ruining people's lives? Is yours so pathetic that this is what you have to do for kicks?"

"She's been doing it a long time, I'd say the answer is yes," a deep voice, full of anger, said.

Darci looked up just as Joe walked in, his eyes on her and Carrie, his face cold with disgust. "Tell me something, Carrie, do you really think you can keep this up and get away with it?" he asked.

"Joe, I really don't know what you are talking about. But maybe you should be at home, trying to repair your marriage, instead of here, trying to blame me," Carrie said, her voice waspish. But her eyes darted away from him, her hands quivering just slightly.

"Now Darci here, Darci is, naturally, very upset. Bad enough she can't seem to keep her indiscretions quiet, and with single men. But she's tried to interfere with a man and his marriage. Of course, if she had learned to think before acting...well, she wouldn't be in the hot water she is in,"

Carrie said, her eyes taking on a kindly glow as she moved to pat Darci's hand. "I understand that she could lose her job—"

Darci caught the older woman's hand before Carrie could touch her and, pressing her thumb on the nerves in Carrie's wrist, watched as Carrie's face paled and her eyes darkened with pain. "Haven't I told you about touching me?" she warned. "Haven't I warned you before to stay away from me? Very, very far away from me?"

Carrie gasped and Darci threw her hand down and stepped back. She cut her gaze to Joe, arching a black brow at him. "I imagine you've been hearing the same tripe that I have?" Darci drawled.

"Oh, yes. Missy is the one who called me this morning, told me how her phone line had been burning all night, people wanting to know if it's true, am I getting a divorce? Are you and me getting hitched..." Joe's voice trailed off as he paused by a shelf, reaching up to pick up a blown glass ball, shot through with threads of red and gold. Tossing it from one hand to another, he turned and met Darci's eyes. "Sorry, sugar. It's not that I don't respect you...but well..."

Darci smiled slightly. "A divorce, huh? That was quick."

Carrie said sweetly, "Now, Joe, I'm sure you and your wife can work it out."

Joe's eyes narrowed. "Cut the crap, Carrie. We all know the truth here."

Joe propped his hips against one of the numerous work counters, staring at Carrie with glacial eyes. "I grew up in this town. I may be twenty years younger than you—but I've been watching your machinations since I was a kid. Reporters are very good observers. After forty plus years of living, well, let's just say, I know you. No acts, please. Otherwise, I'll go front page tomorrow with the phone call I got the other day. How you know information that Becka hasn't shared with *anybody*, other than Darci and her assistant. One has to wonder how you know that. And I just may write that article anyway."

Carrie blinked and the mask fell away. Slyly, she said, "You can't prove anything."

A slow smile curled his mouth and he said simply, "Miz Forrest, I don't have to. Words are everything, as a gossipmonger should know. And people are going to have to wonder what you were up to, what kind of trouble you were trying to cause...when they have proof you were lying. Just how many people did you tell that story to?"

Carrie just smiled cattily. "Nobody knows I lied. And people just love a scandal."

"Well, now that's true...which I'm going to assume means you told quite a few people. But you should have picked a different night." Joe grinned and Darci had to smile at the satisfaction she saw in his eyes. He continued, his voice level, eyes direct. "Because you see, Darci was at a skating rink for a birthday party for my niece. It was thrown together at the last minute because my brother-in-law had to go out of town for the next few weeks."

"And Missy spent the morning getting her pictures from the party developed. She's going to hit the entire town with them, if I know my sister." Joe smiled, reaching up to scratch his chin. "You know how fast she talks, how much she likes to talk. By nightfall, damn near everybody is going to see those pictures — *time-stamped* pictures — of Darci at the party last night."

If Darci wasn't mistaken, Carrie growled. A low, furious sound under her breath before jerking her eyes away and focusing on her mangled leg, rubbing it with both hands.

"I've got to wonder — some people will brush it off, I know, but others? Well, I wonder, are they going to start to ask why in the hell you'd tell such an obvious lie?" Joe moved over to where Carrie was massaging her leg and he leaned down, a sardonic grin on his grizzled face. She lifted her gaze, staring at him with hatred as Joe said, "You should really try to get your story straight and make sure the lady you're spreading rumors about is actually *at home, alone*, before you start telling stories about her."

Darci felt the knot that had been present in her belly since last night loosen just a bit. She breathed out a silent sigh of relief and slid Joe a look of gratitude.

Of course, pictures weren't going to mean a thing to Della. Her ears still stung from her friend's furious phone calls. All the pictures in the world wouldn't mean anything to Della.

Darci lifted her eyes and stared at Carrie, at the smirk in her muddy eyes. The old bitch knew what was circling through Darci's head. Even though the story was falling to shreds around her, Carrie had at least succeeded in one thing. She had cost Darci a dear friendship.

Softly, Darci voiced the words that had crossed her thoughts earlier. "You have got to be the saddest, most pathetic creature I have ever met in my life," Darci said, shaking her head.

Carrie froze, her eyes wide. For a brief second, naked pain shone in her eyes.

Joe chuckled. "Nobody's ever called you out before, have they, lady? Does the truth hurt?"

"Get out!" Her pasty face turning florid with rage, Carrie glared at them hatefully as she shouted, "*Get out! Get out! Get out!*"

Smirking a little, Darci said, "Now maybe you have an idea of just how angry I am, Carrie." Pacing back over to where Carrie sat, Darci snarled down into her homely, hate-filled face. "I've told you this before," Darci said, her voice soft and low. "You didn't listen. I'll tell you once more and I'd advise you to pay attention this time. Stay away from me. Stay very, very far away from me."

* * * * *

Kellan Grant looked up as Darci Law stalked away from Carrie Forrest's house, her face white with fury, twin flags of color riding high on her cheeks. Her head was down so she never even saw him parked just a few yards away from her.

But he saw her...hell, he saw her in his dreams.

Sleek, slender with subtle curves and an ass that drove him crazy, the woman drew eyes everywhere she went.

Damn, but she was a cute thing.

He had thought so from day one when she had moved into town more than five years ago, all big eyes, gamine features and sharp tongue. Pretty mouth. Nice plump little breasts, sleekly rounded hips, nice ass...damn, he really liked that ass. He had been going through a messy divorce at the time and still didn't care to be involved with a woman for more time than it took to get her naked and bury his dick inside her for twenty minutes or so.

His ex had taken him for a ride and he wasn't interested in getting back on that particular roller coaster.

And he knew Darci wasn't about unattached sex, uncomplicated fucks, or a quick lay. There was little about Darci that was uncomplicated.

He ran a hand through the thick, deep auburn hair he had been born with, and hated, most of his life. What in the hell was he doing here? He rested his hands on the steering wheel and told himself he really didn't want to get involved in whatever mess this woman was trying to create.

"I need to have a word with you, Sheriff," Carrie had told him when he'd called her back this afternoon. "It's rather important...but very private. Just some information that you should know."

So what in the hell was going on in her deluded mind now?

Knocking on the door, he waited for Carrie's personal assistant to answer. Or her slave, as she was also known. Kim was basically Carrie's bitch, and everybody, including Kim, knew that. Carrie said *jump* and Kim would only ask how high. Once upon a time, Kellan had seen slavish devotion in Kim's quiet green eyes.

Now he just saw weariness.

She opened the door and said softly, "Carrie really doesn't want visitors, Sheriff Grant."

"Well, I'm sorry to hear that. But she called for me, and if she wants to talk to me in the next few days, now is the time," he said politely. Maybe she'd say, that's fine, another time…and he could go about his job without listening to the complaining of the tired old shrew.

Kim swallowed and Kellan felt his heart break a little for her as he glimpsed the unhappiness in her eyes. What in the hell did Carrie have over her? Or was Kim still convinced that Carrie was the woman she pretended to be?

Kellan knew better. Hell, he suspected half the town knew, but they were so used to the status quo that they didn't say shit. Carrie and Beth…as he followed Kim up the stairs to Carrie's studio, he imagined what the town might have been like if those two hadn't hooked up. They had never really interacted, until the gallery, and life had been sweeter then.

If they hadn't gotten together, maybe people would actually trust each other. Maybe they wouldn't automatically assume the worst of each other.

Kim walked away after pointing to the closed door at the end of the hall, folding her arms around herself, her head down. Kellan walked on, dark auburn brows arched over his hazel eyes as he listened to the stream of hostility coming from the room.

A regular tapping interspersed heavy steps. Carrie was pacing. She had been in an accident when she was a teenager, sitting in the backseat of a car when the friend who was driving ran a red light, and didn't see the oncoming car in time to stop. One friend had been thrown from the car and had died instantly.

Carrie's leg had been pinned and broken in three places, and as a result, she walked with a limp.

"...bitch. I can't believe...damn it, get over here. I don't care what you're in the middle of," she was saying.

Kellan arched a brow, hardly able to believe the harsh, angry voice was Carrie's. Oh, he knew the stoic mother figure she presented to the community wasn't her real nature. But he'd never before heard such clear evidence of it.

He lifted his hand and knocked loudly, right in the middle of her next sentence, and had the honor of hearing superb acting skill as her voice went from shrewish bitch to suffering martyr.

What Kellan wouldn't have given to have been able to see the transformation taking place, and not just hear it.

"Just...just one moment, please. I need a moment," Carrie said, and he heard a very loud, very dramatic sigh. A moment passed and then the door opened, revealing Carrie with a pale but composed face. He wasn't surprised that she still managed to suck people in. She looked entirely too motherly to be the person he knew her to be.

"Sheriff Grant." She stood still, her eyes wide behind the thick lenses, her black plastic frames perched on her nose. "I'm sorry, I wasn't really expecting any visitors—I told Kim I needed some time alone." She smiled that sweet mother's smile before she added gently, "I just...had a falling out with Darci. It's been some time coming, and I don't think we'll be able to repair the rift this time."

Kellan arched a brow and said, "I was under the impression that you two were never friends anyway. What rift would there be to mend?"

His sharp gaze caught the hot fury that flashed for the quickest second in her eyes. But he had to wonder, how bad had Darci pissed her off? Jibes generally weren't enough to faze her.

"Now, that just isn't true, Kellan," she said, her smile dimming a bit. "Just because there's been some strife lately between our gallery and Becka's...well...you know she's never been entirely right in the head."

Kellan arched a brow. "I hadn't paid much attention. But it's never really been my concern anyway." He shrugged as he moved over to the couch and settled down, watching Carrie with waiting eyes. "Exactly what did you need to talk to me about?"

Carrie's eyes clouded for the briefest second, and Kellan watched, wondering if she had forgotten.

Finally, she nodded. With a downward glance at her hands, she heaved a deep, tired sigh.

Twenty minutes later, Kellan was stomping out of her house, aggravated beyond all belief.

Carrie had wanted to let him know that she suspected Darci was guilty of a crime that hadn't even been reported yet. What an absolute fucking waste of time.

Becka had supposedly had money stolen.

And lo, Darci gets a fancy new camera that sells for thousands. Not only *that*, Carrie had seen her skulking around the gallery hours after it had closed.

"Wednesday. Around seven. Then I heard rumors that she was at the Golden Inn with Joe," Carrie had said, her voice rougher, deeper than normal. For once, it wasn't that annoying nasal twang.

"Are you sure you want to go on record with that statement?" Kellan had asked, reaching up to rub his neck. She'd called him here with an obviously contrived story, and now stood there, lying through her teeth. "Sure you want to tell me that she was seen at the gallery? Because if something comes up, I'll be reporting your statement, as you tell it now. And you could be called as a witness."

With her martyr's sigh, Carrie had nodded. "I know that. But right is right, wrong is wrong. It will hurt to stand against

Darci, she's such a unique individual, and I do quite like her a lot. But I have to do the right thing."

Kellan had arched a brow at her and suggested, "Then tell the truth. I really don't think it's wise for you to be telling an officer of the law that you saw a woman skulking around an office when twenty other people saw her at the skating rink. Myself included. And I'd really like to know how she could have possibly been at the Golden with some guy. When she was supposedly at the gallery skulking around, *and* at a skating party. Not just in two places at once, but three. Now, that's impressive."

Carrie's mouth had gone tight as he continued, "Daisy is my cousin, you know. Well, second cousin. Her daddy and I are first cousins and he is going out of town this morning on business. He didn't want to miss her party, so Missy threw one together Wednesday. And Darci met Missy around 5:30 that evening to help get stuff together. They went to the Wal-Mart in Madison for cake and stuff. They even have receipts, with Darci's signature on them. Missy made damn sure that JT, down at the office, saw those. JT is a tad bit upset as well—she is pretty fond of both Joe and Darci. And that's how I know all of this. I had no more than stepped foot in the station this morning when JT was all over me with this information. Took a few minutes to figure out what receipts and pictures had to do with the Golden Inn, but then I figured it out. Of course, this is the first I've heard about her skulking around the gallery."

So what in the hell was going on? he wondered, dragging his mind back to the present. Some bitchy old loon calling him up to tell him obviously fabricated tales. Willing, even, to lie about it on record, it seemed.

And the rumors...hell, the rumors. There were so many, it was a wonder any of them knew what the truth was.

Hell, he knew who had started most of the rumors.

Her name was Carrie Forrest and, in a fit of fury, she had thrown him out of her house after he had informed her that her story—which was really rather pointless, since no crime had been reported—was full of holes. Holes large enough to drive a school bus through.

So what in the hell was going on with Carrie now?

"I hate that whey-faced, bratty little bitch," Carrie whispered, as Beth walked back and forth across the room.

"If you had just made sure she was home," Peggy murmured, shaking her head. "It's a delicious little rumor. She could have lost her job. Nobody wants a tramp teaching schoolchildren, after all. But nobody will believe what's being said about her, after the last one was such a bold-faced lie."

Kim sat curled on the chair, biting her nails nervously.

Tricia Casey sat in the corner, sipping tea, her neatly styled gray hair swept back in a chignon, her eyes watching the tableau before her with great interest. "You told too many tales," she said, shaking her head. "I know we'd rather just see *Dreams* die—" she smirked a little at her own personal joke. "And Becka losing Darci would do a lot of damage to her emotionally. She might not be able to handle it. But gossip is one thing. This wasn't gossip. It was bold-faced lying. You're not as good at that as I am."

Beth scowled at Tricia and said, "Nobody would have listened to you. You're too new here. They like Darci." Beth's lined face looked much older than it really was. Casting a bitter look at Carrie, Beth said harshly, "You caused this mess, Carrie. Damn it, you shouldn't have done something so damned huge. Not with Darci. Too many people like her and she's too damned outspoken. She doesn't take things lying down. You should have figured that out by now."

Carrie slammed her charcoal pencil down and glared at all of them. "Would you shut up? I don't need to hear this from you. Not from any of you," she shouted. A startled look crossed her face and she swallowed. "I-I'm sorry. This is giving me such a headache."

She muttered, "How in the hell was I supposed to know Darci wouldn't be going home? She said she was going home. And I'm not about to just let her get by with the snipes she makes at me. How she treats me like shit, like I was just like anybody else… I'm *better*…" As she spoke, her voice started to take on a little singsong quality, drifting up and down. Lowering herself into her chair, she smiled, and those who saw it took a minute to wonder. That smile was…wrong. Her eyes started to gleam as she whispered, "And that damned gallery. I hate it…I hate all of them."

"Carrie, you need to get hold of yourself," Tricia said quietly.

Carrie blinked, looking confused. Looking from one woman to another, she didn't like the looks she saw, disgust, worry, fear. *Nothing to worry about,* she told herself, turning back to her desk, lowering herself into the chair. *Nothing to worry about.*

Aloud, she said, "I know what I'm doing. I'm doing what's best for all of us, for the gallery." Taking a charcoal pencil in hand, she started to sketch.

"Don't go acting like this had something to do with the business," Beth said flatly. "This was personal. Which means if anybody has problems from it, it will be you. Not us. *You.*"

"There aren't going to be problems," Carrie muttered, her hand moving rapidly over the heavy paper. Her eyes were wide and feverish, locked on the work in front of her.

"I hope not."

Darci was kicking back at the café when Kellan crossed the street, carrying a white sack in his hand.

Dotti's.

His work day was over and he had gone to Dotti's again for dinner. Like he did most every night.

Darci knew, because any time she was in town, she looked for him. And at this time of day, he was usually heading out. Over the past couple of years, she had spent a lot of time studying him.

And the first thought that drifted through her mind was *Damn, but that man has one fine butt.*

The strong columns of his thighs, that firm ass, his back, everything from the back view added up to one fine piece of man-flesh. Yep. There was just one thing to say about him.

Damn, he was fine.

His eyes… She loved those eyes. And his hands — she hummed under her breath as she thought of just what she'd like to see those hands doing.

Darci bet he hated that hair. It was deep, deep dark red, worn a little longer now than he used to wear it, past his collar, brushing his shoulder. His skin was a warm mellow gold, not the pale white she normally associated with redheads. Against that golden skin, his hazel eyes gleamed, glowing green-gold one minute, then amber the next.

You are obsessed.

In response to her silent, self-directed comment, she muttered, "Yep," and chuckled.

Tipping back the cappuccino, she took another savoring sip, humming in appreciation as she swallowed.

A low humph reached her ears and she arched a brow as Clive sent her a narrow look. "Listen, you skinny little white girl, you planning on going home soon or are you going to keep sitting here lookin' purty?" he razzed. "Or better yet, go have some fun. Pretty thing like you needs to be out having fun on a night like this. Not sitting there brooding."

She pursed her lips. "I think I'll just sit here and brood," she drawled, tapping her cup. "I want another, and a biscotti. A chocolate one dipped in white chocolate."

Clive grinned at her and said, "Girl, don't you think you should be out combing the woods and pointing that camera at things? You need to be taking photo-graphs, dontcha? We need some photo-graphs."

She rolled her eyes and said, "I don't feel like taking photo-graphs," drawing the word out the same way he did, mimicking his deep Southern accent. "I'm taking a break. Is that okay with you, buddy?"

He smiled, his teeth white inside the grizzled salt and pepper of his beard. "Sure thing, lady. You're a pretty knickknack to have sitting around my shop, that's for sure." Then his eyes sobered. "I was wondering, though, are you mebbe tryin' to avoid being by yourself, tryin' to avoid doin' any serious thinking? Serious thoughts tend to hurt some when somebody has struck out at ya, somebody who was a friend."

Her eyes drifted away and she sighed. "I don't want to be alone with my thoughts, that's for sure. I figure when I'm less likely to brood, I'll get some work done. I'm too good at brooding though. I don't need the headache it's going to give me."

Clive set her mocha down in front of her, the biscotti on a plate with a lace doily. After patting her shoulder with an arthritic hand, he hobbled away. "Take your time, girl. You just take your time. Like I said, pretty face like yours around here ain't gonna hurt my business none," he told her over his shoulder.

She eventually moved to the padded window seat and pulled out a book, reading until she had a crick in her neck and her hands were shaky from excess caffeine.

Even then, she didn't go home. Closing her eyes, she daydreamed, her mind drifting, chasing itself around in circles. The low hum of conversation around her lulled her, and eased her even farther into her daze.

When Clive came up later and patted her shoulder, his eyes were dark and thoughtful as he studied her. "Girl, I'm almost tempted to just stay open all night. I can tell you don't wanna go home and be alone wit' yourself. But it's late, and I'm tired," he drawled, pulling a chair up. "You know, sooner or later, the people who caused this mess for you are going to get what's comin' to them. What goes around does indeed come around."

"Yeah, well, a couple of these people have been causing this kind of shit for years. And nothing's ever come of it," Darci said wearily. "And they aren't even the worst of it. They aren't the ones who bothered me the most."

"Oh, I know…it's Della. You admired that woman—imagine you still do. It's hard to shut down what's in your heart when ya look up to somebody as much as you did her. I do know that she's got plenty of people who aren't very happy with her."

Her mouth curled up in a sad smile. "I don't want anybody mad at her. That doesn't solve anything."

"No. And it doesn't make you feel any better. Nothing is gonna do that. Nothing changes the fact that she believed somebody's lies," Clive said, his low, soothing voice lulling her frazzled nerves. "Now you listen up. I'm going make you up a special drink, and you don't be tellin' nobody about it. And you can't give me money, cuz I ain't allowed to sell alcohol. But I'm gonna fix it. And then I'm gonna drive you home. You can drink it there."

He patted her hand and stood up. "Once you get there, you're going to go up, get in bed and finish drinking it. And sleep. And put this mess behind you—however you have to do it."

Chapter Two

❧

Kellan's hands moved over smooth, ivory flesh. Silken and sweetly scented, eyes that sparkled green under slanted black brows and a cap of short, black hair. Damned exotic little fairy.

Her mouth tasted like wine under his, addictive and sweet, and her hands moved over his body like butterfly wings, light and feathery. Against his chest, he could feel the hot stab of her nipples, the pounding of her heart.

Rolling her onto her back, Kellan pushed her thighs wide and spread her open, piercing the wet folds with his tongue. She was sweet, spicy…ripe. Ready for him—damn it, he was ready for her, too.

Vicious need pulsed through him and he groaned as she arched up against him with a shriek.

Now…the word circled through his mind. Now…had to have her now.

Moving up her body, he wondered why in the hell he had waited so long—

The buzzing of his pager had the dream falling in tatters around him.

Fuck.

He opened his eyes, his cock throbbing and aching like a bad tooth, Darci's name lingering on his lips. Damn it, he could still feel the echo of the dream as he reached for his pager. Her scent seemed to cling to him and he had to remind himself that it was just a dream.

The most realistic dream he had ever had, but a dream all the same.

But the message on his pager was like a bucket of ice water thrown in his face and his body froze as he finished reading it.

Swallowing, he reached for the phone and called the office, hoping this was some sick joke.

Twenty minutes later, he was standing in Carrie Forrest's house, over the bloodied remains of her body. It was no joke.

This was as real as it got, and about as bloody.

He hadn't seen this much hatred in a long while.

Somebody had a powerful lot of rage built up inside of them, and whoever it was, had let it all loose on Carrie last night.

Beth Morris was downstairs wailing on Peggy Ralley's shoulder and Kim Samuel was sitting on the couch, sipping coffee and staring into the distance, as though she wasn't really there.

Carrie had been beaten to death.

The murder weapon was still in the house. Carrie's cane. The victim's face was hardly recognizable. The cane had broken by the time the perp was done.

Damn it. He felt pity move through him as he knelt beside her body and studied the pitiful mess that had been made of it.

She had wreaked a lot of hell, on a lot of lives.

But nobody deserved to die like this.

"Ms. Morris, you can't— Damn it, this is the scene of a crime—"

"Take your hands off of me, unless you'd like to be talking to me and my lawyer in court," Beth Morris said coldly.

Almost everybody in town had heard that line before. Beth loved to throw it around. Mostly, it was an empty threat, but enough people had actually received papers that most didn't want to push it. The judges at the small county courthouse had tired of seeing her face and had thrown many cases out, so Beth had taken several of her cases to the next level.

It was still a threat powerful enough to evoke fear in some people's hearts.

But Deputy David Morelli wasn't about to let her intrude on a crime scene.

"I don't care if the Almighty Himself summons me to appear in court. I'm not going to let you intrude on a crime scene," Morelli snapped, placing himself between Beth and the studio when the other officer let her go. "Now if you don't take yourself back downstairs, I will. We've already asked you several times. Please don't make us go through this again."

Beth started to sniffle. "How can you talk to me this way? I've lost my best friend."

"And I'd think you'd want us to do what we can to make sure her killer is caught. Including not damaging possible clues," Morelli said levelly.

"I just want to speak with the Sheriff," she said, her voice high-pitched and whining.

From where Kellan crouched, he could almost hear the sigh in Morelli's voice and he figured he owed the man a drink or ten.

"He just got here. He hasn't been on the scene for more than five minutes. Give him some time, Ms. Morris. Now go back downstairs and let us work," he said firmly.

"She did it! I know she did! Everybody loves Carrie but her," Beth sobbed, burying her face in her hands. "Arrest that bitch. You can't let her walk the streets while Carrie lies dead in the ground."

Kellan lifted his head and stared out into the hall as Beth shrieked out, "You put Darci in jail, damn it. She threatened Carrie, just yesterday. Make her pay!"

* * * * *

Kellan left the house some time later, tension settling inside his gut like a leaden fist.

"What's your next step?" Morelli asked quietly.

Turning, Kellan met the older man's dark eyes, scowling. "I'm going to go question Darci Law." And the thought ate at him, like acid in his belly.

Morelli sighed, rubbing his thumb across his lip. "She didn't do it, Sheriff. You know that. Question her, get it out of the way...and when this is over, you really ought to quit mooning over her and just ask her out."

Kellan felt the blood rush to his cheeks. Turning away, he thought sourly, *Well, damn. Been hiding it real well, haven't I?*

Unable to think of a damn thing to say to that, he just scowled at Morelli and stomped away.

This, he decided, just downright sucked.

* * * * *

Darci rolled onto her back, her hand between her legs, a sigh tripping out of her as she dreamed. Oh, she suspected damn good and well it was a dream, but still...

If his hands felt as good in reality as they felt in the dream—shoot, even half as good—she'd climax before he even touched her breasts.

In the dream, his lips were fixed firmly around her nipple, drawing deeply, as his hands palmed her butt, lifting her up against his cock. His hair had fallen free of that short, stubby tail he kept it confined in and it teased her shoulders, her neck. She locked her hands in it, smiling with delight as it turned out to be every bit as silky as it looked. It was the color of mahogany, deep dark brownish-red, shot through with streaks of pure bright red—women would kill to have hair like his.

Damn, a lot of women just might kill to be where she was, spread out underneath that long, sleekly muscled body, that clever mouth moving over her hungrily, that hair wrapped around her fists.

Kellan kissed his way down her belly, pushing her thighs apart. He rose to his knees, reaching up to untangle her hands from his hair before he stroked his finger down her slit, from her clit on down, opening her thoroughly. He moved past the tender patch of flesh between her vagina and her anus to tease the tight pucker of her ass before he lowered his head and placed a full openmouthed kiss against her wet flesh.

"Damn, you're sweet," he murmured, lifting up to blow on her before turning his head to the side and plunging his tongue inside of her.

"Sweet, sweet, sweet..."

Those words were echoing inside her head as she was jerked out of sleep by the persistent knocking on her door.

Darci sat up, her chest heaving, her nipples burning, a throbbing, lingering ache in her pussy...while she played with herself. Her face flushed as she pulled her hand away from her aching cleft and whispered, "Now that was one hell of a wet dream."

She rolled out of the bed and stumbled to the bathroom, washing her hands and then splashing water on her face before she went downstairs, flicking a glance at the clock. Ten o'clock. Damn, what in the hell had Clive put into that drink?

She *never* slept that late.

But she felt—good.

Very good, actually. Of course, that could be the wet dream she had just had. A wicked smile lifted up the corners of her mouth as she opened the door. But heat suffused her face when the open door revealed Kellan Grant. The object of her wet dream.

Slowly, she slid a hand through her hair. *Parking tickets paid...and I don't think Carrie would be stupid enough to press charges for yesterday.*

After all, what can she say? I yelled at her? That I told her to leave me alone?

The dream echoed through her head as she met his eyes and her cheeks heated.

"Good morning, Sheriff," she said slowly. Trying to shove the dream aside, she nibbled on her lower lip as she prayed to God that Kellan couldn't tell what thoughts were running through her head.

"Morning, ma'am," he said, nodding at her. Behind him stood one of his deputies, and the younger man also nodded politely, his eyes moving away from her face.

"I'm afraid I need to ask you to come down to the station, Ms. Law," Kellan said, his voice tight, a muscle ticcing in his cheek. "I've got some questions I need to ask, and I'll need to take a statement. If you wouldn't mind getting dressed…"

Darci glanced down at her nightshirt, confused. No, she couldn't wear the cotton nightie down there. Licking her lips, she looked back up at Kellan and asked, "What do you need to talk to me about? I'm afraid I don't understand, Sheriff."

Kellan glanced at the deputy before he reached up and rubbed the back of his neck with his hand. "Ms. Law, look, this is a pretty…hmm. Why don't you let us come inside? Maybe you can run upstairs and get dressed?" he suggested, his eyes flicking to the front of her nightshirt again.

She nodded slowly as her heart started to quiver in her chest.

Something was wrong.

Bad wrong.

She didn't do it.

Even though he had been pretty certain of it before coming here, the confused look in her eyes only confirmed his gut instincts. She didn't do it.

Okay, yes, he'd known that, in his gut. But another part of him—the cop part—knew that sometimes people did some very out of character things and he just couldn't help but...

But she didn't.

Relief made him slightly lightheaded as he stepped inside. Grady followed behind him and closed the door.

As her pretty little butt disappeared up the stairs, he dragged his eyes away from her and found his deputy grinning at him.

"You should really just ask her out, Sheriff. You've been panting over her since before your divorce. Just do it," Grady said, shaking his head at him.

"Wonderful idea. While I'm asking out a murder suspect, would you like to do anything else damaging to my career? I know, maybe you'd like to plant rumors that I'm selling drugs on the side?" Kellan whispered out of the side of his mouth.

"She's no murderer," Grady whispered back, shaking his head. "I dunno who is responsible, but it's not her." He clammed up the minute he heard footsteps on the stairs and Kellan jerked back around.

But what he saw on the steps wasn't much better than what she had been wearing.

All she had done was draw on jeans and tuck the tails of her nightshirt in. That fine white cotton was much too thin to disguise a damn thing. It clung to the full white globes of her breasts, and the dark shadow of her nipples was outlined clearly.

Darci was too damned sharp not to realize something bad wrong was going on. He could see the nerves dancing in her eyes.

And when a woman got nervous, well, it had similar effects sometimes as that of arousal. She was cold, her skin covered with goose bumps and she kept chafing her arms with her hands, licking her lips as her eyes darted from Grady to Kellan, back to Grady, then focused on Kellan.

And her nipples…they had gone stiff and hard, peaking against the soft white cotton of her nightie and all Kellan wanted to do was drop to his knees and take one of them into his mouth, then the other and see if she tasted as sweet as he suspected.

He suppressed a groan as she seated herself in the emerald green papasan chair and folded her hands in her lap, staring at them. "What's going on, Sheriff?" she asked quietly.

"I need you to tell me where you were last night," Kellan said, lowering himself to the couch and watching her face closely.

"I was at Clive's," she said, lifting a shoulder and staring at them, her peaked brows puckered with confusion. "I usually would have gone out to the park and shot pictures. It was a clear evening, gorgeous…would have been great for some sunset pics, but I didn't feel like being alone with my thoughts. So I went to Clive's."

"So you had some coffee and came home?" Kellan asked, pulling out his notepad. He drew out a pair of glasses with dark gold wire frames and put them on, then just tapped his pen against his notepad, studying her face.

That wasn't enough to alibi her. He already had a good idea of time of death, just from looking at the body. Rigor hadn't set in, there wasn't any smell, and blood had already settled in her body. A little over twelve hours, the way he figured. Carrie had died probably between seven and nine.

"What time did you go to Clive's?"

"I got there around five," she said, frowning.

"And after you had your coffee, you left?" he asked, keeping the urge to swear violently behind his teeth. Not good enough. Not even good to keep from arresting her if they found even the slightest bit of circumstantial evidence.

She shook her head. "I was there until he closed. I didn't feel like being alone." She moved her eyes away, staring out the window over Kellan's shoulder. "Been a long week."

Damn it, she looked like she had been kicked. Like somebody had slapped her. He wanted to go over there and cuddle her, stroke her hair and buss that pretty mouth. And once she was smiling again, he wanted to see how long it would take to make her moan, and make her sigh, and sob with pleasure.

"I heard you've had a rough time—also heard some rumors that Carrie was behind that little ordeal," Kellan said. Bile rose in his throat. He usually loved his job. Enjoyed it. Keeping the peace, seeing justice done when what little crime happened in this quiet town occurred.

But now…self-disgust rose bitterly as he started to set her up and he would have done almost anything if somebody else could have done this.

Anger flared in her jewel-bright eyes and she sneered. "Rumor, my ass. If she's not the bitch behind it, then I'll eat cardboard. She started it, I know it as well as I know my own name."

"She's caused you trouble in the past, hasn't she? Accused you of having liaisons, stealing your photographs from online, a number of things," Kellan said.

"Is that all of it? Hell, I would have thought there was more by now," Darci snorted. "I've no idea what kind of lies she's told about me. I do know that she mentioned to damn near every woman in town that I really am not a wise person to befriend because I'll steal away her man the minute she turns her back. And I'll do everything possible to ruin her life in the process," she said, flicking her spiky bangs back from her face with a silver-ringed finger. "Something's not right in Carrie's head. If she can't have you under her control, she hates you."

"I take it that you wouldn't comply with what she wanted," Kellan said.

Darci shrugged. "I don't kiss ass very well. And I don't tolerate patronization. So no, we never really got along well, if that is what you want to know. I don't like Carrie, I never have. But she's really been jerking my chain a lot lately," she said, shaking her head. She looked back at Kellan and cocked a brow. "You still haven't explained why you are here, what exactly it is that has you wanting to take me in for a statement."

Kellan slid Grady a look. "You got home around nine or so?" he asked, deliberately fudging the time. Clive's didn't close until eleven in the summer. Tourists seemed to think the town should keep big-city hours. So, they kept big-city hours. At least the restaurants and diners did.

"No. I told you," she said patiently, lifting her eyes to the ceiling. "I stayed at Clive's until he chased me out—until closing. Later than that actually." She frowned. "Damn it, my car is there. Shoot. Anyway. I just kept drinking cappuccinos— shoot, I really have to go pee."

Kellan lifted a brow at her and smothered a grin. Damn it, that was one of the things he liked about her. She had to be one of the most open women he had ever met in his life.

She rambled on, unaware of his amusement. "I had been sitting in the window seat, that thing is soooo comfortable. I was reading and then just daydreaming for a while. He let me keep on zoning while he closed up and he told me…"

Then she locked her lips together and her face went red.

Kellan sighed and lifted his eyes patiently to the sky. "Look, Darci. I'm perfectly aware that Clive has a nice little recipe that he hands out every now and then. I don't know what all is in it, and I've never been given one, so while I'm offended that you got one, after only living here for five years, and I was born here, and *I've* never gotten one, you aren't going to get him in trouble."

She arched a brow and whistled *I Wish I was in Dixie*.

"He didn't accept money for it, did he?" Kellan asked, suppressing the urge to laugh.

44

She stopped whistling and laughed. "Damn it, and here I was thinking I was special."

"You are. He only gives that out to a handful of people," Kellan said sourly. "So you got one of Clive's miracle drinks and he drove you home...what time you think that was?"

She shrugged. "He closes around eleven and it was all clean and tidy before he even interrupted my nice little daydreams. Probably quarter after, maybe eleven-twenty. I guess I got home a little before midnight," she said, nodding toward the sparkling river view just beyond the window over Kellan's shoulder. "We talked on the porch, while he made sure I drank my 'goodnight cocktail' as he called it." She slid Kellan a look and said, "He wouldn't let me drink it until we got here, and I can understand why. I had no sooner gone upstairs and gotten into my jammies than I started feeling sleepy. Don't know what he puts in that thing, but it packs a punch. And I haven't slept that soundly in years."

Kellan felt the knot in his belly loosening. "So basically, you were at Clive's all evening. I'm sure other people besides him saw you?" he asked, leaning back and staring at her face. Her brows arched higher as she tilted her head, studying him.

"Yes, I'm sure plenty of people did." Drawing her knees up to her chest, she rested that elfin chin on them and pinned him with a direct stare, one that was totally at odds with her whimsical looks, and that lazy, almost childish pose. "So, tell me, exactly what is it you're worried I did last night?"

"Now you need to be advised that I haven't read you your rights. You're not under arrest, and I don't suspect you of any crimes. However, some people probably do."

Across the room, Grady closed his eyes and just shook his head.

Darci nodded slowly. "Okay," she said softly. "What crime exactly?"

Setting his notebook aside, he leaned forward and said, "Sometime last evening, somebody Carrie Forrest knew was inside her house. They had coffee and she got out cookies, which were left untouched in the sitting room." Kellan stood up and crossed the room, kneeling in front of Darci, not touching her, just watching her face as he finished. "They went upstairs to her studio and then this person killed Carrie."

Darci's mouth dropped open.

She blinked.

Her legs slid down and she shifted on the chair, reaching up to rub a fist across her chest. "What?" she repeated in a soft, weak voice. "I'm sorry. What?"

"Carrie is dead," Kellan said levelly. "She was murdered."

Darci fell back against the chair as though all the energy had drained out of her. The light in her vibrant green eyes dimmed and she swallowed. "You think I could have done it," she murmured, still staring at him.

Yes, one of the most open women he had ever met. She didn't hide a damn thing. Kellan replied as honestly as he could. "I don't think you could have done it. But you are a suspect. Carrie liked to snipe at you, Darci. She did her damnedest to cause you trouble, and you never backed down, especially this last time," he said softly.

In the corner, Grady lifted his eyes to the sky, shaking his head.

"I have reason to dislike her," Darci said coldly. "I don't have reason to hate her. I don't have reason to want her dead."

"Some people might think, after what has happened between you, that you would have every reason to want just that," Kellan said. "She was out to ruin you. Ruin your career."

"Get serious," Darci said, rolling her eyes. "Hatred requires too much energy. And frankly, she's not worth it." Then she paled. "Oh, man. That sounds terrible. She's dead, and...oh, man." She tugged a gold chain from underneath her shirt and worried the charm on it with her fingers, mumbling under her breath. "I didn't like the lady, but my mother didn't raise me to speak ill of the dead. That was mean of me."

Kellan closed his eyes and shook his head. This woman was...unusual. To say the least.

"Ah, I think under the circumstances, your mother would understand," Kellan said softly.

She flashed him a wry grin, her eyes sparkling brightly through the tears. "Ummm, you don't know Mama," she said, her voice thick. "Speaking ill of the dead is just something you don't do. Even of Hitler."

Kellan waited until she took a shuddering breath and her eyes met his once more. "I need you to come down to the station. I need a statement," he said softly.

Her lashes lowered and she sighed, her slim, sleekly muscled shoulders rising and falling beneath the lacy straps of her nightie. "My life seems to be going to hell in a handbasket," she murmured.

Kellan couldn't help it. "Well, it's a vast improvement over the path Carrie's life took last night," he said.

Her eyes widened. Then she slowly agreed, "Well, you do have a point. Although Carrie chose her path a very long time ago."

Well, he might believe she wasn't a killer, Darci thought sourly as she ran her wet fingers through her short black hair. She made a face in the mirror. "It's still not keeping me from having to go down and make a statement," she muttered.

Part of her felt guilty.

Carrie was dead. Apparently pretty brutally. Kellan wouldn't say anything, but she was really good at picking up vibes. And she sensed a terrible rage within him. A terrible rage.

Maybe she was wrong, she thought as she tugged her nightshirt off and searched for a bra in the dresser drawer.

Spying one, she tugged it out and pulled it on, then jerked open her closet and grabbed the first shirt she could find—a waist-length, black sleeveless vest-styled shirt. She stuck her arms in it, buttoned it up and stuck her feet into a black pair of thongs.

Maybe any unjustified death angered him. It would her. Hearing about anybody dying before their time made her mad.

But…still. She couldn't help but think something about this was off. Or maybe she was just letting her emotions toward Carrie affect her. Hell, she thought as she grabbed her purse and keys from the table beside her door and jogged down the steps, she'd been letting her animosity toward Carrie skew her thinking for months.

Why should this change anything?

Except she had decided earlier that she was going to get over this. She wasn't going to let Carrie and Co. matter anymore.

Meeting Kellan at the bottom of the stairs, she looked into his eyes—soft, warm, hazel eyes. He had taken his glasses off. He had looked awfully good with them on, like a sexy scholar.

Of course, he looked good without them too.

He just looked damned good.

She just loved his eyes. She'd love to photograph his eyes, those wide-spaced, heavily lashed, warm, hazel eyes.

Was it her imagination or did they look just a little warmer as he stared at her?

"Let's get this over with," she said quietly.

Her attorney of record wasn't exactly equipped to defend her against a murder charge, but Darci wasn't a fool. As she rode in the back of Kellan's cruiser, she pulled out her cell phone and called Brittany Daugherty.

"Darci, I was just getting ready to come over. I don't know if you've heard anything but—"

"Britt, I'm in the Sheriff's car, riding over to the station," she interrupted. "I think it would be a good idea for you to meet me down there."

"Oh, shit. I was afraid this would happen. Don't say anything, don't tell them anything—"

"I already have told them some stuff, but it was just where I was last night. I was at Clive's all evening. But they want to take my statement, ask some official questions," she said. As she spoke, she glanced up and met Kellan's glance in the rearview mirror.

He was studying her with an arched brow.

She flushed and licked her lips and dragged her gaze away, but she could still feel him staring at her.

"I'd like you to meet me there, Britt," she said, lowering her voice. "The whole damn town knows that Carrie and I had some bad history between us. And half of the town is still convinced she was a saint..."

"The Wicked Witch is more like it," Britt interjected. "But we can't let anybody hear you talking like that. Don't say anything else. And I mean *anything*. Not until I get there. So zip it."

Once Brittany hung up the phone, Darci sighed and flipped hers closed, tossing it into her purse.

"So, what does your lawyer have to say?"

Arching a brow at him, she drew an imaginary zipper across the seam of her lips and turned the lock, before leaning her head back. Damn it. She needed to think.

Because if she thought long and hard enough, surely she'd come up with the reasons she had moved to Vevey to begin with.

At least she'd taken that white nightshirt off. If he had been forced to question her while she had been wearing that nightie, the hint of her nipples teasing him, he was certain he would have gone mad.

He was about to lose it anyway.

Damn it, this was too much.

Kellan had avoided her like the plague for the past few years. And just for this very reason. The scent of her skin drove him insane. The thought of being close enough to touch all of that smooth white skin, yet resisting, was enough to make him want to drag her by the hair to the closest private place and just throw her to the ground and mount her. To see the sparkle of her emerald green eyes and hear the low husky caress of her voice as she spoke —

Damn it. He was going to drive himself crazy.

And they hadn't even gotten started yet.

This was the longest time he had ever spent in her company. And the closest. The scent of her skin was permanently embedded on his memory and he was certain that her mouth would be every bit as sweet and soft as it looked.

Fuck.

He had kept his attraction to her from becoming an obsession just by keeping his distance.

And now that distance had been totally smashed. How could he stay away from her now?

But how could he do anything with a woman who was involved in a murder investigation?

Hell, she hadn't done it. He knew that as well as he knew his own name. But she was involved in it. Somehow. Something Carrie had done had pissed somebody off so much that the person had snapped.

And lately, all her tricks and bullshit seemed to revolve around Darci, Becka, or the gallery.

As Britt sailed in, her bouncy blonde curls secured in a ponytail, she grinned sunnily at Kellan and asked easily, "How's Michaela doing?"

He smiled and said, "Fat and pregnant, last I heard."

"Shouldn't be calling your sister fat. She's just...plump. A baby can do that, I've heard," Britt said as she settled onto the hard chair, flipping open her briefcase and drawing out a yellow legal pad and a pen. After perching a pair of wire-rimmed glasses on her nose, she flicked Kellan a glance and said, "I'll need a moment to speak with my client, if you don't mind."

Kellan sighed and said, "She's not under arrest. I just need to take a statement, ask her some questions."

Brittany smiled serenely. "That is all well and good. But I really should know a few things before you ask her those questions." She arched her brows and waited.

Kellan scowled and tossed his pen down on the table. He pushed his glasses up on top of his head and left the room, shaking his head as he closed the door behind him.

He made a beeline for his office and went straight for the coffeepot, pushing the button, knowing JT already had it ready to brew. She had seen him come in and had huffed her way in here, mumbling about overtime and how a body just couldn't get any sleep.

And she had the pot waiting for him, so he could have coffee as soon as he wanted it.

Loveable old biddy.

As soon as there was enough for a cup, he grabbed the pot and poured one, wincing as footsteps came down the hall, hoping it wasn't JT. If she knew he was letting coffee splatter on the warming unit again, she'd have his hide. But the footsteps went on past, and he sipped at the hot brew and sighed with pleasure while coffee hissed and bubbled on the heating unit.

Oh, yeah, JT would skin him.

But as long as he cleaned up his mess, they'd be fine.

Darci toyed with the cross at her neck as she repeated, almost word for word, how she had spent her night. "Okay," Britt finally said, smiling with satisfaction. "Clive is almost gold around here. If he says you were at his place, then nobody will doubt him."

"Gee, thanks," Darci said sarcastically.

Britt laughed. "Honey, you know by now how things are here. They like you, a lot. But you're still the new kid. Hell, you'll be new after you've lived here fifty years. But Clive, well, he wasn't born here, but his daddy was, and he's been here since he was a kid and around here, he is a fixture. *And* he likes you. All in all, that is a damned good thing. You've got plenty of witnesses and an unimpeachable alibi." Patting Darci on the knee, she said, "Small-town life, babe. Don't you love it?"

Darci groused through the rest of the questions, twisting her rings 'round and 'round on her fingers, replaying yesterday through her mind. *You have got to be the saddest most pathetic creature…*

It was the truth. She knew that.

But all she could see was the bright flash of pain that had appeared in Carrie's eyes for the quickest of seconds. The moment of truth.

It was truth.

For a second, Carrie had been forced to stop hiding from it. And she had hated Darci for it.

"Darci."

Jerking her head up, Darci stared into Brittany's eyes, her own dark and bruised-looking. "She was a horrid, pathetic woman who was getting old before her time," she whispered to her friend. "But she didn't deserve to die before her time."

Britt leaned forward, taking Darci's hand and wrapping her hands around Darci's cold ones. "Listen, honey, and listen good. Malcontent breeds malcontent. Though most people in this town believed Carrie's lies, and few knew the truth, she didn't deserve what happened to her. But unfortunately, the way Carrie liked to live—telling tales, breeding ill will—sooner or later, she was going to set off the wrong person," Brittany whispered. "What goes around does indeed come around. Sometimes, in spades."

Inexplicably, Darci's eyes filled with tears. Britt leaned forward and wrapped her arms around her, rocking her slightly. "Shhh...shhh, don't cry, Darci. She's cost you too many tears already."

Darci forced a deep, somewhat shaky breath into her lungs and then she nodded, pulling back, looking up, letting the tears dry before they fell. "No crying. None. Can we get this over with? I really want to get out of here," she said fervently.

* * * * *

Darci was walking down the two steps that led to the sidewalk when she heard Britt's indrawn breath. *"Don't say a damn thing to her,"* Brittany warned under her breath. "I mean it. Don't get drawn into something with her. Your alibi checks out, you couldn't have done it, we know you couldn't have done it. Don't let her—"

"They are letting you walk out of here?" Beth demanded. Her eyes were bright with anger, her mouth twisted and snarling.

"Beth." The deep voice came from over their heads and froze Darci in her tracks before she could say anything.

And she sure as hell was going to say something, even though Britt's fingers were digging into her arm, about to cut her circulation off.

"Why are you letting her walk out of here? She killed Carrie! Everybody knows it!" Beth spat. A tiny bit of spittle clung to the corner of her mouth and disgust curled in Darci's belly.

"She couldn't have killed Carrie. Not unless she's able to be in two places at once. She's got an alibi for a solid six hours," Kellan said as he came down the two steps, not looking at Darci. "I'm heading out to speak with said alibi and take his statement. But it's pretty much ironclad."

"She probably fucked him to get it," Beth snarled, reaching up and shoving at Darci's chest. "Hell, she's fucking everybody in town."

Darci batted her hand away and said, "Don't touch me again, Beth. I'll make allowances because you're angry and upset. And I'll make allowances because I know you're probably hurting over Carrie, but do it again, and I'll get mad."

She heard a muffled snort from Kellan and Britt snickered. Beth's eyes flamed. "Are you threatening me?" Beth gasped.

"You'd like that," Darci said. "Something else for you to give your lawyer to work on. I'm not saying another damn word to you."

Yep, he was trying not to laugh, she was sure of it, as the odd smothered cough came from Kellan again. Beth lifted her chin, trying to look arrogantly proud. "You think you're going to get away with it," she rasped. "It doesn't matter what alibi you've come up with. You killed Carrie. You're the only one who could have. You're the only one who hates her."

Darci lifted her chin. "Bullshit. Not everybody in this town is blind. She had some people fooled, but there are other people who know exactly what she was."

Then she moved around Beth and headed on down the sidewalk.

"How can you let her walk?" Beth demanded.

"Because she's got a damned good alibi. If it turns out she lied, I'll pick her up. But that's unlikely," Kellan said, moving around her. "Now let me do my job, Ms. Morris."

"You've been fooled by that pretty face," Beth snarled. "I'm not surprised. She's got everybody wrapped around her finger."

Kellan compressed his lips together and continued on down the sidewalk, following in Darci's footsteps.

"See? See? You go following after her, right in front of me," Beth shrieked.

"No. I'm going to talk to Clive. He was her alibi. She spent the evening at his café," Kellan said over his shoulder. "And I thought I'd follow this up with checking with damn near everybody in town, since three-fourths of the population seem to enjoy stopping by his shop for ice cream or coffee on a Friday night."

Kellan didn't see when Beth whispered, "Clive?" or the way her lips tightened afterward.

* * * * *

"Damn it," Beth mumbled.

"It had to have been her. It had to. Doesn't make any sense. Nobody else would have wanted to do it," she swore as she paced around and around her studio.

Her gray hair was messy, oily from many restless passes of her hands. She had never allowed herself to look so unpresentable, but she hadn't been prepared for the sudden knock on the door, and she had been too shaken by what had happened at the police station to go upstairs and try to make herself look as she felt she should.

Her house, damn it. Her house. If she wanted to look a mess in her own home, that was her right.

"It just doesn't make any sense. I don't rightly know why Clive would lie for her, but Darci is the only one who hated Carrie," Beth said, turning and staring at her visitor, her eyes bright and burning with passion.

"Well, I don't exactly see that as being true."

Beth's eyes widened as she saw the heavy glazed urn come crashing down, but she couldn't move in time.

* * * * *

"I guess I should thank him one more time," Darci said quietly, casting a look across the street at Clive's.

"Not now. The Sheriff is about fifteen feet behind us and he needs to get his statement from Clive. Let's let him get it. We can go across the street to the Ice Cream Shoppe. I want a cone—a double, I think—chocolate, with sprinkles. Then I want you to tell me about what happened yesterday when you went to see Carrie," Britt said, hooking her arm through Darci's and leading her across the narrow street.

So, over cold, creamy vanilla—chocolate for Britt—Darci told her. "She pushed me. Too far. But I wouldn't have done this," Darci murmured, her eyes taking on a far-off look. "I might have decked her. But this..." she sighed and shook her head. Then she took a thoughtful lick of her ice cream. "Beth seemed pretty convinced."

"Beth is a woman who is so full of hatred, it's easy for her to think that everybody around her hates as much as she does," Britt said with a shrug.

The bell chimed over the door and a woman with a group of kids came in. Two of them darted toward Darci and she smiled at them, stroking her hand over a towheaded boy, tugging on a red braid. Their mom came up, smiling hesitantly. "Hey, Darci. I heard about Ms. Forrest, glad to see you...well, you know."

Darci arched a brow. "Do I? Do I want to?"

The mom—what was her name…Janna, Janna Harton—leaned over and murmured quietly, "Beth Morris was going around telling everybody you did it. She hadn't even made it home before she was making calls and telling everybody."

Britt's eyes flared. "That's slander."

Darci's lips flattened out and she glanced at the kids. Shaking her head minutely, she told them with her eyes, *not now*. Then she brightly said, "I had the best night last night. Spent it over at Clive's. Went over there around five or so, and did nothing but eat biscotti and drink mochas and cappuccinos until he chased me out when he closed."

Janna's brows rose and she nodded in understanding. "He's got the best chocolate mochas," she murmured.

Her six-year-old twins, Macy and Alan, poked out their lips accordingly. "We can't have them," they wailed in unison.

Macy said, "Mama says we're hyper enough."

"We have to drink steamers," Alan chimed in, his eyes big and pitiful.

"If I remember correctly, hyper doesn't cover it. Maniacal, overactive, bouncing bundles of supercharged energy just might work," Darci said, smiling widely. "I can see why Mama said no mochas."

Macy rested her chin on the table and said, "Mama promised me ice cream, too."

Alan grinned. "Yours looks really good. Can I try a taste while Mama gets mine?"

Darci took another lick. "Hmmm. It is really good," she said. Then she winked at Alan. "Nope. No sharing."

Kellan had Clive's statement, as well as three other customers who had stopped in today for a cup of coffee. They had also been in the mood for some caffeine last night, and recalled seeing that pretty art teacher, as one had called her, perched in the window, just reading away.

"She's a talented thing—taking pictures and teaching kids," Clive had said. "I can't help myself. I keep buyin' stuff from her, even when I tell myself I've bought enough."

Clive had a number of framed photographs decorating his café, most of which Kellan had recognized as Darci's work the moment they had appeared.

He was halfway back to the station when he stopped, blew out a breath and scowled.

If he went over there, it just might save him from having to deal with her later. Head it off at the pass, so to speak.

But damn it.

He really didn't feel up to handling Beth yet.

He turned and headed down Court Street, going left onto Main, then right onto Primrose. Beth's house was a work of art, and she took great pride in that. She preened every time somebody asked to list it on the Christmas Home Tours, but she never let a soul she didn't know inside. And there were very few of those.

He knocked on the door, his eyes studying the woodwork and the molding that was probably over a century old.

While he waited, he studied the woodwork on the door, slapping his hand against his thigh. A minute passed and he knocked again, but still no answer.

He scowled, and glanced at the driveway. That damned pink car was in the driveway, so he knew she was home. Unlike more than half of the population living within the city limits, if Beth was going somewhere, even if it was two doors down, she drove. High gas prices be damned.

If it was in the driveway, she was home.

He turned the knob, and when it opened under his hand, a dread suspicion grew in his gut. He pulled the sidearm out, telling himself he was going to feel awfully stupid when he scared Beth Morris in the shower.

Stupid and scarred for life.

He was turning the corner into her kitchen when he smelled it. Rich, coppery death.

Yeah, scarred for life.

Every death left a scar. But violent death was worse.

And two within two days…in his town.

Something very wrong was going on.

Very wrong.

Beth lay on the floor, her head crushed in. The weapon was most likely the heavy glazed urn that was lying on the thick, pile carpet under his feet. Kneeling, he touched his fingers to her throat.

Her body was just now starting to cool.

Her murderer had gotten away no more than an hour ago.

"What in the holy hell is going on?" he murmured.

Then he stood and reached for the radio at his belt.

Chapter Three

Well, at least this victim didn't have such a good reason for Darci to want her dead. While Darci didn't like Beth, Beth hadn't made it her life's mission to make Darci's life hell.

Kellan worked through the interview gently, aware that Darci was more than a little shell-shocked.

Britt said quietly, "You know she didn't do it, Kellan," after Darci just sighed when Kellan went through the round of questions one more time. She rubbed soothing circles on Darci's back, feeling the tension mounting as Darci breathed in and out in harsh, shaking motions. "Her time is alibied, most of it with you."

Kellan gave Brittany a narrow look. That didn't matter. What mattered was that he had a murderer in his town, and he had to find the bastard.

But yeah, he knew she didn't do it.

Didn't change what he had to do, though. He sighed as he studied the river outside Darci's window. "It wouldn't be a bad idea for you to hang around tonight," he said to Brittany.

He was planning on driving by a few times himself.

Britt arched a brow and said, "Already taken care of, my friend. Why else would I be here this late?"

Darci mumbled from the circle of her arms, "Would you two stop talking as though I'm not here? And I don't need a babysitter."

The words sounded loud in the silence of the brightly lit kitchen. What was it about the midnight hour? When words were spoken at such a late time, it just made everything seem so much more vivid, so much louder.

By the time he had finished at the crime scene, it had been after eleven. After taking care of notifying the family and dealing with the paperwork, he had started home.

But then he'd turned, driving past Darci's house and he had seen lights blazing, and Britt's car. So he had stopped.

Maybe it had been more to unravel this knot of worry in his gut, though. Not police business. Technically, he should have done this interview at the station, not in her house. She had given him permission to do it, as well as record it—although he suspected she really wasn't too connected right now. She was in shock, plain and simple. The pupils of her eyes were dilated and she kept rocking back and forth, holding herself.

He had been scared, coming here, worried he might find something he wasn't ready to handle. He knew, deep in his gut, that these killings had something to do with Darci.

Somehow.

Once Darci had opened the door, and he had seen her weary, shell-shocked face, he had felt…better.

Still battered, still enraged, but better.

"Do you have any idea who would have done this?" he finally asked, pulling his glasses off and tucking them inside his jacket.

Darci looked up at him, resting her cheek on her arm. "I don't understand hatred, Sheriff. You're probably asking the wrong person. Whoever did this had a lot of hatred. I think we kind of discussed that about Carrie. This takes more hatred than I'd give anybody." She lifted a shoulder in a weak shrug. "I'm lazy. I don't want to give anybody that kind of energy. I get angry fast, I've got a short fuse, but it burns itself out pretty quickly. Just don't like to waste my time with it for too long. I just don't understand hatred. It's too…violent. Too dark."

"You don't strike me as being somebody who'd be afraid of violence," Kellan said, quirking a brow as he lifted a cup and sipped at his steaming coffee. He was remembering how she'd batted Beth's hand away, that angry threat in her eyes, in her voice.

"Just because I'll use force to defend myself doesn't mean I like violence," Darci said, resting her chin on her hands, staring straight ahead. "And understanding hatred and not being afraid of violence are too different things."

"Point taken," he said, inclining his head. "So you've never hated anybody? An old boyfriend? Ex-husband? The cheerleader in school who stole everybody's guy?"

A tiny smile tugged at her lips. "No. I don't think I've ever expended the energy to hate. I might hold grudges, and I hold them well. But old boyfriends weren't worth the time, otherwise, they'd not be old boyfriends. They'd still be in the present. And there are no ex-husbands. As to the cheerleaders, well, I was one, but I didn't need to steal boyfriends."

He grinned. "I bet they probably flocked to your door," he said, a grin cocking up the corners of his mouth.

She shook her head. "No. I was the tomboy cheerleader. Boys weren't worth my time back then," she said. "So there was no reason to hate the cheerleaders who did steal the boys."

"Okay. So you don't have a clue who might have done this," Kellan said, blowing out a sigh. "Maybe there's a lady who believes some of the rumors that she's heard about you. Thinks you might have been sleeping with a man she's involved with."

"So she kills two women just to try to get me in trouble? It would make more sense if she just came after me."

"Murderers don't always understand logic," Kellan said, shrugging. "I'm just trying to understand why I have two women dead — and one of them is somebody who has a history of causing you a lot of grief."

Darci shot Britt a look. Britt shrugged, her lips pursed.

Spreading her hands wide, Darci said, "I just don't know... I just don't know," she repeated, closing her eyes and burying her face in her hands.

She was so tired.

Achingly tired.

But she couldn't sleep.

Rolling onto her side, she stared through the floor to ceiling windows just inches away from her bed. The river was no more than a hundred yards away—usually watching it roll by made her feel a little more peaceful than she felt now.

There was no peace inside her tonight.

What was going on?

Darci closed her burning eyes.

There were no answers in the river. No answers inside her throbbing head either.

Two women dead.

And her last words spoken to both of them had been in anger.

It was with a heavy heart that she finally fell asleep, hours later.

* * * * *

Restlessness plagued the small town of Vevey, Indiana over the following weeks.

Carrie was laid to rest, and then Beth, two days later. Carrie's house was sitting empty, but already people from the State Registry were in town making noises about trying to get Beth's house.

Darci couldn't quite believe it. The lady hadn't even been resting a week when the first call came, from what she could tell.

Now they had people in town, all but ambushing anybody who so much as walked by. But Kellan had finally put a stop to it when he strode up to the small group of people who had practically camped in front of it. Britt had gone into great detail about it, her eyes sparkling with laughter.

"Well, sir, you see, we're from the Historical Society and this house is of great interest to us—"

Kellan had cut off the pompous, florid-faced geek of a man who'd spoken with a thick Southern drawl. Darci had dealt with that man when he had come into the gallery and she had wondered if maybe some people took historical reenactments just a little too much to heart.

From what Britt had repeated, Kellan had interrupted him by saying, "It's of more importance to me. A lady was murdered there and until I've decided I'm done with it, nobody can do a thing with it anyway. Now stop badgering everybody who lives here before I get annoyed. Do any of you have homes? Jobs? You've been here nearly two weeks, almost around the clock and the house isn't even for sale."

"Now see here—"

Kellan had lifted a straight auburn brow, and Britt's imitation of him had Darci giggling. Britt said, "The guy shut the hell up. They cleared off the street although they passed out their cards and some of them offered money to the neighbors to contact them if so much as a For Sale sign went up."

Darci scowled. "Hell, I'm tempted to buy the house to keep those idiots from getting it," she said. "He came into the gallery. I don't think I've ever met a bigger idiot in my life."

"Well, I have," Britt murmured, her eyes rolling. "He's on his way in here." She ducked behind the counter and slid into the back room as the door opened. Bryce Bishop came in, his dark eyes roaming over Darci's face as he handed over a handful of mail.

"This came to Dark Destinies instead of here," Bryce said, dumping the pile on the counter, missing Darci's outstretched hand like he hadn't even seen it. "You all getting back in the swing of things?"

Darci lifted a brow. "We never got out." Raising her voice, she called out, "Becka!"

Bryce looked toward the beaded curtain that hung over the door to the private part of the gallery, a small smirk on his mouth. "Oh, yeah. Guess y'all didn't see much point taking time off to mourn some old friends."

Darci coolly said, "If they had been friends, that would have been different. Lives violently lost will always be mourned. But prostrating myself on the sidewalk doesn't change anything."

One of the more vocal ladies who had art displayed at Dark Destinies had done just that—dropped to the ground wailing, tears running down her face as she screamed and lamented as Carrie's casket was carried out. Her miniskirt had revealed her lace thong to everybody around.

And she'd repeated the performance the next day.

Bryce snickered. "No. That's true. Although I wouldn't mind seeing you flash some skin," he said, his eyes dropping and lingering on her neckline.

Becka came through the curtain, followed by Brittney, and when she saw Bryce, her mouth twisted down in a frown. Ignoring him, she looked at Darci, impatience in her eyes. "What?"

Darci reached for the pile of mail and held it out to Becka. "You really do need to make that call to the post office. Destinies received some of our mail again."

Becka rolled her eyes and said, "All right...all right. I'll go call them now." Without even speaking to Bryce, she turned around and moved back through the curtain.

"Well, isn't she in a good mood," Bryce smirked.

Flashing him a brittle smile, Darci said, "Hmm. Thanks for the mail. You can go now." Dismissing him, she looked back at Brittney and said, "So has there been anything new?"

Britt made a noncommittal response, not wanting to talk in front of Bryce, Darci guessed.

The silence stretched out for a moment while Bryce's eyes lingered on her. Then he murmured, "Be seeing you around, sweet thing."

As the door closed behind him, she whispered, "I certainly hope not."

"That guy is such a jerk," Britt muttered as she came around the corner. "How many times has that place gotten your mail?"

"Three that I know." Lifting her shoulder in a shrug, she said, "Probably nothing to it."

"Complained?"

"Becka has to," Darci said. "I tried. They took the information down, but since I'm not the owner, they aren't going to take me too seriously. Becka needs to talk to them, and I've reminded her. A number of times. Today was probably the tenth. Dunno if she's listening to me."

"Hmmm…" Britt said, that noncommittal sound that could say everything and nothing. Then she waggled her eyebrows at Darci, her voice teasing as she said, "Soooo…are you aware of the fact that the Sheriff can't keep his eyes off of you?"

Darci's hands stilled and she froze. Studying Britt through the veil of her lashes, she asked, "What?"

Britt smiled a cool little cat's smile. "He's got the hots for you. I can tell. And you watch him like he's a hot fudge sundae and you've been on a six-month carb diet." Fluttering her lashes, Britt said, "Too bad you're a suspect."

"You bitch," Darci said, groaning and falling back against the wall behind her. That was *so* not what she needed to hear—not when she had been fantasizing about the sexy sheriff for years, ever since she'd moved to Vevey.

Britt laughed. "Well, it's not like it's a forever thing. And if it was such a serious thing, you could have done something about it before now. And maybe you're not really a suspect. Maybe he's already found the person," she offered, trying to be helpful. "Maybe he's arresting him even now. Then you two can celebrate with dinner and an all-night fuck fest."

With a narrow glance, Darci muttered, "You are messed up."

With a snicker, Britt said, "Well, maybe you should go see a movie first."

They both jumped when Becka hollered out from the back, "Forget the movie. Just get laid."

Britt and Darci looked at each other and started to giggle.

Bryce Bishop had his eyes on that little bitch. Staring down her nose at people, twitching that tight little ass of hers and then expecting people not to comment. Hell, she was sharing it with half the men in town—he'd be damned if he was going to miss out.

He sauntered into his house and came up short when he caught sight of a familiar head bent over the newspaper spread out on his table. The house had been picked up, too. And unless he was mistaken, there were cookies in the oven.

"What in the hell are you doing?" he snapped, kicking his shoes off and tossing his wallet down.

"Just wanted to see you."

"Yeah, well, have you forgotten? I kicked your ass out a long time ago," he reminded her.

Her eyes filled with tears and she sighed, shakily saying, "Okay, I'll go."

She was on her way out when he caught her hand. "Hey, why don't you hang around a few minutes?" he asked, as he reached for the zipper of his fly, pushing down on her shoulder and smiling as her mouth closed around him.

He started to pump his cock in and out of her mouth, shuddering as her fingers cupped his sac. "You always did know how to suck cock, sweet little bitch," he muttered. "I've missed that."

She wasn't there in bed wrapped around him like a lamprey when he got up late that night. That was pretty odd. She usually clung, hanging on him like a little puppy. Hell, even her eyes were puppy-dog eyes, watching him soulfully.

He sat up in bed and reached for the pint in the bedside table, swigging down a few drinks, waiting until he felt the familiar buzz before he took a few more. Once he was in that warm, pleasant haze, he sighed, took another sip and sat up.

The room danced dizzily around him and he grinned. Should have gotten drunk before he fucked her earlier. Would have helped a little.

Climbing out of bed, Bryce scratched his chest as he left his room. Bright light flashed in his eyes and he flung his arm up, squinting through the glare to see her standing by the front door, wearing his shirt, staring at him. Whiskey splashed on his arm and chest from the bottle he had thoughtlessly tipped sideways as he blocked the light.

"You called me Darci," she said, her voice husky.

Bryce scowled. "So what? It's not like I'm taking you back," he muttered, raking his hand through his tumbled hair. "You're a good fuck, but you're too damned clingy."

She swallowed, a sound so loud he heard it from several feet away. "Well, I'm sorry I'm so clingy," she whispered. "I've gotten a lot better. But I guess it isn't good enough."

He flopped onto the couch, lifted the remote, and stared at the tube as he took a swig from the bottle. Tuning her out, he settled on the porno channel, his hand closing over his semi-rigid cock. Behind him, he heard her moving around and he just wanted her out of there. Maybe he'd dig out a few of the pills he'd hidden away and...

"Bryce," she whispered as she leaned over him.

"Wha—" Something cold, icy...then a hot liquid spill. He saw red fountaining out from him... What was...

Behind him, she watched as Bryce's head slumped, blood pumping from him with thick, liquid gushes of crimson red. His hands lifted, trying to close over the gash in his throat. She laid the knife down on the table behind the sofa before she walked away. In the bedroom, she knelt down and reached for the case under the bed. Pulling it out, she studied the labeled tapes closely. She'd watched them, unwillingly, a hundred times. She took the two that were stacked haphazardly on the top. One she needed. The other, she hadn't seen before. Better make sure he hadn't been running the video camera some night when she hadn't realized it.

Then she carefully wiped the box clean and pushed it back under the bed, grabbing her purse and tucking the tapes inside it before returning to the living room. She eyed the knife for a long moment before she picked it up, staring over the edge of the couch at Bryce's still body.

"Later...bitch," she whispered as she wiped her fingerprints off the knife before tossing it down. She'd already wiped the room down and with quick, economical motions, she shed his shirt and got dressed. Dropping the shirt by the door before she slid through, she tucked her head low as she headed down the alley behind his house.

Chapter Four

ဢ

Darci's heart stopped.

Somebody was outside her house. She had lifted her lashes, just barely, and stared at the window, trying to wake up.

It was unnaturally silent outside and her mouth went dry with fear.

The moon shone silver, reflecting off something white — something that didn't belong there.

A face.

But before Darci could take a closer look, the person was gone.

She jerked upright in bed, her heart slamming in her chest, breath rushing out of her shakily. "Damn it…"

The house was quiet — too quiet. Darci couldn't tolerate that sort of silence. Slowly, she swung her legs around and put her feet on the cool wooden floor. The chill in the air raced up her back, tightening her nipples, her skin roughened with goose bumps. Her heart slammed against her chest as she walked across her darkened room and reached for the light switch. Nothing.

Her breath started to wheeze in her chest as she rushed out to the hall and tried the light switch there. Nothing. With her back pressed flat against the wall, she walked along it back into her room, closing the door silently behind her. Licking her lips, she reached for the phone by her bedside, suppressing a sob as it came up dead.

Nothing. Damn caller ID — why in the hell had she ever replaced her regular land line with a portable? Because she liked knowing who was on the other line, liked being able to carry the phone with her to the basement as she developed her negatives.

My cameras —

Get a grip, there's probably somebody in the house. Call the damned police, her common sense demanded before she could fly out of the room to run and check on her equipment.

Okay. Cell phone. Where is the damned cell phone...purse! The purse was lying on the chaise lounge under the window where she had thrown it as she slid out of her shoes. With shaking fingers, she turned it on, and then she stifled a cry as she couldn't remember the number she wanted to call. Swallowing, she pushed the buttons 9-1-1 and hit send, sinking down into a darkened corner and waiting, staring at the door with unblinking eyes.

As the call came through, Kellan was just waking up from a sweet, hot dream...and the call was like a splash of icy water, clearing his head and tightening his gut with fear.

Rolling out of bed, he grabbed his jeans and shoved them on, stepping into an untied pair of work boots on his way out of his room. The T-shirt he had tossed aside the night before was still hanging on the doorknob to the laundry room and he grabbed it with one hand as his other hand scooped up his weapon, which he had left hanging on the back of the barstool at the breakfast bar.

Under his breath, prayers he didn't even realize he still remembered were being spoken. *Damn it. Not her. Don't let me find her...*

As he sped down the highway toward her house on the river, he cut off that train of thought. In his rearview mirror, a pair of headlights appeared, and sirens flashed on top of the patrol car. He heard their distant wail. One of his deputies. God, please let somebody already be there...don't let her —

Snarling, Kellan slammed his fist on the leather seat, rasping out, "Stop it!"

The sirens behind him went silent just as they turned onto her road. He slammed on his brakes in front of her house and jumped out, running up to the house as he drew his gun, swearing and praying from one breath to another. The front door was unlocked. Gritting his teeth, he pushed it open, some subtle tension inside him relaxing as he breathed in the soft, vanilla-scented air, like potpourri—or candles.

And paint?

But there was a distinct smell that simply wasn't there...
Thank You, God.

"This is Sheriff Kellan Grant..."

Darci heard his voice and sobbed in relief, rising from the floor and stumbling out into the hallway. She swallowed a scream as she came against a hard, hot body. Big hands came up to cup her arms as she slammed her foot down on his, hearing a muffled grunt, followed by...

"Damn it, Darci, why in the hell do you need the police? You're dangerous."

"Kellan!"

"Is there anybody still here?" he asked, moving up against the wall and pulling her with him.

"The lights are out," she whispered, stuttering, her body starting to tremble. "I woke up...saw somebody..."

"Okay...okay. Take a deep breath. Calm down, listen to me. We have to check out the house. I want you to go back in your room and stay there," he said, his voice changing to a firm, no-nonsense tone as he guided her back into her room. The broad band of light from his flashlight moved over the room and he checked the entire area out before he urged her down on a chair, snagging the blanket from her bed and wrapping it around her shoulders. "Stay here, sweetie. Okay?"

And then he was gone. She muffled the sob that rose in her throat as the door clicked shut, then the doorknob shifted a little as he checked the lock.

She couldn't take her eyes off that door. The brass glinted ever so slightly in the dim light of the room and she stared at it, fascinated.

If it moved...was the person still here? What if he killed Kellan? What if he was waiting...a frustrated, frightened sound escaped and she pressed her hands to her eyes. "Damn it, stop! He's a fucking cop, he knows what he is doing."

But an odd little whisper in her head kept repeating, *So does the killer...*

Darci jumped as the lights flashed back on. A few minutes later, outside her door, Kellan said, "Darci, it's me." She watched as the doorknob started to turn. "Unlock the door."

Swallowing, she forced herself to stand up and walk over to the door. Her hands shook uncontrollably as she turned the little latch, unlocking it and stepping back from the door.

As he came inside, she rubbed her arms, violently cold.

"Somebody tripped the power in the garage, and came in through the front door," he said, lowering himself to sit on her bed, his eyes watchful. "No signs of forced entry. But we can see signs that somebody stood outside your window, where you said you saw someone as you woke up. A few other things... And the perp left a note."

Darci read the script through the clear plastic he had tucked the note inside. Her heart tripped as the words started to make sense.

Don't worry, Darci.

I'm not coming after you — even though he gave me a good reason to kill you tonight.

"You have any idea what that means? Who *he* is?" Kellan asked, once she had dragged her eyes away from the note and looked back at him.

"No," she whispered, her throat tightening, vising down until swallowing was nearly impossible. She stared at the note again, until her eyes ached from the strain.

"Kellan," she murmured, her heart slamming painfully against her ribs. "What is going on?"

Tears started to burn their way down her face and she lifted a hand to wipe them away. "Damn it, look at me, I'm shaking so badly," she muttered, dashing the tears away. "Crying…and *nothing even happened.*"

"That's bullshit," Kellan said, reaching out and taking her hand, rubbing it between his hands. "You could have been hurt tonight. Worse. We've got a maniac on our hands, and most likely he was the one in your house."

"She…" Darci murmured, remembering the writing.

"What?"

She jumped, startled at how close his voice sounded. Turning her head, she looked into his eyes, only inches away from her face. Sweet heaven, those eyes… Licking her lips, she concentrated and said, "She. The handwriting looks kind of feminine to me. Although I've seen men who do write prettier than women. And vice versa. But it's not just the handwriting. It's the note itself. A man isn't very likely to want to kill a woman because of something another man did."

"Unless he thinks you've been doing something with that man that you shouldn't," Kellan said, but a brow rose and he smiled in approval. "So…you sure there aren't any jealous boyfriends?"

Her heart slammed against her chest as his eyes dropped to her mouth. Running her tongue over her lips, she whispered, huskily, "No. No boyfriends."

He muttered something under his breath and then he reached out, cupping his hand over the back of her neck and drawing her close. Darci went, hypnotized by the look in his eyes. His head started to lower and she could feel his breath on her lips as he whispered, "I can't believe I'm doing this."

As his mouth slanted across hers, Darci gasped, reaching up and curving her fingers into his neck, feeling her nipples tighten as he pushed his tongue deep inside her mouth, one hand coming up to cradle her face.

A moan caught in her throat.

Seconds later, he had pulled away, his eyes dark, turbulent. "I shouldn't have done that," he murmured, reaching up and rubbing his thumb across her full, damp lower lip.

"I kinda wish you'd done that long before now," she said quietly, leaning down and pressing her lips to his, this time sliding her tongue into his mouth, seeking out that sharp, unique taste of man. She closed her eyes in appreciation as she slid off the lounge to kneel in front of him.

One heavily muscled forearm wrapped around her waist, bringing her flush against his body. Her breasts flattened against his chest, her nipples drawn into tight, hard little buds that seemed to ache and throb for his touch. Wrapping her arms around his neck, she dipped her fingers into his hair, delighted to find it hanging loose and free, nearly to his shoulders. Thick, silky, it twined around her fingers, just like she had thought it would.

He tipped her face up, slowly drawing back and moving his lips along the line of her jaw, her ear, and her neck. "Damn it, you smell so good," he whispered gruffly, and his low, heated voice sent shivers down her spine. "Taste so sweet... I've driven myself crazy wondering."

Against her belly, she felt the long, rigid length of his cock and she whimpered as one big hand cupped her butt, holding her still as he pumped his hips against her, his cock cuddling into the softness of her abdomen. "Maybe you shouldn't have just wondered," she teased, pulling her head back slightly, staring into his eyes.

He chuckled. "Darci, babe, you're a bit more than I know how to handle," he mused, staring into her eyes.

Footsteps sounded out in the hall and her body cried out in disappointment as he pulled away, easily lifting her to the lounge before he settled back on the bed, linking his hands between his knees, staring at her with brooding, unreadable eyes. The door opened just as he lifted the note from the floor, studying it through the plastic cover. "A woman," he said quietly, his eyes thoughtful.

Darci pulled a robe on over the thin, white chemise before following them out into her home. "You sleep pretty soundly, Darci," Kellan murmured, sighing as he studied the walls and the ugly red paint that smeared them.

"The paint is still tacky. She must have done it right before she went outside. I wonder what she was doing," Kellan muttered, reaching up to run his fingers through his hair. It floated loosely through his fingers and he absently told himself he needed to get it cut.

"Maybe she wanted to scare me," Darci said softly.

Her eyes were locked on the wall, at the stain of red that smeared it. No words…just an erratic line, right down the middle, and palm prints pressed to each of the matted photos that adorned the wall.

"Well, that's a given," Kellan sighed. "You find out somebody opened a door you're certain you locked, and slid inside your house…you're going to be scared."

"I'm starting to get pissed as well," she said, lifting her shoulders restlessly, a muscle ticing in her jaw as she stared at the ruined pictures.

Kellan suspected he knew what was going through her mind. Certainly, she could throw the frames away, get new ones—the glass over the photos had protected the pictures she had shot. But he knew, even if she did that, they were ruined for her.

As if in echo to his thoughts, she quietly said, "Some of these are the first photos I ever took. More than fifteen years of my life invested in them. And now they are ruined. I can't ever look at them again without seeing those bloody handprints."

"I'm sorry, Darci," he said quietly, dipping his hands into his pockets to keep from reaching out to her.

A dry laugh escaped her. "Yeah. Me, too. But maybe not for all of it," she replied.

And the look she sent him from under her lashes had his blood pounding heavy and hot through his veins.

No fingerprints.

None. The handprints on the glass and the walls were smooth, like a mannequin. They discovered why later as a deputy searching the grounds had found a pair of vinyl gloves lying beside the mailbox, stained red with paint.

"Who in the hell are you?"

"Sheriff?" one of the deputies asked from behind him.

As he tossed the bag containing the vinyl gloves onto his desk, he muttered, "Nothing. I'm just talking to myself."

Grady finished reading the report and asked, "Think it's the same person?"

"Almost has to be. This town is too damned small. You don't go all this time with hardly any crimes and then suddenly have two nutcases show up at once," he said, rubbing his eyes. He hadn't slept, not even for twenty minutes, since the night before...when he had kissed her.

And then she had kissed him.

The echo of her taste still lingered in his mouth. She had been so sweet, so hot...the scent of her arousal had flooded the air and he had wished he had more time...time to push her back onto the ground and find the source of that hot, musky scent, ripe and female.

Nearly thirty-six hours had passed.

And he still couldn't forget the feel of her satin skin under his hands.

"What in the hell are we going to do?" Grady asked, sighing and leaning back in his chair. "We don't have the men to watch her full time. And this all has something to do with her. Doesn't it?"

"'Fraid so," Kellan replied, turning to stare out the window. The small sheriff's office had more traffic in it than it usually saw on a weekend. Late Sunday, yet the small parking lot was full. Those who weren't there because he had called were there because they wanted to know what in the hell was going on.

Even the police got curious.

He'd love to be able to tell them something. Anything.

Anything more than, *No, we don't know what's up…*

He was getting pissed.

* * * * *

Kim stared at Tricia Casey with tired eyes. "Bryce will be in sooner or later—you know how he is. Why—"

"We need him here *now*," Tricia said icily. "I've lost two of my best artists. I've got business to do. I do not have time to stand around the gallery. That is why I hired you two and I'm tired of him not doing his job." Her eyes narrowed shrewdly and she added, "You make an art of avoiding him—why is that?"

Why don't you go and find him? Kim thought nastily. But she didn't dare say that aloud. Not to Tricia.

Kim really didn't want to go looking for Bryce. His golden boy blond looks, the way he stared at her, it all made her feel tight and itchy. But Tricia wasn't going to go looking for him.

And the only person left was Peggy. Not likely *she'd* do anything. Even though she was part owner of the gallery, she never did anything beyond work in the small studio in the back. Kim wondered if she even knew who Bryce was.

Kim trudged down the steps, turning to the right. She could always drive over there—it was nearly a half mile to his apartment, but she had no desire to hurry back to the gallery.

Resentment brewed in her belly as she remembered the look in Tricia's eyes. She knew. That knowing, disdainful look... Kim wanted nothing so much as to knock that look off her boss's face. Like *that* was really going to happen.

She had to keep getting her paychecks, didn't she? Carrie was no longer there to run interference. For the longest time, Carrie had made sure Kim would be around because she liked having a lackey. But Tricia couldn't care less about Kim. And there was no reason to worry about keeping Carrie happy now.

Turning right on Main Street, she jogged across the intersection before the light could turn green, muttering under her breath.

Kim do this...Kim do that...

Cutting across Preservation Park, she hit Lyle Street, scowling as she saw Bryce's black truck parked in front of his apartment. *Jerk.* He was home, likely hung over or stoned. Just ignoring the phone.

As she plodded up the stairs to the small apartment he rented from Letty Miller, she mumbled under her breath. "One of these days, I'm going to get extremely tired of doing everything I'm told," she groused, banging on the door.

She realized he wasn't going to answer. It was too quiet in there. Even when he was hung over, he didn't sleep that soundly. He should have already yanked the door open.

Kim was even braced for him to yell at her. But there wasn't a sound in the apartment.

Pulling up the doormat, Kim grabbed the key and unlocked the door.

The smell struck her like a fist.

Kellan settled down across the table from Kim, studying her pale face. "He's been dead a couple of days," he said quietly. "It will be a few days before I know for certain. But there's nothing you could have done."

She nodded jerkily. "That smell…" Lifting her eyes, she said softly, "I still feel sick."

"Were you and Bryce friends?" he asked gently, steering her mind away from that. He'd found her kneeling in the grass after Letty heard her stumble down the stairs and the old woman had gone to investigate.

Now, Letty was fine, her bright eyes snapping almost joyfully. Oh, she'd be infamous now, he knew. She'd had somebody murdered in her apartment. Nothing like that to get people to talking.

People were weird. Some of them had a morbid fascination with death. Letty was one of them. She followed every murder story that happened in the local area, from Louisville, to Madison, to Indianapolis and back. She knew more about local murders than a news reporter could ever hope to dig up.

And now one had happened on her property.

Kellan imagined it would affect her differently if it had been somebody she liked. And she *had* taken the time to bring Kim a cold rag and a glass of lemon-lime soda to wash the taste of vomit from her mouth, patting her back kindly before she led Kellan to the apartment.

Letty wasn't a bad person, just…unique.

Kim's hesitant words snapped Kellan back to attention, listening as she slowly said, "No. We weren't really friends. I knew him, but he didn't like me." She gave a humorless laugh. "I honestly don't think he liked women at all, if you want the truth."

"You mean, you think he was gay?" Kellan hazarded, a little confused by her words.

"Oh, no. I don't think he is gay. He loves...ah, using? Maybe that's the word. He loves to talk about all the women he's slept with, and he can be pretty demeaning toward them. Never around Peggy or Tricia—or anybody else who might try to make him eat his words. Tricia would cut him down without blinking...and Peggy could fire him," Kim said. Then she gave a watery laugh. "I'm still talking about him as though he's alive. *Damn it.*"

Kellan gave her a minute, watched as her hands closed into tight fists and she took a deep breath. Once she had settled, he asked, "You mean an authority figure? Both Peggy and Tricia were his bosses." Kellan scratched his head. He had known Bryce Bishop, distantly. And the guy was definitely down on the female race, a chauvinistic pig if ever he'd met one.

"Maybe," Kim said, tucking a lock of hair behind her ear. "He likes—I mean, he liked—to push around the women he knew he could push around. But he never seemed to try it with those he couldn't intimidate."

"Was he seeing anybody that you know of?"

Kim chuckled. "Sheriff Grant, you seem to think he actually thought me worthy of confiding that sort of thing," she said, forcing a tremulous smile. "I wasn't anything to him. I know how he acted around women just because I saw him at work all the time. But he wouldn't talk to me about his life. Wouldn't talk to me about anything."

Sighing, Kellan pressed his fingers to his brow. This wasn't adding up. Darci's break-in, this latest murder... *Even though he gave me reason to kill you last night...*

Through his lashes, he studied Kim's face. "Where were you, Kim, on Friday night?" he asked softly.

She blinked. "Friday night?" Shrugging, she said quietly, "Same place I usually am on Friday nights—home alone." He heard the bitter acceptance in her voice and stifled a wave of sympathy for the girl.

Running his tongue across the inside of his teeth, he ran the idea through his head. "What are your thoughts on Darci Law?"

Now she cocked her head, staring at him with a line of puzzlement between her brows. "Darci? We're not exactly friends..." her voice trailed away and she shrugged. "She doesn't much care for the people I work for. And Darci has a funny set of rules. She won't talk to people she doesn't trust. And since I work for people she doesn't trust, well, that means she can't trust me."

"Rather astute observation," he drawled.

Kim flushed red, her eyes turning sad. "Not an observation," she mumbled. Licking her lips, she looked down at the table, scratching at the surface with a nonexistent nail. "Darci told me that. Every once in a while, when I worked at Becka's place, we'd go out for lunch. I tried to get her to go grab a bite with me, once, after I started working for Peggy and Tricia. That's when she told me that."

"How did you feel about that?" he asked. Was there something here?

"Kind of down," she admitted. "Darci is...well, she's Darci." She flashed Kellan a smile, her nose wrinkling. "You know her. She's..."

"She's Darci," Kellan finished, chuckling, nodding. "Yeah, I know her. She's Darci, all right."

Kim nodded, rubbing at a small nick in the table. "I was pretty hurt at first. But I wasn't really surprised. Darci's got a way of looking at things—black and white." She swallowed, and when she spoke, her voice was softer, a near whisper. "Beth and Carrie did some kind of underhanded things to Becka."

"If it was underhanded, why did you go with them?"

"Carrie. She...she went. Carrie is how I got my job with Becka in the first place. When she told me, I guess I felt I had to," Kim whispered.

"Did you have any reason to be mad at Carrie? Or Beth?"

Kim sighed. "I don't know. Carrie wasn't the nicest of people, I know that. But she got me my job, helped me get the apartment after I got divorced," she said, frowning. "But she could be kind of mean."

Hell…Kim wasn't stupid, Kellan thought, leaning back and sighing. If she had killed any of these people, she would be protecting herself. Not leaving herself wide open like this.

"I'd like to do a formal interview, Kim. Just procedure," he said, studying what few notes he had made in his notepad. "Is that okay with you?"

She shrugged. "Whatever you think is best, Sheriff," she said quietly.

* * * * *

Damn.

Helluva lot of blood, Kellan thought, surveying the blood pattern. It had sprayed from Bryce's neck in a geyser before the man had reached up, trying to staunch the blood flow. No defensive wounds…didn't see it coming?

He'd died pretty quickly.

An empty whiskey bottle lay on the floor, splattered with dried blood. How much had he drunk before she cut him?

He paced into the bedroom, and studied the rumpled blankets. The air was stale. Couldn't recognize any particular scent beyond that of death. Using his pen, he tried to edge back the sheets a little. Stains…maybe recent. The coroner would be able to tell him if Bryce had had sexual intercourse before he died.

Was this the he who had been referred to in the note?

Maybe.

Bryce had liked to watch Darci. Kellan knew that because *he* liked to watch Darci and tended to notice when other guys were doing the same. But Darci wouldn't go for Bryce, Kellan suspected. Not her type. She'd cut him to shreds with her tongue, especially knowing Bryce's penchant for chauvinistic remarks.

This might be the he, he thought, nodding slowly. Made sense. Darci was something Bryce had wanted. Would make a woman jealous. But why hadn't the woman killed Darci?

And if it was the same killer...why kill Beth? Carrie?

Those were people who had caused Darci problems. Killing them, then Bryce, just didn't make any sense. Bryce hadn't really caused Darci problems. He wasn't worth her time, Kellan suspected.

So why had he been worth the killer's?

"This doesn't make any sense," he muttered, shaking his head.

The formal interview with Kim hadn't yielded anything.

Kim was a lonely, fairly simple woman without a lot of friends. No, she didn't know if Bryce was seriously seeing anybody. Yes, she knew a lot of people who could be mad at Bryce, but Bryce had been pretty much a bastard. He'd pissed off almost everybody he met at some point in time. Yes, she was at home Friday night, all night, alone. No, she didn't have a boyfriend.

Kim didn't have the spine to do any of this. Wouldn't have the spine to sneak into Darci's home, try to scare her...hell, Kellan doubted she had the brain.

Or the fire. Although the murders had been quick, there was something...heated about them. Kellan couldn't get past the thought that whoever had done this had some deep hatred inside of her.

Kim didn't seem to have that kind of passion.

Somebody with heat inside them...he ticked through the people in his head whom he knew were acquainted with all the victims. Well, Darci had heat, but he knew she hadn't done it.

The murders had left her sick.

Plus, he also believed what she had said... *I'm too lazy...hatred requires energy.*

Yes, it did. A lot of energy.

Tricia? Hell, that woman was an icicle. She didn't have heat inside of *her*. Hatred was heat.

Maybe Peggy...but he dismissed that idea before it even formed. She was a listless, lifeless being, the only heat he'd ever seen from her was in the paintings and sketches she sold.

Della.

He couldn't think of a reason for her to kill Bryce, but maybe if he looked... There was certainly reason for Della to be angry with Carrie, *if* Della had finally figured out how badly Carrie was using her, how Carrie had lied. Somebody unbalanced would have a hard time dealing with anger in a logical manner.

Was Della the type to fly over the edge with her rage?

Possibly. She had certainly lit into Darci, from what he had heard, when she thought Darci was screwing Max. And he'd seen signs of her temper, knew she could sometimes react...irrationally.

Maybe it was time to talk to Della a little bit.

Chapter Five

ഌ

"Where was I?" she repeated, staring at him with flat, dark eyes. Della Bennett ran a hand through her dark, curly hair and lifted a cigarette to her mouth, puffing twice before blowing out a stream of smoke through her nostrils. "Here. In bed, with Max," she said, shrugging. "Why, you think I killed Bryce? That worm?"

"I didn't say anything of the sort, Della," Kellan said, tapping his pen against his thigh.

"Mmm. Maybe not, but you're trying to pin down my whereabouts for the night he was killed. Can't think of any other reason why you might be asking," she drawled. "Max is at work, but you're welcome to check with him."

"Oh, I will," Kellan said.

She shrugged. Couldn't care less...he read the body language, the look in her eyes, and even though he finished running through his questions, he added everything up to one simple fact. She couldn't care less about Bryce.

She wasn't his killer.

His killer had cared, maybe obsessively so.

"What about the day Carrie died?" he asked.

Her lips curled up in a wry smile. "Max can tell you about that, too. I was busy ripping him a new asshole for daring to mess with another woman," she said, tapping her cigarette against the ashtray. "He told me I was crazy and he didn't know what in the hell I was talking about." An odd look passed through her eyes and she added softly, "He was telling the truth. I didn't admit that to myself until just a few days ago. He wasn't messing around on me, not with Darci, not with anybody."

"So you know Carrie was lying? Mad about that?"

"Of course, she wasn't lying." Della frowned at him. "Hell, I don't know who started the rumor. Carrie was just telling me what she thought was going on. I don't know where she came up with the story. Can't ask her, either," she said sadly.

"You don't think Carrie made it up, to cause trouble with you and Darci?"

"Hell, what's the point in that?" Della asked.

Kellan shrugged. "Darci admired you. A lot. Liked you," he said, watching as she flinched at his words. Losing that seemed to bother her some. "That's changed now. Hurt you a little...but I think you hurt Darci a lot. And that's what Carrie was after."

"Why in the hell would Carrie want that? She likes...liked Darci. Damn it, it's still too hard to believe," she muttered, rubbing her temple. "But she liked her. She'd tell anybody that. Even if Darci did run her mouth a lot."

Kellan laughed. "Della, I never thought you were naïve enough to believe everything somebody tells you. Now...I know people pretty well," he said, tossing his pen on the table. "And I can assure you, Carrie didn't have fond feelings for Darci. She hid it well, but she did not like Darci. At all."

With a brittle laugh, Della demanded, "How in the hell do you know?"

He shrugged. "Same way I know Carrie didn't like you either. You two women are things Carrie wasn't...vibrant, passionate women. Everywhere you two go, people like you. People want to be like you. People flock to you," Kellan said. "In order for Carrie to get people to like her, she had to lie, make them think she was something other than what she was. She was a tired, bitter old woman."

Her hands started to shake. Minutely shaking her head, drawing on her cigarette. "That's not true," she finally snapped, her voice rising.

"Yes, it is," he said, cocking a brow at her. "And you've suspected it for a long time. You just don't want to admit it—because then you'd have to admit why Carrie went out of her way to befriend you from the get-go. She wanted to use you. Now, that, normally, wouldn't be unusual—I think a lot of people have tried to use you—you're famous, talented. But you're also smart, and quick. Usually you can spot a user from ten miles away. But not with her—you *let* her use you. That must really burn."

"Fuck. You," Della said coldly, enunciating each word slowly and carefully. Smashing her cigarette down into the ashtray, she stood and stomped out of the room. "Let yourself out."

Strike two, Kellan thought wearily, rubbing his eyes.

He headed down River Road, telling himself to stop getting so antsy.

Darci was fine.

She had a deputy there watching the house, and she'd call if anything seemed the slightest bit odd.

No reason for him to go by the house.

Except for the fact that he had to see her. Touch her.

It was close to seven-thirty, which meant the deputy would maybe want a bite to eat.

But Kellan hadn't planned it that way. Well, not completely.

As he pulled into the driveway, he ran his tongue over his lips, remembering the way she tasted, how she felt. How she had burrowed against him and pressed her breasts up against his chest, so that he had felt the hard nubs of her nipples stabbing into his flesh. The way her belly had cuddled his cock. The hungry little moans in her throat.

He paused by the deputy's car and knelt down. "I've got to talk to Miss Law some more. You want to go grab you a bite to eat, Hank?"

The older deputy slid Kellan a telling glance, but he didn't say anything, just lifted his stooped shoulders in a shrug. Nodding at Kellan, he started the car and shoved it into reverse, an odd smile dancing on his mouth.

"I'm as transparent as glass," he muttered, straightening back up and pushing his hand through his hair.

Kellan glanced down at his clothes and then scowled as he realized what he was doing. The button-down and blue jeans were standard work clothes for him, topped with a blazer when he absolutely had to. If it was good enough to wear to work, then it should be good enough to go and talk to somebody related to his case.

Related, my ass. You just want to get your hands on her body again. Well, yeah. He knocked on the door and tucked his hands into his pockets so that he wouldn't grab her the second she opened the door.

Still, when she glanced through the window and he saw that smile bloom on her face, he still had to fight not to grab her. She was too damned adorable for words, so soft and sweet and sexy. All big eyes, kissable mouth, and soft skin.

All he wanted to do was bite her.

"Hey," she said quietly, leaning against the doorjamb, folding her arms under her breasts. Kellan's eyes lingered on the smooth swelling mounds, the little nubs of her nipples pressing against the thin, white fabric. His mouth was watering. And if he didn't do something or say something, he was pretty sure he'd be drooling in a few more seconds.

"Hi. I let Hank go get a bite to eat. Mind if I come in?" he asked. He even managed to keep his voice halfway level.

89

"Sure. Don't suppose you've got anything new, do you?" she asked, standing aside and letting him move past her. Heat sizzled up his arm as his biceps brushed against her breasts. Her eyes flew up and met his. Electricity flew between them.

Reaching behind him, Kellan closed the door, watching as she braced her back against the wall with her hands tucked behind her. His eyes dipped once more to her breasts and he swore roughly. "If I tell you that I'm not here about anything related to the case, are you going to kick me out?"

One black brow rose and she shrugged. "Well, that depends. On exactly why you came. If it's because I didn't pay a couple of speeding tickets, then yes, I'll probably kick you out."

He grinned at her as her lids drooped low over her eyes, a cat's smile dancing on her lips. "A lawbreaker, huh? Always knew there was something shifty about you, Miss Law," he murmured, bracing a hand on the wall beside her head and leaning down to stare into her eyes.

She widened her eyes and gave him an innocent stare. "I'm really sorry, officer. If I promise not to do it again, will you be gentle with me?" she teased, her pretty green eyes sparkling at him.

He smiled as he lowered his head, slanting his lips across hers and pushing his tongue into the sweet cavern of her mouth. As she moaned, he breathed the sound in, reveling in the soft female pleasure it implied.

Pulling her against him, he pivoted so that his back was braced against the wall and the soft weight of her body was leaning into his. Pulling back just a little, he whispered, "I don't know. Hardened criminals emerge all the time because somebody decided to be gentle with them, instead of giving them their just punishment."

Sharp little teeth nipped his lip. Kellan groaned as he buried his fingers in her hair and whispered, "I think that's assaulting an officer of the law, Darci." All playfulness left him then as he brought her mouth back to his and feasted on the soft silk of her lips, drowning in her sweet taste.

His cock throbbed like a bad tooth, aching and sore. The scent of her rose in the air, hot and female. Running his hands down her back, he cupped the round curve of her ass in his hands. She moaned — a broken, hungry little sound that echoed in his ears.

Moving his lips to her ear, he whispered, "I've been driving myself crazy, wanting you the way I do. I'm tired of fighting it."

Darci laughed as she pulled back just a little, running her widespread palms down his chest, toying with the buckle of his belt. "Well, I'd hate to be responsible for driving anybody crazy."

With a chuckle, he murmured, "Now why don't I believe that? I think you enjoy knowing you drive people insane..." He caught the hem of her shirt and pulled upward slowly, keeping his eyes on hers, watching as he slowly bared the pale skin of her torso. That hot female smile lingered on her lips and she stepped back, lifting her arms over her head and letting him tug the shirt away.

Her breasts lifted and fell as she breathed, her hands hanging relaxed at her sides. Small, round little globes, topped with deep pink circles. Lowering his mouth, he traced his tongue over first one pink nipple and then the other, smiling against her flesh as she trembled.

"You taste good," he whispered.

"So glad to hear that," she said, her voice trembling as she reached up and cupped the back of his head in her hands, holding him against her.

He arched her back over his arm, suckling the beaded bud deep in his mouth as he swirled his tongue across it. Cupping one knee in his hand, he drew her leg up, opening the soft folds between her thighs. Through the soft cotton of her pants and the sturdy denim of his, he felt the heat of her pussy, hot enough to scald him.

"You're hot," he groaned, straightening up and spinning around, pinning her against the wall. He cupped her other leg and guided it around his hips, shuddering at the damp heat there between her thighs. "Are you planning on calling a stop to this? Because if you are, do it now. Wait much longer and I think I might have to arrest myself later."

His teeth closed over her nipple and he heard her breathless laugh just before she asked, "Why would you have to do that?"

"Well, I just don't know if I'm going to be able to stop." He slid his hands inside her pants and cupped her ass, the naked skin feeling like silk in his palms. "You taste so fucking good."

"Hmmm…I don't want you to stop, so don't worry," she murmured.

"Fuck," he groaned against her breast. Dropping to his knees, he tore her pants away, finding her naked underneath. Staring at the lips of her pussy, a soft growl escaped him and he pressed his mouth against the smooth, naked mound, stroking his tongue down the slit and groaning as the hot, spicy taste of her exploded on his tongue.

He pushed her thighs wider apart, angling his tongue so that he could fuck it in and out her tight sheath, feeling her hands bury in his hair as she screamed. Her knees buckled and he caught her against him, easing her down to the floor. Kellan wedged himself between her thighs, draping one thigh over his shoulder.

He stroked one finger down the dew-slicked flesh of her pussy, spreading the lips apart before he leaned back and studied the glistening pink folds with hungry eyes.

"Since you don't plan on calling a stop to this, you don't mind if I spend some time—right here."

Darci sobbed out his name as he pumped two fingers in and out of her pussy while he teased her clit into aching readiness with his lips and teeth. Fisting her hands in his hair, she arched up against him, wrapping her thighs around his head and holding him against her.

Holy hell, his tongue was magic. Breath locked in her lungs and she fought to breathe past the fire that burned in her belly. She whimpered and finally the band around her lungs unlocked and she sucked in air. His fingers slid wetly over the flesh of her pussy and she shuddered. His hands cupped her ass and she shrieked as he pulled the cheeks of her ass apart, letting the cool kiss of air dance over her body.

As the orgasm ripped through her, he shifted lower, pressing his mouth against her as though he was drinking her up. Her back arched and she pumped her hips against his face, whimpering, feeling tears spill out of her eyes, leak down her cheeks.

Her eyes drifted closed as he lowered her hips back to the floor. She felt the cool tile of the foyer under her ass, her body feeling boneless and limp.

"Darci?"

She forced her lashes to lift, fighting the languid feeling that had saturated her entire body. "Hmmm. In a few more hours, I might be able to breathe and respond, Kellan," she murmured, watching as he levered himself up over her. His mouth and chin were wet, his eyes hooded, hungry.

"Well, I'm not waiting a few hours," he whispered, a devilish grin curving his lips up. "You can just lie there...and think of England."

Her heart bumped against her chest as he straightened up, reaching for the buttons on his shirt. Her heart bumped again, slamming just a little harder as renewed lust stirred in her belly. She pushed up onto her elbow, interested in the broad wedge of muscled chest he was revealing.

She stroked her finger across the muscles of his belly, watching as they rippled under her touch. "I think I can find something more interesting than England," she whispered, smiling as he hissed out a breath between his teeth.

His body crushed hers into the floor and she sucked air into her lungs, digging her fingers into the thick muscles of his shoulders. His hand moved between them and she whimpered as she felt him tugging at his belt, unbuttoning his jeans.

His cock brushing against her belly, and as he moved lower, brushing against the naked mound of her pussy. The broad head pushed against her and Darci groaned, arching up against him, feeling one large hand cup her ass, tilting her hips upward. Big, thick…she sucked air in as he pushed deep inside the tight clutch of her body, pulling back and surging deeper inside.

"Damn it, you're tight as a fist," he groaned.

Darci squeezed her eyes closed, feeling a burning pressure that bordered on pain arc through her as he flexed his hips and pushed deeper. Tears stung her eyes and she sobbed.

His mouth covered hers just as she started to push against his shoulders, certain she couldn't take any more. His tongue stroked across hers, one hand coming up to cup her breast, rolling the nipple between his thumb and finger. At the same time, he shifted position, moving higher on her body so that he brushed against the swollen bud of her clit with each slow thrust.

The sensations had her gasping, making her body relax the tension that she hadn't realized had flooded her. As that happened, he pushed deeper inside and the head of his cock stroked over the notch buried in her pussy by the mouth of her womb. Heat sizzled in her belly and she screamed against his mouth as he pulled out, pushed back in.

His hair felt cool and silky under her hands as she clutched greedy handfuls of it. Sweat slicked his flesh as he drove inside her, the thick pillar of his cock tunneling through her pussy as she clenched around him. Dizzying bursts of color exploded before her eyes as he raked his teeth down her neck. As his teeth closed around the swollen bud of her nipple, she threw her head back, not even fazed as it slammed into the hard tile beneath her.

"Kellan, oh, please...right there," she whimpered as he shifted again, working a hand between them and circling his thumb over her clit.

It felt like a tight band had been strung between her clit and her nipples. Every stroke of his tongue on her nipples, and every circling caress of his thumb on her clit drew that band tighter and tighter, while the slow, purposeful strokes of his cock had her lifting up against him with each stroke.

"You like that?" he growled against her lips. "What else would you like?"

She shivered at his words, at the low, sexy growl, the sensual threat she heard in his voice. "Hmmm...from you? Just about anything," she whispered.

His fingers dug into the soft flesh of her ass and she sobbed out his name as he traced his finger down the seam between the cheeks of her bottom. "Anything?"

The orgasm hit her with the force of a lightning bolt, setting every last nerve ending to sizzling as he circled one finger around the tight pucker of her ass.

"Kellan—"

His mouth covered hers and swallowed down the scream as he started to probe the small hole, pushing just the tip of his finger inside. The muscles in her pussy started to convulse around his cock and she cried out as the burning heat inside her swelled, pushing the air from her lungs, making dark pinwheels and rainbows flash behind her eyes.

The slow, thorough probing of his finger inside her ass had her arching against him, unable to decide if she liked it or not. Just as she was deciding that she did like it, though, he pulled away and she groaned in frustration, reaching for him.

His hands caught hers and she twined her fingers with his, trying to hold him to her as he pulled away. His hands went to her hips, guiding her over onto her hands and knees. Darci felt the punch of need explode through her as he jerked her hips back against him. She felt his cock cuddle between the cheeks of her ass, felt his hands stroke down the rounded flesh, and she whimpered as one broad palm smoothed over her rump. Her body tensed in anticipation as his hand left her flesh.

When it slapped down on her ass, Darci all but jumped out of her skin. She pushed back against him, and sobbed as he spanked her again. And again, until the flesh of her ass burned and she was so damned aroused — her clit aching, her pussy weeping.

"Such a pretty ass," he purred roughly, stroking one hand down the curve of her rump, before slapping again with the flat of his hand. "Look at how pink your skin gets…you like that, Darci?"

Sobbing, she barely had the breath to answer. "Yes…" And then his hand landed on her butt again, striking first one cheek and then the other. He teased the sensitive folds of her pussy, stroking back and forth over her.

"Damn it, Kellan, please…" she whimpered.

"Please what?" he asked, his voice dark and low.

"Fuck me!" she wailed, pushing back against him, feeling just the tip of his cock breach her folds.

She heard a low, rough growl from Kellan and then he slammed into her with one long, bruising stroke and she arched up, ecstasy ripping through her with violent intensity. She threw back her head, screaming, the tissues of her pussy clutching at his cock as he pulled out and worked back inside, fighting the tense muscles of her sheath as she climaxed. Her hair fell into her eyes, wet with sweat, limp, as she lowered her head to the floor, gasping for air as he tunneled back inside of her.

"I'm not done yet," he rasped, reaching down and taking her hands, guiding them into place at the small of her back. "You aren't done yet, either, Darci. You've no idea how long I've wanted you, how many times I've dreamed of fucking you until you screamed yourself hoarse. No, it's not done yet."

Her wrists secured at her back, his big body crouched over hers, Darci shook her head. Every muscle in her body felt as limp as spaghetti. The hard, brutal digs of his cock in her pussy left her body shaking and tense, and she didn't know whether she wanted to beg for more.

Or beg him to stop. "Kellan," she whimpered. "Kellan, please..."

"Hmmm. You're not screaming," he teased, pulling gently on her arms, reaching around and brushing the sweaty hanks of hair away from her face. She felt his eyes on her — blood rushed to her cheeks.

Then his fingers trailed between the globes of her ass and she bucked. His hand came around her hip, gathering the slick cream from her pussy and then returning to smear it over her asshole. "I wasn't planning on this," he whispered. "Not exactly. But if I had...I think maybe I would have been more prepared. Fuck me, I've dreamed about burying my dick inside this sweet little ass of yours."

His finger pushed inside and she keened, a low rough sound, her back arching, tension slamming into her. She wanted to brace her body on the floor, but he still held her hands. Tugging against the hold he had on her wrists, she whimpered, couldn't decide whether she wanted to fight harder to get away from him or come just from how damned hot he was making her.

He started to fuck his finger inside the snug confines of her ass, letting go of her wrists with his other hand. He stroked that hand down her butt and she screamed as he spanked her again, that light slap on the flushed, tender flesh of her ass closing a fist of agonized pleasure around her that wouldn't let go.

Kellan slammed into her, harder, harder. His hand went back to grip her hip, holding her steady for the double penetration of his cock in her pussy, and his finger in her ass. His strokes picked up and she pushed back, sucking air into her lungs past the tight fist of lust.

She exploded around him, her pussy clutching around his cock as she screamed out his name. Black dots exploded behind her eyes and she felt the hot splash of his seed deep inside her pussy.

His hands clutched at her hips as he pulled out and burrowed back inside with one final thrust.

With her arms sprawled limply beside her head, Darci groaned. "I think I'm dead," she whispered hoarsely.

He bent over her and she felt his head come down and rest between her shoulder blades. "Ummm...no. Not dead. Most definitely alive," he said. Little tremors rippled through her pussy as his cock jerked. "And when I can breathe again, I plan on enjoying...this...again."

This was accompanied by his hand reaching around and cupping her pussy as he eased back and urged her to the ground, cuddling her up against him. His body was hot, damp, his heart slamming against her back where he held her tight against him.

* * * * *

Anger boiled in her belly as she lingered outside the window.

Bitch.

Whore.

Damn it, how could she be in there getting laid when Bryce was dead? His own fucking fault, calling her Darci again, but damn it, didn't the bitch have any compassion?

She should be sobbing, crying, sad at least that Bryce was gone. The whole world should be mourning him.

But she wasn't mourning. She was getting fucked within an inch of her life.

Darci's screams were audible even through the windows. With her hand pressed against the glass, she listened, rage and a twisted form of greedy desire lurking in her belly as she watched.

He'd turned the light on. She watched as the sheriff rose up on his knees, looming over her as he cupped her slender hips in his hands.

She couldn't see well enough. She wanted to see his cock, wanted to watch as he pushed inside Darci's pussy.

With a whispered curse, she turned away, sliding through the bushes and the trees until she got down closer to the river. Then she headed west to Cole's Landing where she'd parked her car.

Her feet moved silently over the ground, barely stirring the branches and the leaves as she passed.

Not right. The bitch shouldn't be enjoying life so much when Bryce was dead, his body forever cold. She wanted to *hurt* Darci. So much she could taste it.

But damn it, this wasn't about Darci.

Shame and grief rose in her belly as she remembered Bryce's hands on her, his gruff voice in her ear as he barked out orders and insults, the feel of his hands on her flesh as he fucked her, as he punished her. Nobody had ever made her feel the way he had—hot, depraved, the humiliation and hunger twining inside of her until she couldn't tell one from the other.

She'd never feel that again. But it was his fault. Damn it, his fault.

"You got distracted," she muttered, digging her keys out of her pocket. "Distracted. And see what it did? Remember the plan. Keep the plan in mind."

Chapter Six

ಐ

A week of uneasy silence passed. Bryce's messy apartment had shown them nothing but that he was definitely a bachelor, with empty pizza boxes cluttering the kitchen, empty beer cans and a stash of uppers. With a wry twist of his lips, Kellan studied the small assortment of pills and wondered why he hadn't figured Bryce as a user.

Of course, he hadn't really seen Bryce as somebody who would be involved in bondage games either. But the porn mags in his house were all of the darker variety, and the box under the bed had revealed an assortment of chains, handcuffs, and ball gags.

And videos…the videos sent a surge of excitement rushing through him. This was personal. Very personal. And there was nothing in the world as personal and intimate as sex.

Would those videos show anything?

Licking his lips, he counted them and recorded them on the inventory list. Well, he had been planning on a movie tonight, but he had hoped to get Darci to meet him in Columbus and maybe catch one together. Then maybe find some secluded area to park and fuck her brains out.

They couldn't risk being seen together right now. Not with this investigation going on, but he wanted her so badly that he couldn't breathe.

"Better this way," he told himself, plowing a hand through his hair before gathering up the videos. *I'll spend the night watching a bunch of videos and then I'll go jack off in the shower and get some rest.*

And hopefully, these videos would yield a clue. Some sort of clue.

* * * * *

Darci moved through the gallery in a daze. Her mind didn't want to realign with her body. All she could remember was *that* night. He'd left sometime before ten o'clock.

"I wish I could stay," he had whispered, brushing her hair back.

"Me, too."

"This damned case...damn it. When I get this thing solved..." then his voice had trailed off as he'd jerked her against him, pressing a ravenous kiss against her lips, his hand fisting in her hair. Before she could start to kiss him back though, Kellan had pulled away and left without another word.

Her lips buzzed now, just thinking about that kiss. Pressing her fingers to her lips, closing her eyes in memory, she was caught by surprise when the door opened.

Turning, she found herself staring into Tricia Casey's bland green eyes. Arching a brow at the older woman, she said, "Well, I usually don't get to see you in here."

Tricia laughed, her eyes twinkling as though she knew what sort of things were running through Darci's mind. With a shrug of her shoulders, she said, "I don't have much time for visiting. Not with running the gallery, hunting down new artists...and it's terrible, but we are busier now than we ever have been. Violent death has done wonders for Carrie and Beth's sales. Peggy and I can hardly keep up."

"People are a macabre bunch." Folding her arms across her middle, Darci asked, "What can I do for you, Tricia?"

She smiled, causing the few lines in her face to deepen. One wasn't likely to guess her age. For a woman of sixty-two, she looked remarkable. Reaching into her purse, she drew out a small stack of envelopes. "We keep receiving your mail," she murmured, holding it out to Darci.

Darci arched a brow. "I'll have to complain again. Tiresome, never knowing where your mail is going. Especially since one or two times the letters looked like somebody had tried to open them. Not the bills, of course, but the ones that come from customers."

A cool smile curved Tricia's lips and she shrugged. "Bryce was always terribly nosy, I'm afraid. Wouldn't surprise me in the least to hear he was reading other people's mail."

Folding her hand around the envelopes, Darci took them and sauntered back behind the counter. Calmly, she said, "Well, that being the case, I assume I don't need to worry about people looking at my mail anymore. Seeing as how he's gone."

Tricia sighed, a sad look crossing her face. "Indeed. Such a tragedy. He was so young. I just don't understand what is going on," she murmured.

Darci lifted a shoulder. "Probably the only person who does understand is the one behind it," she finally said, idly flipping through the envelopes. *No sense…Beth…Carrie…Bryce…* Hell, Bryce wasn't connected to her at all. Hadn't ever done more than check out her ass when he thought she wasn't looking.

The only thing they had in common was Dark Destinies.

* * * * *

Kellan had reached the same conclusion, although he would have disagreed with Darci's thoughts on Bryce.

He was connected to her. Because the man had wanted her. A near obsessive want, judging by how many times he had fucked a woman and told her she'd answer to Darci's name if that was what he felt like calling her.

Dark Destinies…and Darci… Well, there was one other thing they had in common.

Kim.

Bryce had his own little harem, and Kellan was a bit surprised over some of the faces he had seen. Married women, dumpy women, women he would have pegged as being too smart to want anything to do with Bryce.

But he knew what it was like to have a need for something dark. He had dark, obsessive fantasies of his own, all centered around Darci. These women who had been with Bryce wanted the pain and the humiliation and the sex he doled out with a fair amount of skill.

He liked to spank them, cane them, tie them down.

Often he would gag them, or pull a hood over their heads before applying the whip.

The blonde who was currently chained to the floor and giving Bryce a blowjob was one who took him by surprise.

Another link between the dead people.

She'd been Beth's fetching girl. Carrie's whipping girl...

"Say it, Kim, say you're my fuck slut," came Bryce's voice from the TV as he pulled his wet dick from the woman's mouth.

She stared up at Bryce with rapt hunger, whispering obediently, "I'm your fuck slut."

And she had been the lover of one of the murder victims. Well, Kellan had to amend that as Bryce backhanded her across the face before jerking her by the hair and forcing his dick halfway down her throat. Maybe *lover* wasn't the right term.

Casting a glance at his watch, he vacillated. Did he really want to go and question Kim about this? At seven p.m. on a Saturday?

No. He didn't.

But that didn't keep him from climbing into his car and flipping through his notebook to find her address.

As he pulled out of the drive, he tried to turn it over in his head.

Could she have done it?

Damn it, he just didn't know.

She was so quiet, so timid. Had she just been pushed too far?

* * * * *

Kim screamed, throwing her hands up over her face as the poker came crashing down toward her. With desperation, she kicked out and knocked her attacker's feet out from under her.

She hit the floor with a crash and Kim scuttled backward on her hands and feet, grabbing hold of the coffee table and shoving herself up. Had to run…had to get out, get away…

The pain in her ribs and in her chest was ungodly. Breathing was torture.

"Damn it, you bitch." The words were rough, ugly with hatred. And getting closer.

Kim grabbed the door to the balcony and jerked it open, stumbling through and slamming it on the arm that came through behind her. A furious howl lit the air and she could have sobbed with relief as a voice from above called out, "Damn it, what's going on down there? Kim? Is that you?"

"Going to fucking beat the shit out of you, bitch."

She flinched away from that voice, backing away as the door slid open. The poker raised and she screamed.

"Damn it, what the fuck? I'm calling the cops, damn it…"

Lights glared in the front of the apartment parking lot. Kim turned her head, time slowing down to a crawl as she saw the familiar car pass under the lights, then the door flew open…the blue of the swimming pool just below her…

Turning, she blinked, waiting for the poker to fall one more time. But her attacker had frozen, eyes locked on the car pulling into the lot. With a whispered prayer, Kim gripped the railing and swung one leg over. As she moved the other, those malevolent eyes swung her way.

Taking a deep breath, she leaped just as the poker started to come swinging down.

The cold water closed over her and then oblivion.

Kellan nodded as Grady finished reading off the witness reports.

Somebody wearing black. A hood.

But nobody had seen the attacker's face. Nobody could tell if it was a woman, a man, or a seven-foot Martian with green skin. Pressing his fingers to his eyes, he tried to tune out the antiseptic smell of the hospital, tried to forget about the blood on his hands.

Pulling that broken, battered body from the swimming pool had filled him with shame and anger.

He had gone there planning to question Kim, but he had all but laughed at himself halfway there. Too weak. Too timid. Too stupid.

And her plunge off the balcony had probably saved her life. While he'd pulled her still body out of the pool, the assailant had gotten away. Only moments later, deputies had arrived on the scene in response to the calls from several of Kim's neighbors, but their search hadn't turned up anything.

"Damn it, what in the hell is going on?" he muttered.

The waiting room doors swung open and the doctor stepped out, her face weary but satisfied. "She's going to be fine, I think… I was worried about head trauma or possible spinal injury, jumping into six feet of water, but God was smiling on her," Dr. Winter said. "The MRI looks okay."

Her blue scrubs had blood smeared on them and her shoulders were slumped with weariness. "She's got some internal bleeding. Broken ribs. But she's responding, at the moment, and right now just needs to rest." She glanced down at herself before flicking Kellan a look. "And so do I. I need a shower, a new change of clothes and a nap. I usually don't have trauma cases like this show up in my hospital, Sheriff. But I figured you wouldn't leave until you heard something."

He nodded, and forced himself to smile slightly. "I'm putting a deputy on her door."

Dr. Winter said shortly, "Good."

He left soon after talking to Grady, reassuring himself that Kim was still alive.

Grady was a good cop. He'd do his damnedest to make sure the girl stayed that way.

Which meant allowing nobody in that room. She had been the best suspect, even if she was the most unlikely. And she'd almost died.

So he still had a killer out there. Somebody who was striking out in an irrational manner. No sense. Damn it, it made no sense.

None of it. He stalked outside, jerking open the door to his car and dropping into the seat. He left the door open, leaving the dome light on as he stared at his hands. Blood stained his clothes, and he couldn't get it out from under his nails. The bastard had caught her across the chest with the business end of the poker. Not all of her injuries were from blunt force trauma. The pointed end had torn open a nasty gash diagonally across her torso.

"Damn it," he muttered. Closing his hand into a fist, he slammed it against the steering wheel and rasped out, "Who the fuck are you?"

* * * * *

Kim slept through the day.

Everywhere he went, Kellan heard the same damn thing. "Who could have done that? Kim is harmless." A hundred different variations of the same question.

In the county hospital cafeteria, Kellan poured himself another cup of bitter, overly strong coffee.

"That stuff will eat the lining out of your stomach."

Turning around, he stared into Darci's wide green eyes. "Hey," he murmured.

She smiled slightly, arching a brow at him. "Hey," she whispered. Heat flooded her eyes and Kellan felt that look as solidly as if she'd reached out and touched him. Her eyes looked bruised, sleepless. And the sigh that shuddered out of her sounded terribly defeated. "I heard about Kim. Came by, but Grady says he can't let anybody in."

He sipped at the coffee, his eyes widening as the caffeine started to sing in his system from the first sip. The minute it hit his empty belly, he winced. "Damn. Probably *will* eat the lining away," he muttered before taking another sip. "Kim can't tell me who it was. Nobody can give me a description, other than dark clothes and a hood. And since we don't know…Kim is in a lot of danger."

"I don't get it." She moved away from him, dropping into one of the chairs, resting her elbows on the round table as she massaged her temples. "Maybe this is why I'm not a cop, but I don't see much connection between any of these people. The only thing they have in common is they all worked for the gallery."

Kellan took the seat across from her, arching a brow. "I imagine Tricia is getting pretty desperate. Peggy spends more time working in her studio than in the gallery, her two employees are gone, and two of her artists."

She shrugged a shoulder. "Apparently, Beth and Carrie are more popular now than they ever were. Talked to Tricia recently — she says she's never been so busy."

In the act of lifting his coffee to his lips for another stomach-searing drink, Kellan froze, lowering the cup back to the table. "People love a scandal. And the bloodier, the more notorious, the better," he murmured. "Three murders... I imagine her gallery is hopping."

He kept his voice level, but his mind was buzzing as the pieces finally fell together. *Stupid...stupid...stupid*, he said to himself silently. Money. Not Darci... But Bryce...that didn't make any sense.

The videos from the past night flashed through his mind. Yes, Kim had been there, but then so had a number of other women. Jealousy. Somehow, that was how Bryce played into it, and the fact that he worked for the gallery, increasing the already notorious reputation.

Three murders. Would have been four, except Kim had gotten away. Had it all been about money? Had the scene just been staged so that it looked personal? He felt eyes on him and he looked up, seeing Darci staring at him with a confused, curious look.

"What?" she asked softly.

He shrugged. "Nothing." He pushed his cup away and forced a grin. "You're right. That coffee will tear up a belly. I've got to get back to the station, go over a few things," he said. Leaning forward, he put his mouth by her ear and said, "Go home. Stay there. Don't talk to anybody."

Arching a brow at him, she opened her lips to ask a question and he reached out and pressed his finger to her lips. "Don't ask questions. I can't answer them. But do this for me. I'm going to advise the deputies to be extra careful, but you do not go anywhere."

Chapter Seven

❧

Tricia ignored the knock on the door.

Bryce's chauvinistic attitude aggravated the hell out of her, but he knew how to get the paperwork done. Kim could do it, screwed it up in the process, but at least Tricia didn't have to deal with it.

So until Kim got out of the hospital and was able to come back to work, Tricia had to do it herself again.

But the fist pounding on the door just banged again. And again. Finally, she tugged her glasses off and left the office, staring through the door at the grim outline of the Sheriff.

Opening the door, she stepped aside. "Hello, Sheriff Grant. Gallery isn't open on Sundays. And I'm behind now," she said wearily. "So much paperwork. I've got a million things to get done, including trying to hire some more employees."

"I'm going to have to intrude for a while," he said.

She sighed and let him enter, pushing the door closed behind him before she walked back to her office, his feet soundless on the plush carpet behind her.

"I don't have much time, Sheriff. Can we make this fast?"

The Sheriff's hazel eyes looked blandly back at her through the lenses of his glasses. "I can try. I need to know where you were last night and when Bryce was killed. Then where were you three weekends ago."

Air trapped in her lungs and she blinked once, frowning at him, "Excuse me?"

"Can you answer the question, Ms. Casey?"

"You're trying to get my whereabouts for the nights my friends were killed," she said, amazed, staring at him with wide eyes. She dropped down onto the chair just inside the door, the strength leaving her legs as she stared up at him. "You're serious."

"Ms. Casey…"

She passed her glasses from one hand to another as she hollowly said, "Last night, I was home. Alone. But the night Bryce died…well, I've told you that. I was in Columbus for a dinner meeting with several other gallery owners. I've been thinking of expanding and…" her voice trailed away and she realized she wasn't going to be able to do that right now. All of her plans—this would ruin her. Having a gallery where her employees and contract artists were being murdered was one thing.

But nobody would want to do business with somebody accused of murder.

"And I was with Beth the night Carrie was killed," Tricia whispered. "But you can't ask her, can you?"

No. But Kellan did have the reports from the deputies who had done the questioning of Carrie's friends. Fuck. He flipped his notebook open and jotted down a few notes. "You heard about Kim, right?"

He watched as she nodded slowly. For once, she actually looked her age. Normally, she never let a line show on her face, but right now, she looked totally shell-shocked. He left the gallery a few minutes later, plowing a hand through his hair.

He couldn't focus. First, he had thought it was Kim. Then Tricia. Oh, he'd check her story out, verify it. But already he had a bad suspicion that her story would check out.

Idiot. He was letting Darci skew his thinking. Worrying about her, so convinced it was about her. "It's not, is it?" he muttered as he returned to his car.

Totally unaware of the eyes that watched him.

Tricia was still sitting there, staring dumbly at nothing when the door opened. Sliding Peggy an evil look, she said waspishly, "Well, your plan is working. We've got more business than we could ever dream of, Carrie is out of the way and she can't cause us any more trouble. Beth's constant bitching is over with and we've made buckets off of the works of our artists who were so tragically killed. But now he *knows*."

"He doesn't know. He may suspect, but if he knew, you'd be on your way to the station," Peggy snapped. Her salt-and-pepper hair hung in careless ringlets around her face as she tossed her head, rolling her eyes at Tricia.

"I want to know about Bryce."

Peggy arched a brow, her mouth flat. "Excuse me?"

"Why did you kill Bryce? And Kim? That's what is causing the trouble. Damn it, if you had just stopped — "

Peggy sneered. "Oh, don't go acting like you had nothing to do with any of this. Don't forget who killed Beth. You're just as much involved in this as I am. And Kim, hell, she's a whiny whelp. Useless. What does it matter?"

"What about Bryce? He wasn't in the plan. And he was just as annoying as Kim is," Tricia snapped, control fading fast. She wanted to shout and scream and pummel Peggy's face. Damned irrational bitch had gotten her into this mess.

"Bryce was *not* annoying."

Tricia lifted her head, studying Peggy's face. "Damn it. You were fucking him," she whispered, narrowing her eyes.

Peggy moved away, her motions jerky and stilted. "Bryce and I were lovers for a time."

"Then how could you kill him?"

Tears rolled down her cheeks as she collapsed to the floor. "I wasn't going to. I missed him — he pushed me away, told me I was too clingy. I went to his house that night and we...we..."

"You fucked," Tricia said snidely.

111

Peggy's face flushed and she snarled, "I loved him. It was more than just fucking." Her eyes took on a glassy look as she stared at her hands. "But then he called me Darci again. I hate it when he does that. Hate it. I saw the knife. And he was just sitting there with his back to me, ignoring me...always ignoring me. He'd started fucking that bitch, Kim. I saw them together, damn it. Fucking her as though she actually was something special. She didn't appreciate him. She just wanted somebody to fuck her sorry ass."

Tricia closed her eyes, shaking her head. "Damn it, you let emotions get in the way. You attacked Kim because you're fucking *jealous*."

Peggy sneered at Tricia. "No. I did it because it was good to keep going and because I didn't like her. Sooner or later, I'll finish the job."

Tricia pressed her fingers to her temples and muttered, "You're nuts."

She never heard Peggy stand up as she herself rose, walked around the small office, and tapped a finger against her lips. "We have to get everything hammered out. Kellan knows I was home alone. I think he believes me. You need to come up with an—"

She stopped in mid-sentence as the cold pain sliced through her. She stared down at the silver glint of the knife piercing her chest. Blood bubbled out of her lips as the knife was withdrawn and she slowly sank to the floor.

"I've already got it hammered out," Peggy said to the still body at her feet. She nudged her ex-partner with her foot and said, "I'm going to be remembered. I may not be the best artist in the world. But at least my art will be remembered."

Chapter Eight

ℬ

Kellan parked at the station, drumming his fist on the steering wheel.

His cell phone rang and he tugged it off his belt, recognizing Grady's number and frowning. Kim was stable. He'd made sure of that.

"This is Grant."

"You need to get down here," Grady said shortly. "Peggy Ralley just walked in and she's got blood all over her."

"She's been attacked?"

"Ahhh...boss, I don't think it's her blood."

Understanding dawned in his mind and he threw the car into drive. Peeling out of the parking lot, he said, "I'm coming, but County is about twenty minutes from me. She got a weapon?"

"Can't tell. The nurses are talking to her...she looks kind of weird in the eyes."

Shit. "Keep her out of that room, Grady. Do *not* let her in there," he snapped.

"Well, gee, I kind of figured that out," Grady drawled and Kellan could almost see the sarcastic roll of his deputy's eyes.

"Son of a bitch." Not Tricia. Peggy. The quiet, colorless woman who faded into the background, except for her art. He punched the gas and shot through the red light, hitting the lights and sirens, swerving to go around the pickup in front of him. The two-lane highway opened up ahead of him as he sped for the hospital.

113

"Boss. I think I should get off the phone. She's heading my way."

The cell phone went silent and Kellan threw it down, swearing viciously. *Blood...* A snarl escaped his lips and he grabbed the phone again, punching in Darci's number. Three rings...four rings...five... A sick fear bloomed in his gut, duty warring with the need to make sure Darci was safe.

The relief that flooded him when Darci answered the phone on the seventh ring was unlike anything he had ever felt.

"Damn it, what in the hell took you so long to answer the phone?" he demanded. "Are you okay? Where is Hank?"

Her voice, low and amused, came over the line. "Nice to talk to you, too. I was in the studio, developing some negatives. I'm fine and Hank is sitting in his car, singing along with some cry in your beer music."

"Thank God." Damn it, he wanted to see her, touch her. Kellan hadn't ever been that afraid before and he suspected his heart wouldn't start beating normally until he had touched her, held her close against him and felt her heart beating against his, the way it did when he had her naked and wrapped around him.

"Listen to me. Do *not* let anybody in your house other than me or Hank. Nobody, you understand me?" he said intensely. "Stay away from the door, stay inside. Got it?"

She was silent for a long moment and then she said, "What's going on, Kellan?"

"No time. I've got to go." His hand clenched around the phone and he bit back the words that were dancing on his tongue. "Do what I said, okay?"

"Sure. Are you—"

He took the turn into the hospital at fifty miles an hour, tires squealing. "I've got to go... Darci, I think I'm in love with you."

Then he hit the *end* button and tossed the phone down, slamming on the brakes in front of the emergency room. He ran through the automatic doors, down the hall that led to ICU, fear and anger a metallic taste in his throat. Whose blood?

Grady's voice rang out down the hall. "I will *not* tell you again, Miz Ralley. Step back or I will shoot."

The laughter that came from her was unlike any he had heard before. High, maniacal, and wild. He slowed to a stop as he veered around the corner, staring at Peggy's back. No blood… But then she turned around and he saw the chilling smile on her face. Bright red blossoms stained the front of her paint-splattered shirt.

"Peggy."

She smiled at him, a brittle smile. "Things are all messed up. I should have killed Darci that night, and then maybe Bryce would have stopped thinking about her all the time. I wasn't going to kill him. Not until he called me Darci again. The bastard."

He flicked Grady a glance, but then looked back at Peggy when he saw that the deputy was slowly moving closer to the woman's back.

"Bryce?"

Peggy laughed. "I thought you were smarter than this," she said, shaking her head. "Took you long enough to figure it out. I thought you might put it together after Beth, but you were too busy fucking Darci. Della was going to be next. But then Tricia started to freak out…" her voice trailed off and she wiped a hand down the front of her shirt, lovingly caressing the blood splotches. "Well, she made me mad."

"Mind if I ask why you did all this?"

Grady was just a few feet away now, gun raised. "Well, not for money. I know that's why Tricia did it. All the great artists died tragically," she said with a wide smile. She started to reach inside her shirt.

"Keep your hands where I can see them!" Kellan barked out.

But she didn't stop and when he found himself staring down the business end of a Beretta, he finally figured it out. All of it. She wanted them to kill her. She wasn't here to kill them, but to force them to kill her.

Suicide by cop, the coolest way to kill yourself… He drew his gun because he sure as hell wasn't going to let some crazy-ass self-important artist kill him.

"Put the gun down, Peggy."

She laughed, but whatever she was going to say died as her eyes went wide and then fluttered shut. There was a thud as Grady's gun came down on her skull, a soft thump as her body crumpled to the floor, and then all fell silent.

Kellan sucked in air, blood roaring in his ears as he lowered the gun, watching as Grady kicked her Beretta away and knelt down, tugging out his cuffs and securing her hands before touching his fingers to her throat. He rose and blew out a breath, his mahogany skin gleaming under a thin coat of sweat, his eyes wide.

"Son of a bitch. This woman is nuts," Grady whispered, shaking his head.

* * * * *

Tricia's body was already cool by the time Kellan and two of the deputies broke down the door to the gallery. Peggy Ralley had had some fun before she left. None of the art in the gallery that wasn't done by her hand had survived her rampage intact. Sculptures lay smashed on the floor. Canvases sliced by a knife, and a few, the two closest to Tricia's body, had bloody splotches.

"She used the knife she killed Tricia with," Kellan murmured quietly.

Grady knelt by the door, studying the shattered pieces of a rich purple vase. "Why didn't we see it before now?"

"No rhyme or reason. We were looking for something that made sense." Kellan shook his head, straightening over Tricia's still body. He met the coroner's gaze as Drake Stillman stepped inside, looking around the gallery with vague surprise in his eyes.

Things like this didn't happen in their county.

Kellan suspected that this past month had been the busiest of the county coroner's life. He gestured to the bagged knife lying on the table.

"I'm fairly certain that's the murder weapon," he said. "I think she used it to slice up the paintings. We found it on the floor by Tricia's body, like she'd tossed it away before she walked out. Then she showed up at the hospital with blood on her clothes."

Drake's question was cut off by the ringing of Kellan's phone. He checked out the number and said, "It's the hospital," as he thumbed the *talk* button. "This is Grant," he said, turning away from the curious gazes.

He listened to the low murmur of the nurse on the other end of the line and then hung up the phone, turning back to meet Grady's eyes. "She's awake. I've got to get back there."

* * * * *

Darci paced the floor, shooting evil looks at the silent phone. Four hours had passed since Kellan had called and she hadn't heard another thing from him.

She stood at the window in the dining room, staring out at the silvery moonlight reflecting off the river. *I think I'm in love with you...*

"Jerk. How in the hell can you say that and hang up, and not call back?" she muttered, running a hand through her already tumbled hair. It stood up in messy spikes and curls from a hundred nervous passes of her hand. She rested her forehead against the cool pane of glass, closing her eyes and murmuring, "Where in the hell are you?"

Worry was a gnawing thing in her belly, making her gut churn, tightening her shoulders, aching in her head. Her fingers itched to pick up the phone and call, but she forced herself not to. Calling him, interrupting him...what if he was finding out who the killer was?

What if...if...what if the killer had gotten to him?

Panic blossomed in her mind and she turned around, bypassing the phone and heading out the front door, jogging down the steps. She heard Hank's door slam and he met her on the sidewalk.

"What's going on, Miss Law? What's wrong?"

"Where's Kellan?" she demanded.

"Darci, he wants you to stay inside," Hank said flatly, taking her arm and trying to guide her back up the walk.

She jerked her arm away and planted herself in Hank's face, poking him in the chest as she demanded, "Tell me where Kellan is. What in the hell is going on?"

His face softened and she felt a flush rise in her cheeks as the sympathy darkened his faded gray eyes. "He's probably back at the hospital. Talking to Peggy Ralley."

Darci's jaw dropped and she felt her shoulders slump. "Not another one. Damn it, what is going on?"

Hank patted her shoulder. "Maybe I didn't make that clear, Miss Law. He's questioning Peggy Ralley. She showed up at the hospital this afternoon, blood splattering her shirt. Pulled a gun on the Sheriff. Turns out the gun wasn't loaded. Possible that she wanted him to shoot her. They disarmed her somehow—I don't know the details. But I'd say it's over."

The phone finally rang. Five and half hours after he'd told her that he thought he was in love with her, and then hung up on her. Oh, it had rung a few times before, just shortly after Hank told her about Peggy.

118

But it had been everybody *but* Kellan. Becka, Clive, Brittany…each time, she'd gotten off the phone with a curtness that bordered on outright rudeness, not wanting to talk to anybody but Kellan.

The phone rang again and she grabbed it, the strength leaving her knees as Kellan's low voice murmured in her ear, "Wasn't sure if you'd still be awake."

She laughed shakily and said, "Well, I could have tried to go to bed. But I doubt I would have gotten any sleep, considering what you said right before you hung up on me."

"Well, everything kind of went down pretty fast," Kellan said softly. "I need to talk to you…but I know it's late."

She stared at the clock as the hour hand finally ticked to midnight and she shook her head. "I don't care how late it is. I want to talk to you, too."

Moments later, she lowered the phone, the dial tone sounding. Softly, she whispered, "I'm pretty sure I'm in love with you, too."

Spinning around, she went to the bathroom, and stared at her reflection. Her hair stood up in wild spikes and she winced, grabbing some hair goop and slicking it through her hair, taming the wild tresses, smoothing the sides, fluffing the top a little.

Darci licked her lips nervously. *Maybe I should go put on something…well, something more than a tank top and boxer shorts.* But lingerie was so predictable. And she wasn't sure she wanted to wait for him naked.

Makeup?

No. Not when it was past midnight. She turned away from her reflection and stomped out of the bathroom. Food. Food was good. Chances are, he hadn't eaten, and come to think of it, she was kind of hungry.

There was stuff for lasagna, but that took so long. Spaghetti? No, not in the middle of the night.

Sandwiches. That would work. She grabbed the bread and tossed it on the counter. Roast beef, tomatoes, cheddar cheese, mayo, spicy mustard. Did he like spicy mustard?

She stared at the ingredients spread out in front of her for a long moment and then buried her face in her hands.

"I'm in love with a guy and I don't even know what he likes on his sandwiches."

Blowing out a breath, she washed her hands and then grabbed a couple of plates and a butter knife. If he liked spicy mustard, then he could add it to the sandwich himself. Right?

Right.

Her stomach screamed noisily at her as she finished the sandwiches and stood at the counter, eating hers. Maybe her belly would stop jumping if it wasn't so empty.

She hoped.

But then the knock came on the door and she pressed a hand to her belly, the butterflies still raging. Nope. Didn't work. But at least she wouldn't pass out from hunger, right?

Nerves, embarrassment, panic…but not hunger.

Dropping her half-eaten sandwich on the plate, she left the kitchen, muttering to herself, "Why am I so nervous?"

Because she hadn't once thought about what would happen beyond today. Hell, with all the insane things happening right now, and the nocturnal visits from nameless people, she had thought a time or two that maybe she wouldn't have a tomorrow.

And this was much more nerve-racking than the memory of that pale face in her window. After all, she knew what that person had basically wanted. To scare her to death.

But Kellan…what did he want?

She opened the door slowly, staring at his face with wide eyes, catching her lip between her teeth. He looked exhausted. Stepping aside, she asked quietly, "Have you eaten anything?"

He grimaced. "No. Haven't had time to think about it," he said, shrugging.

Catching his hand, she led him into the kitchen and took the second sandwich, pushing the plate into his hand. A surprised look entered his eyes, a smile slowly edging up the corners of his mouth. "Thanks," he murmured. He dropped into the chair and for a moment, just rested his elbows on the table, weariness in every line of his body.

Her heart clenched when he lifted his head, meeting her eyes as she stared at him from across the room. Something dark and hungry entered his gaze and then he looked away, reaching down to pick up the sandwich.

She spun away, that look striking her to the core, heating her belly, tightening her nipples. Flipping open the fridge, she grabbed a bottle of wine. "I'm going to have some wine. You want a glass? Or a soft drink?"

Kellan studied her bent head, his eyes running over her and settling on the fine tremor of her hands. "You seem a little nervous," he murmured, lowering his half-eaten sandwich to the table and leaning back in the chair, watching as she pressed her hands to the counter, her shoulders rising and falling as she took a deep breath.

"Ummm...maybe a little." She tugged the cork out of the half-empty bottle of wine and he was silent as she poured herself a glass and upended it, drinking half of it and then topping her glass off before she poured a second glass and turned around.

Kellan rose from the table and met her halfway across the room, taking it from her, lifting it to his lips, holding her stare all the while. He could see the pulse in her neck fluttering wildly. The wine slid down his throat, warm and smooth as liquid gold, and he took one more sip before setting it down and taking hers away, putting it on the table as well.

"Why?"

She blinked, staring at him owlishly, licking her lips. "Why what?" she whispered huskily.

"Why are you nervous?" he murmured, lowering his head to brush his lips against the pulse in her throat.

"I—" her voice squeaked and then a shaky sigh slipped out of her.

"Because of what I said on the phone?"

"A little."

He trailed a gentle line of kisses up her neck, nuzzling the sweet-smelling hair just behind her ear before he asked, "Good nervous? Or bad nervous?"

"I haven't decided yet... I've never done this before."

"Done what?" he asked before he brushed his lips over her mouth. The scent of her skin flooded his head, making it hard to think beyond the scent and the feel of her.

"Been in love with anybody."

His heart beat a rapid tattoo in his chest but he kept his voice level. "Are you in love now?"

"I think so...and I'm scared to death," she said shakily.

Lifting his head, he smiled slightly, cupping her face in his hands as he stared into her emerald green eyes. "Me, too. I tried pretty damn hard to stay away from you, Darci. You are more than I'm prepared to handle," he said quietly. "I knew this would happen."

She scowled at him, a frown drawing her brows low over her eyes. "Well, I didn't exactly force you into anything," she muttered.

Kellan laughed. "No...and I was losing anyway. You sneak into my dreams, haunt my thoughts," he whispered. "This was inevitable."

Her body melted against his as he added, "I feel you with me even when you're not around. And I ache...I want you with me all the time." Slanting his mouth across her, he pushed his tongue into her mouth gently, sipping at her lips until she opened for him, wrapping her arms around his neck and arching against him with a soft moan.

Trailing his fingers down her spine, he caught the hem of her shirt, raising it slowly, flattening his palms against her sides, stroking them upward, letting the movement of his hands draw the shirt up.

He stepped back just a little, pulling his mouth from hers just long enough to slide the shirt off completely. He felt the soft mounds of her breasts flatten against his chest, her nipples tight little beads, as she wrapped her arms around his neck, her mouth pressing eagerly, hungrily to his.

"Shhh...this is going to be slow. I want to take my time with you right now," he said. Taking her mouth again, he slowly danced her over to the table. He slid his hands inside the waistband of her boxers and slowly stroked down her hips, letting the silk fall to her ankles in a puddle of blue. Then he boosted her hips onto the table, stepping back to stare down at her body.

Skimming his hands up her sides, he cupped the pert little mounds of her breasts, bending low to catch one between his teeth, smiling against her flesh as she arched up against him with a rough moan. Her hands moved restlessly over his shoulders, dipping into his hair to pull him against her, roaming down his arms. Her nails dug into his biceps and he grunted at the sharp little pain.

Lifting his head, Kellan stared down into her dazed eyes, smiling as she stared blindly back at him, licking her lips. Her breasts rose and fell unsteadily as she gasped for air. He trailed one finger down the center of her torso, circling around her navel, skimming lower to trail between the dew-slicked folds of her pussy.

He watched her face as he circled the tender opening, pushing just a little inside that tight passage. Her lids drooped low and her upper body went boneless as she collapsed back against the table, hands curled into loose fists at her sides. The satiny tissues resisted his slow caress and he gritted his teeth, remembering how hot and tight she had closed around his cock.

The organ in question jerked demandingly, trapped in the tight confines of his jeans and underwear. Throttling down the urge to tear his clothes away and drive his dick deep inside her, Kellan leaned over her, bracing his hand by her head, staring into her eyes as he slowly pushed his finger inside her pussy, withdrawing as she arched against his hand. He added a second finger, watching as her eyes flew wide open, harsh pants falling from her lips.

"Come for me," he whispered gruffly, shuddering as the creamy heat tightened around his fingers.

She sobbed aloud and he circled the tight little bud of her clit with his thumb and repeated, "Come for me. Come on, Darci, let me feel it."

Her entire body bucked under the touch of his hand, pearly white teeth sinking into the full lower curve of her lip. The scent of her arousal was heavy in the air and he couldn't breathe without it flooding his head, couldn't close his eyes without her image flashing behind his lids. She climaxed into his hand with a rush, the hot cream wetting his palm.

Catching her hips, he dragged her to the edge of the table, sinking to his knees before her and pushing her thighs wide. As he pressed his mouth against her, she screamed and he plunged his tongue inside her folds, using his thumbs to spread the lips of her pussy wide. Her sheath was still convulsing and he groaned against her, his entire body hardening, clamoring with the urge to fuck her hard, fast, deep.

She tried to draw her knees up, but he shifted his grip, keeping her thighs pressed flat against the table as he fucked his tongue in and out of her pussy, drinking down the hot, musky cream, nuzzling his nose against her clit. Darci screamed out his name and at the sound of it, his control started to snap. Slowly, he rose, staring down at her hungrily. He reached up, removing his jacket and shoulder holster, tossing it on the floor, and laying the holster and gun on the table.

Her eyes locked on his hands as he unbuttoned his shirt. A hot, hungry look entered her eyes as he shrugged the shirt off. Pride rippled through him as she stared at his torso and arms with an almost drugged fascination. He unbuckled his belt and freed the buttons at his fly as he kicked off his shoes.

His cock sprang out as he shoved his jeans and shorts down to just past his hips. Her eyes dropped to linger on his sex and Kellan shuddered as her tongue appeared, slicking across her swollen lips.

Her heart slammed against her ribs as she stared at his cock, the ruddy head jerking under her gaze. It curved up thick and straight, nestled in a bed of dark, springy curls. Her mouth watered but before she could shift position and slide off the table, he bent over her. She pouted, poking her lip out as she reached down and trailed her fingers across the iron-hard length of his cock. A pearly bead of fluid dampened her fingers and she lifted them to her lips, sucking the pre-come with a satisfied smile.

"Witch," he growled, nudging her thighs wider and stepping between them.

Darci chuckled huskily but the sound died away as he pumped his hips, dragging his cock across her wet folds, burrowing against her. Her clit throbbed as he rubbed against it. Bringing her knees up, she gripped his hips and arched into him.

The blunt head nudged against her entrance. Digging her nails into his arms, she shifted the angle of her hips, groaning as he slipped just the merest fraction of his cock inside her. Hunger pulsed in her belly. Tipping her hips higher, she tried to draw more of his length inside her.

His hands, hot and hard, cupped her hips, stilling the frantic movement easily as he slowly pushed deeper.

"Slowly," he teased her.

"Damn it, Kellan," she cried out, clenching her muscles around him. A smile spread across her face as he stiffened over her, dark flags of color appearing high on his cheekbones, his lids drooping low over his eyes.

She did it again, clenching and then releasing the muscles in her pussy until he growled and plunged deep, burying his cock completely inside of her. She screamed out his name, staring blindly up at the sky as he pulled out and pushed back inside with one long, hard plunge. Her womb throbbed. Her clit burned.

His weight crushed against her, pressing her into the table as he moved higher on her body, one hand cupping her ass and lifting her. Now each stroke of his cock had his pelvis rasping across her clit. Desire, need, and hunger built inside her with every thrust of his cock into her pussy.

"Look at me," he growled.

She met his gaze, staring into his eyes, the stark burning hunger in his face adding to the hot, burning hunger in her gut. He moved lower down on her body, so that his mouth was only a breath away from hers. Caught in the hot, hungry depths of his hazel gaze, she sobbed out his name as he started to shaft her slowly, with short, powerful digs of his hips.

"I love you, Darci," he rasped just before his mouth caught hers. The words *I love you* were trapped in her throat, smothered by his mouth as he plunged his tongue into her mouth, mimicking the rhythm of his hips.

The driving hunger in her body finally exploded and she shuddered as the muscles in her pussy seized around his cock, clenching at his flesh as he pulled out and worked his cock back inside. She screamed into his mouth as he started to pound harder against her, his cock swelling within her pussy. A roar rumbled out of his chest, the sound of it mingling with the short, staccato sounds of her cries as she worked her hips against him. Her skin felt too hot, too tight to contain everything that was exploding inside of her.

Bright pinwheels of light exploded in front of her eyes, and her breath felt trapped in her lungs. The hot splash of his seed spurted within her pussy and she whimpered as the convulsions in her sheath finally started to slow. Her body went limp under his and her hands smacked into the table as her muscles went lax.

His body collapsed against her, his weight crushing her into the table. Kellan's chest rose and fell like a bellows, his breath moving the hair just behind her ear. Stroking one hand up his side, she whispered, "I love you, Kellan."

His head lifted and he stared sleepily down at her face, a slow, hesitant smile creeping across his face. "You do, huh?"

She grinned at him. "Well, why else would I be nervous? If I was just using you for sex, this would be easy. I can handle easy. Don't handle more complicated stuff very well."

A cold chill raced across her flesh as he pushed himself up, straightening over her body and tugging his jeans back up. He stroked his finger down her cheek, his eyes soft and gentle. "I guess we're going to have to fumble our way through it together, then."

Chapter Nine

෨

"Peggy."

One brow cocked up over his hazel eyes as he said, "You know that's the fifth time you've said her name." They lay in her bed, her hand pressed against his heart, his cupped over hers.

"I can hardly believe it. She's so…well, Peggy. She fades into the background. Okay artist, but nothing spectacular. That's just her…she just—blends."

"I guess she was tired of blending," he murmured. She shivered as he lifted her hand to his mouth and pressed a kiss to her palm.

"Why?" Darci asked, staring out the window.

"She wanted to be famous. And she never stood out. In any way. This was her way of making sure she stood out from the rest," Kellan said, lifting one shoulder in a shrug.

"Umm…maybe she should have dyed her hair purple or something. This was kind of extreme."

Kellan turned his head and brushed his lips across her forehead. "That's the sanity in you speaking. Her and sanity had a breakup a while ago."

* * * * *

In the silence of the cell, Peggy's hand raced over her sketchbook. A giggle escaped her as she added the finishing touches to the sketch, Kellan and Darci, wrapped around each other, his back arched as he drove inside her, Darci's eyes wide, her mouth open in a silent scream.

And a knife, long and wicked, pierced his flesh, entered through his mid-back, exiting through his belly and impaling Darci. Though the sketch was in pencil, she could see the gleam of sweat on their bodies, the bright emerald of Darci's eyes, the copper and red strands of Kellan's hair.

And the bright red of the blood that puddled under them.

"I'll be remembered..." Peggy whispered, a smile lighting her face.

"I'll be remembered..."

HIS EVERY DESIRE

෩

Dedication

ஐ

I'd like to credit KB with the phrase…
Keep your friends close…and your enemies dead in the
ground.

Trademarks Acknowledgement

ஐ

The author acknowledges the trademarked status and trademark owners of the following wordmarks mentioned in this work of fiction:

Armani: Giorgio Armani S.p.A. Corporation
Benz: DaimlerChrysler AG Corporation
Beretta: Baretta is Italian made
Browning: Browning Corporation Utah
Jaguar: Jaguar Cars Limited
Porsche: Dr. Ing. h.c. F. Porsche AG Corporation
Taurus: Ford Motor Company

Prologue

℘

The blood was everywhere. The thick metallic scent of it in the air, the darkening stains of it as it dried in puddles on the floor.

He was trapped in the dream again, a dream more than twenty years old, and he knew it. Knew that if he could just wake up, the dream would fall apart...until the next time.

But he couldn't wake up. Walking through the hall of the condo, he felt trapped. Everything seemed smaller now — he was just a kid when he found her, and then everything had seemed so much larger — so large he felt lost.

Now he felt trapped, the walls closing in on him as he moved down the hallway.

She lay there, her pretty, dark blue eyes, just like his own, staring sightlessly up at the ceiling, her face a mask of blood and bruises. She was naked.

Twenty years ago, he'd stood there, staring at the battered, nude body of his sister, the scream forming in his throat as his young mind tried to make sense of what he was seeing.

With age, he could now make sense of it, although it didn't lessen the fury or the pain any, not in the dream. Not when he was awake.

There had been blood on her thighs. Lots of it.

Dried blood on her arms, her belly, her legs, and numerous little cuts. Bruises on her legs, her arms, from where she'd been held down.

Twenty years ago, he had turned away, run away, as though maybe he could outrun it and maybe it wouldn't be real.

She had whispered to him. He had heard her voice—it had terrified him and comforted him at the same time as she had murmured to him. *Run. Run away, baby. Hide and don't look back.*

He had run. Fast and hard, furiously. There had been nights when her voice had come to him, waking him from a fitful sleep and he had started to run again. *Time to go, baby. He's looking for you again…*

Finally, that had stopped. And he had stopped running and started planning.

In the dream though, he hadn't run away. In the dream…

He moved to kneel at her side, took the blanket from the couch and covered her before he reached up and gently closed the sightless eyes.

And he whispered, "They will pay, Carly. Every last one of them. I won't stop until I see it happen."

It was the sound of his own voice, a hoarse whisper, as he murmured those words that woke him up.

Joel lay in bed, his gut churning from the aftereffects of the dream.

Twenty years later, three of the men who had raped his sister were dead. They had paid, just as he had promised Carly.

The temperature in the room dropped and Joel tugged the tangled sheet so that it covered him better. "Carly, some rest?"

She laughed. The laughter had sound, and he glanced around the room, wondering if she would appear this time. He saw just the faintest white glow hovering in the corner. "You were awake before I showed up, baby."

A cool breeze seemed to drift toward him and the white glow came closer. "Let it go—Grainger doesn't matter. Not to me. I'm past caring about him."

Joel scowled. "If you didn't care about him, you wouldn't be here, would you?"

The glow solidified into an actual form and he felt a fist wrap around his heart as he saw her face. She was so damned pretty. So determined to get him away from the hellhole they had lived in with Mom.

"It's not Vincent Grainger that's keeping me here," she murmured. "It's you. Once I know you're going to be okay— I'll be fine."

Joel smiled tightly. "I am okay."

Carly just sighed. "Baby, you haven't been okay a day in your life."

He sighed, shoving a hand through his hair. "Look, I have to do this. You don't understand that, but I have to. Once I deal with him, I'll...I'll do..."

His voice trailed off because he didn't know what he was going to do.

Carly smiled at him. Reaching up, she touched her hand to his face. The ghostly touch felt cool against his cheek. He met her gaze as she said, "That's just the problem, though. You don't know what you're going to do. You have to look for a life beyond this. I didn't get a chance to live mine. Don't waste yours on hatred, Brother."

Then she faded away.

Joel closed his eyes.

Hatred had eaten away at him for so long—it was just a part of his life. He lived with it. Breathed it.

He couldn't just shove this aside—not until it was all done.

The men who had killed his sister would die. Three of them were already dead in the ground, but there was at least one more — Vincent Grainger.

The bastard who had given the order. The bastard who had stood over her while his men raped her. Had them hold her down while he took his turn.

He'd made a mistake. Two of the men he'd killed early on, without learning if there were others. They'd been bragging about it, the dumb shits, talking about Carly and other men and women they'd killed, just because Grainger had decided he wanted it done.

The third one, though, Robert Ellingsworth, that one, Joel had questioned before he'd killed him. Not that it had done much good. Ellingsworth had been certain, to the very last second that Joel wouldn't kill him, and he was more afraid of Grainger than he was of Joel, and he hadn't talked.

Not when Joel had beat him bloody, not when he'd damn near twisted the bastard's balls off.

Ellingsworth had been dead a little less than a year now, and Joel had run out of resources. It was time. Time to move in on Grainger.

Time to ruin him. And when the bastard understood how it was to feel helpless, caught, trapped, then Joel would kill him.

But first…first…there was something else.

Chapter One

හ

"I want your wife." Joel stared coolly at Vincent Grainger, showing no sign of the worry that he might to fuck this up.

But he couldn't take it anymore. If he saw one more mark on her...

Grainger had shark's eyes. Empty, expressionless pits of black in his face that had terrified more than one man. He was a man of average height, average weight—he worked out religiously, and the tailored Armani suits he wore covered a body that was lean and fit. There was nothing at all intimidating about the man...except those eyes.

There was no sign of life in them, no sign of a soul of any sorts. And it often seemed as though his eyes could see clear through a man.

Grainger stared at Joel, with those flat shark's eyes as he said, "I beg your pardon?"

Joel laughed, a low, mirthless sound. "You heard me. You understand, too. You asked what it would take for me to become a...business acquaintance of yours, and I want your wife. Otherwise, I'll take my business elsewhere."

Vincent laughed. "No piece of ass is worth gambling a fortune on, Joel."

A small smile crept across Joel's face and he shrugged. "Well, since you like dick more anyway, you probably wouldn't know. It's not like she's exactly your type. She can still be your little trophy wife—but I want her in my bed."

Very few people knew Vincent's Grainger's secrets the way Joel did, and he knew damn near all of them, including the fact that the crime lord was homosexual. If it had been anyone else who had laid it on the line like that, Grainger probably would have killed him.

But they both knew Grainger was scared of Joel.

A lot of people were. And Joel did every damned thing he could to foster that fear.

He didn't have the shark's eyes, although his face was more often than not an expressionless mask, and he hadn't ever invited a man to dinner and shot his guest in the forehead before going on to dine, the corpse bleeding on the table, as Grainger had.

But he had killed before, often enough, brutally enough, that none questioned his ability, and willingness to do it again.

"One of these days, Joel, you just might push me too far," Grainger whispered, his lips barely moving as he spoke. A dull red flush of anger stained his cheeks and those normally flat black eyes glinted.

Joel grinned arrogantly. "Maybe. But not while I still have some things you really, really want. A few pieces of land, several building contracts. Among other things."

The other man chuckled. "You know, it's a damned good thing I like you."

Actually, it was enough to make Joel sick. Not that he hadn't been aiming for this for twenty years.

To see Grainger dead—that had been his goal since he had been all of twelve years old. For the past ten years, he had had been moving toward that goal with slow, but steady determination. Working his way first into Grainger's notice…then gaining his trust.

He hadn't just been biding his time though—Grainger wasn't the only one Joel wanted dead. There had been three men, including Grainger, possibly four, he didn't know for certain.

Three of them were already dead.

The only thing that had kept Grainger alive was Joel's need to make sure he had all of them.

All of the men who had raped and killed his sister. Once he knew for certain, Grainger was dead.

Joel had lied, killed, cheated, and slept with the enemy, figuratively speaking, fucking his way through every last female around Grainger who could share the slightest bit of information. Killing some of the scum who stood in his way. Befriending the human garbage who flocked to the crime lord.

Lying—lying was a way of life for him now, and had been since he was twelve. He'd cheated and stolen most of the money he'd used to buy his first piece of land, a slice of beach that Grainger had been looking at. And when Grainger had sent a man to...*convince* Joel to sell, Joel had killed him.

The world wouldn't mourn the men Joel had killed. Joel knew that. Joel, in his gut, knew that. Even if it did give him some uneasy moments, and even if it did sometimes bring him out of a restless sleep, his body soaked with sweat, his stomach roiling, the need to puke choking him.

He'd killed, and he'd kill again if that was what it took to get rid Grainger. It was every bit as ruthless as it sounded, Joel knew.

Grainger respected ruthlessness. It was one of the few things, other than money, the bastard *did* respect. And Joel had become damn near as ruthless as the man he wanted to kill.

Sometimes—only sometimes—he had a brief flicker of regret over what he had become. Over the things he had done.

Move in closer to Grainger, gain his trust, find out what he needed to know...and kill him.

His sins were myriad, never mind he had committed them in the name of revenge to reach his goal, and it was a damn understandable goal.

Of course, some might consider killing Grainger a sin as well.

Joel didn't.

There was murder...and then there was justice. And the world would be a better place without that sick fuck in it anyway.

But still, Joel wondered, once Grainger was dead, would his sins keep him awake, screaming into the night, as the self-hatred took a deep hold on his soul?

Right now, he could ignore the voices of his conscience. Focusing on the goal made it easy to wear blinders.

After though—he didn't know how he was going to cope after.

When he had started, none of that had mattered. Nothing had mattered except reaching his goal, completing the plan.

Until Tracy.

For twenty years, he had operated in a vacuum, unaware of anything that didn't pertain to the mission, uncaring of the world around him.

Until he had seen her, seen the fear in her eyes, seen the fragile prize that Vincent Grainger kicked around like a puppy.

One look. That was all it had taken, one look into those large, dove gray eyes, looking so lost, so battered in the delicate features of her face.

One look—and the blinders he'd worn for twenty years were viciously, brutally jerked away, and he found himself wanting something other than vengeance.

Something other than justice.

Right now, *she* was what kept him awake at night.

Not screaming, but sweating and hard and aching...and furious. The bruises he saw on her silken skin, the ghosts he saw in her eyes, the fear and the way she cringed when Vincent spoke to her in that low, silky, deadly tone.

Joel hoped he wasn't screwing up the plan, but he couldn't take seeing one more bruise on Tracy Grainger's lovely face. Couldn't take seeing her move carefully, holding herself rigidly so nobody saw the pain each move caused.

Although Grainger was gay, he still fucked his wife. But rumor had it that he could only get it up with a woman when he was violent. And the more violent he got, the more he liked it.

Vincent was big into doing things he liked.

The first time Joel had seen Tracy, she had been slowly sitting up on the floor, tears rolling down her face as she smoothed her robe over her lower body. She hadn't moved quickly enough to hide the small traces of blood on her thighs, and she hadn't ducked her head quickly enough for him to miss seeing the busted lip or the bruise spreading across her face like an ugly stain.

That had been the first time Vincent had invited him to his elegant coastal mansion in Maine for a weekend of business and pleasure. Vincent operated mainly out of New York—the mansion was for play, and for the times he wanted more privacy.

Joel had since learned that it was also Tracy's prison.

There had been plenty of females around, both professional and otherwise, if Joel had wanted to fuck.

But he hadn't.

Not even when he saw the delicate, battered form of the brutalized woman lying on the ground. What he had wanted was to kill, to maim as Vincent smirked insolently down at her and slowly zipped his pants.

Joel had watched as Vincent licked the blood from his fist, and rage had torn through him—hot, potent rage, unlike anything he'd ever felt.

But then she had glanced at him, not at her husband, but at Joel, with those wide, frightened eyes, and for the first time in years, Joel had felt true guilt.

Because as she sat there, bruised and shaking from her husband's rape, he had wanted her. Not because of the violence that hung in the air, but because of her. He had looked at her, and had wanted her…and had looked at Grainger and had hated him more than he had ever hated him before.

It shouldn't have been possible, but it was, and as time passed, that hatred festered and grew until it was like a great, black sickness in his gut.

So had the need. A need to feel that soft, slender body against his, to ease the fear he saw in her eyes, to hold her and promise her that she'd never know another moment's pain, another moment's fear.

That had been close to two years ago, and over that time he'd seen repeats, or caught glimpses of her face before she turned away to hide more bruises.

He wasn't going to see another mark on her. Not ever.

Allowing a slow, sardonic grin to curve up his mouth, Joel said, "Well? What's your decision?"

* * * * *

Two weeks later

Tracy sensed them approaching and part of her wished she was swimming in the ocean, instead of the warmed indoor pool. In the ocean, in some toxic, polluted lake or the piranha infested Amazon—somewhere that she could just keep swimming, and swimming. Someplace away from Vincent.

At least she didn't have to worry about him hitting her right now. Vincent had never hit her in front of another person—likely, he wouldn't start now. He didn't give a damn if anybody knew he beat her, if anybody knew he raped her, but he did prefer his violence to happen without prying eyes.

But as she approached the shallow end of the pool and started up the steps, a hot flush spread up her face.

It was Joel Lockhart, her husband's newest partner, or would-be partner. So far, from what she knew, Joel held out, refusing the subtle gifts, and the not so subtle bribes with a disinterest that only strengthened Vincent's desire to forge a partnership with the man.

Moving out of the pool, she dutifully crossed to Vincent, kissing his cheek and accepting a towel from him. Her robe lay just a few feet away, but she didn't dare move to get it, not yet.

There was something in the air…something odd, something she didn't like.

Vincent turned away from her and she breathed a silent sigh of relief—maybe it was nothing.

But then tension crawled up her spine as Vincent faced Joel and said, "I assume you already like what you've seen of the package. But let's let you see the rest of it."

When Vincent turned around and stared at her, Tracy would have given anything, *anything* to have just never been born. "Take off your swimsuit, Tracy."

"What…?" she asked slowly, licking her lips, flicking her eyes nervously from Vincent to Joel. This was some sort of joke. Although she knew of her husband's personal sexual preference, he always displayed an insane jealousy anytime somebody seemed to notice her as a woman.

And he was telling her to strip? In front of *Joel*?

Interest from men like Joel always inspired the worst jealousy in Vincent, spurring beatings and bruisings that would have her hobbling around for weeks. Joel was pure male, strong and arrogant, broad-shouldered, lean-hipped with that loose, lazy stride that seemed to proclaim he owned every last inch of the land he walked on, wherever he went.

She'd seen the hot male interest in his eyes on more than one occasion, just like she had seen the anger in his eyes the few times he had seen her with a bruise on her face. But he had never once moved in her direction—and now Vincent wanted her to *strip* for him?

Vincent narrowed his eyes at her. "Don't make me repeat myself."

Fear fluttered in her belly. Slowly, she reached up, peeling one black strap down, then the other, but before she pulled the suit down, she looked back at Vincent, her face hot. "Vincent, what's going on?" she asked thickly.

"Joel has agreed to become my partner in several future endeavors. In exchange, all he wants is you," Vincent said, smiling. *Smiling,* like they were talking about getting a new car or something.

Humiliation bloomed in her. Her skin went hot and tight and nausea roiled in her belly. He had fucking *sold* her? That was what this was...*her,* in exchange for the money and power that Joel could bring him.

Tracy shook her head, slowly backing away. "No," she whispered, almost soundlessly, unaware of how frightened, how tormented her eyes looked.

Vincent moved toward her and she cowered as he raised his fist, but the blow never came.

When Joel spoke, she finally dared to open her eyes and she saw him holding Vincent's wrist in a grip so tight that Vincent's fingers were going bloodless. "Mine, Vincent. Remember that, and while she's mine...there will be no marks on her, no bruises, no rapes."

Vincent jerked his hand, but Joel never once let go. "I can fuck my wife when I chose—and I don't remember me not touching her being part of the deal."

Joel dropped Vincent's hand, and as he moved a little closer, she saw something in his eyes that she'd never seen before. Hate. He hated Vincent. What game was he playing?

"You want to fuck, go fuck Jamil. Tracy's clean...*now.* You both took the blood tests." At that, Tracy's face flamed red, remembering when the doctor had woken her out of her sleep thirteen days ago and jabbed a needle in her arm, all without saying a word. And Vincent hadn't touched her since...how long had they been talking about this? "As long as she's mine, you won't touch her. I want to fuck *her*, not everybody else you've fucked."

"You can't fucking tell me what to do with my wife!" Vincent shouted.

"I can. You gave her to me. And if you think you can back out...*try*. I'll fucking gut you. I get what I want, Vincent. Remember that."

Vincent's face flushed an angry red, but then the color drained out of his face as he stared into Joel's face. He meant it. And he was too fucking afraid of Joel to do what he normally would have done to somebody who threatened him. He'd tried, several times, to kill Joel. And each time, it had cost him men. Lots of men.

Tracy didn't know what in the hell to think as Vincent gave one terse nod before turning to face her. He couldn't touch her...but that meant...*Oh, God*, she prayed. *This wasn't exactly what I meant when I asked for a way out!*

But there was no answer, divine or otherwise, just her husband moving up to take her swimsuit and ease it down over the mounds of her breasts. "How...how long?" she asked, her voice a tight, nervous whisper, jerking her eyes to meet the dark blue gaze of the man standing behind her husband.

With his long legs splayed and his arms crossed over his chest, Joel stared at her. Those midnight blue eyes were hungry, hot as blue flame as he watched Vincent strip the black tank suit down her belly, over her hips, and push it down until it fell into a puddle around her ankles.

A harsh sound left him and she stared at him, half terrified, as he seemed to feast on her with his eyes. They almost seemed to gleam with hunger—Joel's dark eyes rarely showed any emotion—seeing that emotion in them, directed at her, suddenly made her feel weak. "For as long as I want you," he whispered, moving closer as Vincent backed away. "Damn it, you're lovely."

Automatically, she started to bring her hands up to cover herself, but he caught them, holding her wrists gently in his as he sank to his knees in front of her, nuzzling the damp valley between her breasts. Her skin crawled—jerking her gaze up, she realized Vincent was staring at them, his eyes hot with lust, but it was Joel he was focused on.

Not her.

Hell, if Joel saw that look…but all thought fled from her brain as Joel closed his mouth over her nipple and started to suck. Not bite. Not pinch. Just suck, slow lazy motions that had needs she had forgotten she had suddenly springing to life. A soft cry escaped her and her legs wobbled.

As she started to crumple, he stood quickly, catching her against him as he whirled around, bracing his hips against the low stone wall that ran along the edge of the pool.

"Touch him, Tracy. He's paying handsomely for this— make sure he gets his money's worth." She stared at Vincent as he spoke, her face flaming, confusion raging in her. Damn it— what in the hell was this? The heat spilling in her belly was too new, too hot, she couldn't think…

"I said touch him," Vincent said quietly. She met his eyes as he purred, "However he wants, wherever he wants. You'll give him his every desire. Be his pretty little whore, and make sure he gets what he's paying for."

She flinched at Vincent's words, tucking her chin as tears of shame burned her eyes. Joel's head lowered and he whispered against her ear, "This isn't about money, Tracy. You're mine now…"

As he took her hands in his, placing them against his chest, Tracy kept her face lowered. But she couldn't help but watch. She'd noticed him, noticed him watching her, noticed that strong body under the suits he wore…and for once, a man was touching her without trying to hurt her.

For one panicked moment, the thought circled through her head…*I can't do this!*

If she backed away from Joel, her gut told her he would let her go. He didn't have that sadistic streak in him that would make him want to hurt a woman. She could back away from him and he wouldn't force himself on her.

But her husband was staring at her, watching them greedily, and he *would* hurt her. Tracy had learned long ago to adapt to her situation. Otherwise, she'd die.

This was one of those times.

That made it just slightly easier to admit that she *was* curious about how he felt, what he looked like under those Armani suits.

Hard, strong... Tracy had learned the hard way to fear a man's strength and some panicked voice inside her whispered, *He's a man...he'll hurt you sooner or later.* Even though every other instinct in her shouted that he wouldn't hurt her.

Slowly, she loosened his tie and tugged it off, carefully placing it aside before reaching for his shirt. As she unbuttoned it, he shrugged out of his jacket. His movements brought him closer and she gasped as she felt the hard ridge of his cock brush against her naked belly. Even though blood rushed to her face, she never once looked up, just kept unbuttoning his shirt until she could spread it open.

The open shirt framed a hard, muscled wall of skin that gleamed a soft gold, a thin line of dark hair that ran like a silken ribbon between the dark copper of his flat nipples, curling around his navel. His abdomen was hard and lean, and as she stared at him, the muscles in his belly quivered just a little.

Almost as if he liked the way she stared at him.

Tracy found herself wanting to touch him, curious to see if his skin felt as hard and tough as he looked. Before she could lay her hands on him to find out, he shrugged out of his shirt and hauled her against him.

She stiffened at the hard feel of his body against hers, the taut, strong muscles that banded her to him. Her breasts were pressed flat by the wall of his chest. She could feel his heart slamming against her chest and his hands — his hands held her tightly to him, and she could feel the reined power in them.

A shiver of fear ran through her, surrounded by all that heat, all that male power.

But his mouth, when he lowered it to hers, was achingly gentle. He traced his tongue over the seam of her lips and she sighed shakily, letting him push his tongue inside her mouth. A rough groan rumbled out of his chest, the vibration of it tightening her nipples and making her belly clench.

"You're so damned sweet," he muttered, drawing back and staring down at her. Thick black hair tumbled into his eyes as he stared down her, the lean planes of his face hungry and intent, dark flags of color high on his cheeks.

She tried to look away, but his hand caught her chin and lifted her face back to his. "Mine," he said gutturally, and she shivered at the possessive, rapacious look in his eyes. His eyes stared into hers as he cupped her face, pressing a gentle kiss to her brow, moving down to buss her lips gently. "My every desire… You are all of that, and more."

The gentleness in his voice, the sincerity of his words made her head spin. Damn it, it had been too long since she had dealt with these kinds of emotions. Not just interest, but *need*, coupled with a need to please as well as be pleased.

All she knew how to handle anymore was fear. Tracy was so damned tired of being afraid.

She swallowed and moved her hands to his chest, gliding them down and reaching for the buckle of his belt. As she unfastened it, she heard his rough gasp. Behind her, she could almost feel the hot, heavy breaths of Vincent as he watched them.

Blocking Vincent out of her mind, she focused on the goal. That was how she survived. Focusing on the goal. Right now, it was making sure that Joel was pleased with her. If she made him angry…Vincent would make her pay. If she disappointed him, Vincent would make her pay.

So she did what she guessed was expected, and unzipped his slacks.

The hard, heavy length of his cock jerked as she freed him, the ruddy head already glistening with moisture. Tracy swallowed as she reached out, capturing that bead of moisture and slicking it over the head of his cock. His sex bobbed under her touch and she started to jerk her hand back at the sudden movement, only to have Joel close his hand over her wrist, guiding her back to him. He pumped his hips against her hand and she automatically closed her fingers around him, staring at him with wide eyes as he started to shudder.

His eyes met hers and she looked away, nervous, embarrassed. Staring at his cock seemed a little safer, oddly enough, than staring into those hungry eyes. Another drop of moisture seeped from him and unconsciously, she licked her lips as she watched it roll down the crown of his cock.

As she started to sink to her knees, she heard Vincent, his voice harsh and raspy, as he said, "Suck on his dick, Trace. Tell me how it feels."

Tracy's face flushed, blood roaring in her ears so loudly that she barely heard Joel snarl at Vincent. "Shut the fuck up. You want to watch, I don't give a damn. But stop talking."

His hands caught her hair and he forced her face back up to his, shaking his head. "No, Tracy," he murmured. "Just what you want…" but she ignored him.

Focus on the goal…focus…focus…it had been her mantra for so long, but rarely had the path to the goal caused such urges to arise within her.

As she closed her lips around the fat head of his cock, she was startled at the hot, *hungry* urges that suddenly flooded her.

This wasn't the first time she'd given a blowjob. Vincent liked it when she sucked him off…it was the only thing she could do that he actually enjoyed without having to hit her. But she'd never enjoyed doing it before. Never...the rush of heat that hit her belly as she slowly pumped her head up and down was foreign. She sucked on him, moaning softly at the hot, rich taste of his skin, the way he jerked in her mouth and the soft, almost ecstatic moans that slid from him.

"Tracy..."

She continued moving, reaching up with one hand to wrap her fingers around the base of his cock. He was so wide that it stretched her mouth to suck on him. Wet, slurping noises filled the air and part of her realized how frantic her movements had become.

His cock jerked again in her mouth, but then her mouth and her hands were empty and she felt as though she was flying through the air. His hands closed around her, lifting her up and planting her naked ass on the waist high garden wall. A soft hungry moan escaped her and she didn't even realize she was reaching for him until he caught her hands and moved them down, holding them flat against the stone upon which she sat. "Fuck, Tracy..." he muttered, staring down at her, his chest heaving up and down. "Look at me. Listen...*he* doesn't exist right now. You do what you want, not what he expects of you."

But she had been. Licking her lips, she tried to find her voice, but she couldn't speak.

She was too damned hungry for him. All that escaped her was a soft, hungry little moan, and when Joel heard it, his eyes narrowed and he hissed.

His hands let go of her wrists and he pushed her thighs apart. She was dimly aware that he stared at her as he sank to his knees in front of her. Tracy's head was still reeling, her mouth watering for another taste of him, and nothing she saw made any sense. She couldn't focus...had to focus... had to...

But then he put his mouth on her. She was *wet*. Oh, shit. Wet...aroused...she hadn't actually wanted a man's touch in what seemed like forever and when he slid his tongue over her clit, she exploded, her fingers buried in the thick black curls of his hair, and she screamed.

He drew the tender little bud into his mouth and pumped two fingers inside of her as she climaxed, and another one hit even before the first one had ended. He groaned against the mound of her sex and the vibration of it had her shivering.

"You're sweet," he muttered, pulling back just a little as he pushed her thighs wider apart and shifted his angle.

Then he plunged his tongue inside her core, fucking it in and out. Her eyes flew wide, one leg coming up to hook over his shoulder and hold him tightly against her.

She came again and again as he feasted on her pussy and by the time he rose, she was limp and exhausted, staring at him with huge dark eyes, her mind clouded, her body one big ache of satisfaction.

But he wasn't done.

He reached for the pants that he had kicked off at some point and she watched dully as he donned a rubber. Blood rushed to her face as she caught sight of Vincent standing to the side—staring at them. He was masturbating, his pants unzipped, cock out, his hand pumping up and down his length while he watched them greedily.

"Stop," Joel whispered, catching her face. "Don't look at him. Look at me...you're mine now. He knows this...and you will, too, soon enough."

As he moved between her thighs, she stared up at him, her gaze held captive by his as he slowly pushed inside her. "You're so damned sweet," he grunted. "So tight."

He was stretching her—but oh, it was glorious. Tracy whimpered in his arms as he pulled out and slowly worked a little more of his cock inside her. "Am I hurting you?" he rasped.

Soundlessly, she mouthed, "No," as her head fell back, limp. Her flesh was slicked with sweat and as he buried his

151

cock completely inside her, he brought her fully against him, his chest rubbing against the tight buds of her nipples.

"Good...this sweet little pussy won't ever feel pain again," he crooned as he pulled out, surging back inside her with just a little more force. "Say my name, Tracy...I want to hear you scream it as you come again."

"Joel," she whispered automatically, her eyes closing. She didn't see the look of disappointment that crossed his face as she arched against him.

She was tight, slick, hotter than anything, so hot she burned him even through the thin barrier of the rubber. He hated that latex barrier—soon, soon, he'd fuck her without a barrier. Feel the silken, slick skin of her pussy clenching around his dick...damn it, he couldn't wait. His balls drew tight against him with the thought and he gritted his teeth as he fought not to come.

Not yet.

He wanted her to scream out his name because she couldn't help it...not because a man had ordered her to, and she was too afraid not to obey. No more. He wouldn't see fear in her eyes again.

Cupping one slender thigh, he drew it up over his hip as he circled against her, smiling painfully as she gasped out a startled "Oh". Aware that her bastard of a husband was still watching, he lowered his head, keeping his voice low as he crooned against her ear, "I've been dreaming of this...dreaming of the day I'd get you in my arms, when I could bury my dick inside your sweet little pussy, your body moving against mine. The dreams don't even come close...this is the closest to heaven I'm ever going to get."

She shivered as he spoke and the snug little sheath of her pussy started to flex around him. He watched as those pretty, dove gray eyes darkened. When she came, she opened her mouth and breathlessly screamed out his name. A hot blaze of satisfaction rolled through as she climaxed, his name falling from her lips a second time, her eyes wide and dazed. As she shuddered against him, he exploded inside of her, roaring out her name as vicious, gut-wrenching need tore through him.

Everything around him faded away, and for a few minutes, he was aware of nothing more than her—her gasping cries, the way she shivered against him, the way her pussy flexed and squeezed around his cock.

Just her…

* * * * *

It had worked.

Joel still couldn't believe it, damn near two weeks later as he lay behind Tracy, his cock cuddled against her ass while she slept peacefully in his arms. Vincent had come into the room again, watching them.

Tracy had seen him and froze, but Joel had simply eased her back onto the bed and moved down her body, kissing his way down until he sprawled between her legs and used his mouth on her.

She loved that. A slow, sad smile curved his mouth. He understood why—Vincent's only pleasure in her body was when he could hurt it.

Stroking his hand up and down the smooth skin of her hip, he pressed his lips to her shoulder. "Not anymore, Tracy," he promised. "Not anymore."

Vincent had fucked up. A man never gave away his greatest asset so easily, so blindly. Maybe Vincent hadn't realized how much Joel had wanted her.

His every desire…

Those words echoed through his head and he buried his face in her hair.

In his arms, he held what his heart had desired for years. He just hoped that once he was done with what he had to do, he could keep her.

But even through the satisfaction, and the slightly dismayed awe that he had for her, he was afraid.

Before, if he had fucked up and ended up dead, it would be only be his life that was lost.

But now—if he messed up now, if Grainger somehow figured out who he was, Joel would pay.

And so would Tracy.

Chapter Two

ဢ

Tracy shook her head as Joel repeated himself. "Divorce him. File for divorce. I'll come with you. Then I'll take you home with me. He won't hurt you."

"I can't," she said softly, shaking her head again. She still couldn't fathom it—even though she was still trapped, the same way she had been before, she was happy.

At least, happier than she had been in a very long time.

Vincent never touched her anymore. Hardly ever spoke to her. And Joel was always there, it seemed, pampering her, coddling her, taking care of her.

And now he was offering yet more protection—he *could*. He could protect her from Vincent, was possibly the only person who could.

But she couldn't risk it—not yet.

As though he was following her silent train of thought, he asked, "Why not?" As he took her hand, he sat down on the rock-strewn beach, tugging her down until she cuddled on his lap. As he wrapped his arms around her, she rested her cheek on his chest, listening to the steady sound of his heartbeat.

"I can't, Joel. He's told me what will happen if I ever try to leave…and I've tried. But the last time…"

Joel knew about the last time. She'd ended up in the hospital with a broken jaw. That had been seven months ago, two months before he'd made his decision and told Vincent that he wanted his wife. And for five months, he'd had her. And she hadn't been hurt, not once.

Surprisingly though, he was. Hurt that she wouldn't leave her husband for him. Even though he understood how afraid she was.

"I won't let him hurt you, Tracy," he whispered against her brow, hugging her fiercely.

"I know." She drew back a little, and Joel felt his heart clench as she stared up at him with those big gray eyes, her soft, blonde, tousled locks framing her elfin features. "It's not me I'm worried about." She swallowed and he watched, rage already brewing inside him. What had Vincent told her?

"Last time I tried to leave him, he sent a man to my mom's house. While she was sleeping, the man raped Mama's nurse. And he told me next time, he'd find somebody who liked them old and feeble."

Joel clenched his jaw, fighting back the need to bellow out the rage inside him. Quietly, he said, "I can take care of your mama, Tracy. And you. I don't want you living in that house anymore."

As she tucked her head under his chin again, he felt his hopes die. But then, an insane delight ripped through him as she murmured, "Let me think about it, Joel. Okay? Just let me think…"

He was silent for a few minutes, his head whirling with thoughts. Over the past few months, he had been making moves that would eventually bring Vincent's world crashing down around him.

Soon, Joel knew, he would have to make the final move. Reveal his hand, so to speak.

When that happened, information he had been gathering would be in the hands of people who desperately wanted to bring Grainger down. Letters, memos, videotapes that Grainger was completely ignorant off, all of which would be sent to the New York City DA, the FBI, and every major news station.

Grainger would have no place to turn. Too many of the people he'd walked on to get where he was would only laugh if he tried to get help. He'd be alone—and that was exactly how Joel wanted him.

He wanted the bastard to feel alone, helpless.

Wanted to see that look in Grainger's eyes before he killed him.

But when that happened, Joel didn't know what in the hell would happen with Tracy.

Joel was tired of lies.

He'd tell her the truth. But when she knew what he had done, the lies he had told, lives that he had most likely ruined, the people he had hurt—and the blood on his hands—what would she do?

Shoving the thoughts aside, he muttered, "Think later." Tumbling her onto her back, he slanted his mouth across hers. "Think later," He repeated, his voice harsh and guttural. Right now, I want to make love to you."

Under the cloudy gray sky, as the surf crashed against the rocks several hundred feet away, he stripped her naked, worshipped her body with his hands, his mouth, adored her with his eyes, and etched every last nuance of her on his memory.

The clock was ticking...the game would be over soon.

* * * * *

From the cliffs, Vincent watched as his partner fucked Tracy.

He licked his lips hungrily, wishing he was the one taking Joel's cock into his body.

It wasn't a new thing. He'd been having fantasies about Joel Lockhart almost since he'd met the strong, intimidating bastard years earlier.

Joel had confused the hell out of Vincent. It was pretty damn obvious that the bastard wanted something, but what in the hell it was, Vincent still didn't know. It couldn't just be Tracy. And if Joel just wanted in on the more lucrative aspects of Vincent's businesses, then he would have acted years ago.

No, Joel had waited years before even accepting an offer from Vincent. Vincent had made easily half a dozen proposals before had Joel accepted even the simplest one.

And all the while, Joel had moved in silence, taking bits and pieces of land that Vincent had wanted. Buying up businesses that Vincent hadn't even realized were on the market.

A damn shark. A deadly opponent. Normally, Vincent would have him dispatched and never blinked twice.

But Vincent didn't want to be rid of Joel Lockhart.

Vincent *wanted* him.

He knew damn good and well that Joel wasn't into men. That didn't stop the fantasies though.

And they had become more frequent, more intense lately.

Hell, there were even times when he fantasized about taking Tracy, driving his dick inside her tight, dry pussy, as Joel fucked him. Jealousy ate him alive. Not because his wife was fucking another man. But because she was fucking the man *he* wanted.

Jamil's appeal had palled, and Vincent had kicked his longtime lover to the curb, but now he wished he hadn't. His balls ached, his cock hurt, and he needed to get fucked.

Or fuck...narrowing his eyes, he focused on Tracy, watching as Joel pulled her to straddle him. Hell, that just might be the closest he got to Joel, fucking his whore.

That's all she was—she hadn't made a sound of dissent when Vincent had turned her over to Joel. Didn't have a qualm about committing adultery.

Vincent was unable to comprehend just how badly frightened Tracy was of him, how terrified she was of telling him *no* on anything.

The jealousy eating at him was tearing a hole inside him.

And he had to fill it.

* * * * *

Joel smiled gently at her as he stroked his hands down her arms.

"I'll miss you," she said softly, forcing herself to smile at him.

His gaze held hers, burning with intensity. She went willingly as he pulled her against him, his lips moving against her hair as he said, "It will be just a few days. Stay at my house —"

She shook her head. "No. I want to, but…if I do — he's paranoid enough. I don't want to give him anything to get suspicious about."

The intensity in his eyes seemed into ignite, the deep midnight blue of his eyes lighting, burning as he stared down at her. "You're leaving him, aren't you?" he whispered into her ear.

Tremulously, she nodded. "Mama's gone, now… I was going to anyway…" tears appeared in her eyes as she recalled the sudden death of her mother three days ago.

"Shhh. It's okay," he whispered, stroking his hands down her back. "You'll be away from here. *Soon.*"

That was what she kept telling herself. Over and over.

* * * * *

As one day without Joel stretched into two, she worried the string of pearls around her throat and paced the house. He'd given her the necklace on Christmas day, and she'd worn the pearls to her mother's funeral, knowing she would leave Vincent.

He had nothing to control her with now.

Nothing.

Finally—*finally*—she started to hope for some sort of future. She was too afraid to daydream that it just might be with Joel. She was falling in love with him. Tracy didn't know what would happen with Joel, if he would tire of her, or if— please, God—if he wanted her the same way she wanted him.

She could dream about it though—something she hadn't done in years.

Tracy would have a *life*. Once she left Vincent.

A life. She hadn't dared dream of happiness, not for years, and she could now. Dream of happiness, of safety…of a life free from fear.

But it would definitely be away from Vincent. Away.

That was what mattered most. Away where she could make love to Joel without him coming in and watching.

When the door creaked open behind her, she didn't jump and spin around at Vincent's voice. After all, he hadn't touched her for months.

And he wouldn't now…

Chapter Three

ஐ

Wrong.

She had been horribly, horribly wrong.

As she sat alone in the living room, a glorious black eye blooming across her face, she watched the digital clock as midnight struck. A new year started. And she made a resolution.

She was getting away from this.

And she wasn't waiting for Joel to come back and get her either. He was going to be gone for three more days, and she was leaving *now*.

For three years, her husband had kept her locked in a world of terror. She had tried to leave. Many times. But the bastard always found her. Somehow.

He wouldn't find her this time. Even if she and Joel didn't last forever, Joel had given her something priceless.

Strength.

She wasn't the weak, spineless woman that Vincent had tried to make her into. And she was no longer destitute either.

Although she'd made a pile of money when she was modeling, in that life long before Vincent had seduced her into believing he loved her, all that money was gone. Well, not gone. She had no doubt that Vincent had doubled and even tripled it.

But she hadn't been able to get to it. The bastard gave her less than fifty dollars a week—enough for gas so she could drive to the gym, and of course, she was followed.

She was penniless. She was married to a rich mobster, and she was penniless. Her car had barely enough gas to get her to town if she wanted to shop a little, but if she wanted clothes, she had to ask, and then the fucking housekeeper would go with her.

Well, until Joel.

Joel had taken her shopping. He'd taken her ice skating — he'd taken her for snow cones at the county fair in August. But that had been with his money.

Now Tracy had money of her own. Mama — bless her — had left a very large amount of money to Tracy. In trust. Which meant Vincent couldn't get it unless she let him.

That had pretty much pissed him off. But he'd held his temper while she went through the heartbreaking process of burying her mom. Regardless of his treatment of her, there were limits to what Vincent could allow the public to see. He had an image to maintain, and sometimes it was the only thing that saved her. And he wouldn't hit her when Joel was around. But that time was over — her safe time was gone. That was very clear.

When he had come to her room today, he had told her, in very specific terms, what would happen to her if that money wasn't transferred to him. Originally he had wanted it transferred when the banks reopened on Monday, but he had decided to give her a few extra days after he'd busted her eye.

She hadn't once mentioned Joel's name, although part of her had screamed out for him as Vincent hit her, as he took her to the floor, tearing the clothes from her struggling body.

She had hit him that time. And he'd responded by closing his hands around her neck. Even as he squeezed the air from her lungs, she had fought. Two of his bastards had ended up coming in, holding her down and laughing while he raped her.

But they hadn't taken turns.

Vincent had offered them the chance, but as she curled away from them, touching the pearls at her neck as if they were some sort of talisman, they had looked at her with fear in her eyes. Fear of what Joel would do.

She knew what she was supposed to do now, while Vincent was out partying. She was supposed to put ice on her face to keep it from swelling. That way, when she had to cover the nasty bruise for a few days, or a week, the swelling wasn't so noticeable.

But she didn't want to. She was tired of trying to hide what he'd done to her. Hell, it didn't work anyway. Vincent could play the respectable businessman all he wanted, but they all knew what he was.

Scum.

A thug.

A mob boss.

Everybody in the small seaside village of Rockfort, Maine knew what he had done to her. They turned a blind eye for the most part, but they knew. She even understood why, in some ways. Vincent Grainger was a dangerous man. People who crossed him often ended up dead.

Tracy decided that having police reports done on your potential mate should just be a way of life. If she'd done that...God, if only somebody had told her. Would she have believed them?

Damn it, she didn't know.

Tracy wanted to think so, wanted to think she would have been smart enough to see the truth. She wanted to think, if somebody had warned her, she'd still be living a relatively happy life in New York, instead of trapped here, all but a prisoner.

Even when Vincent wasn't around, and that was often, she was watched. The four days a week he spent in New York City should have been a little less stressful, but it was worse...because all the servants watched her. He paid them well—everything she did was reported back to him. Every trip to the gym, everything she wore, everything she ate, everything she said.

Closing her eyes, she felt the tears as they slid down her cheeks. If she had to fall in love and marry a criminal, why couldn't it have been Joel? She didn't know what kind of business Joel was in, but it couldn't be completely legit. Legit businessmen didn't do business with men like Vincent Grainger.

At least Joel didn't seem to want to see her hurt. And...he seemed to care. She saw something in his eyes when he looked at her, something...soft. Something sweet. He wanted her, but sometimes, the way he looked at her, she wondered if it was more.

All Vincent wanted was to hurt her. And take everything that she called her own. Like Mama's money.

The money...hell, he wanted the money. Maybe she'd give it to him. So long as it was in the form of a remembrance gift. She'd scatter the money on his grave.

Reaching up, she touched her fingers to the nasty bruise, wincing as pain streaked through her. There was another ache, deep and low in her belly. The tender flesh of her vagina felt bruised and torn. She wasn't bleeding this time, although he had put her in that condition before.

Part of her wondered, wasn't he even the slightest bit worried about Joel?

Swallowing, she shoved that thought out of her head. *She* had to do this. By herself. If she was ever going to be strong enough, she had to leave Vincent on her own.

She'd been planning for months, ever since that cloudy day when Joel had asked her to come to him, to leave Vincent.

She'd planned on doing just that, letting him take care of her and Mama.

Part of her, even then, had known that she would leave Vincent. Joel gave her strength. But it was important that she do this alone. She had to know she could.

Because while Joel wanted her now, he may not want her forever, and then she'd have to know how to take care of herself.

And Vincent—as soon as he thought she was helpless, he'd come after her.

So she'd been planning, researching...and now it was time.

Rising, she moved to the elaborate curio cabinet across from her and took down one picture. Their wedding picture.

The étagère across the room held two photo albums, things the housekeeper liked to put together, pretending that this was a nice, normal home. Three years of marriage...and her mark on this house was in a handful of photo albums, and the blood that washed down the drain after Vincent was done beating her.

Taking those few things, she left the living room, moving tiredly up the stairs—soon. One way or another, soon it would be over.

* * * * *

Joel's skin prickled as he sped closer to the Grainger mansion.

He'd been gone five days. It should have been safe. Hell, Vincent spent most of his time in New York anyway. It *should* have been safe.

There was so fucking much he had to do, he should have stayed longer—but fear had made him rush back.

Tracy...she'd been hurt.

Insane fury went through him at the thought, and he prayed he was being paranoid. Not because he didn't want to hurt Grainger. He did. Badly. But he didn't want to see her bruised...he'd promised her.

As he used his personal key at the front door, he could hear the voices.

Simmonds wasn't there to open it, and that alone meant something was wrong.

The very first thing he heard was Vincent's low voice as he said, "Tracy, you are going to be very, very sorry for this...and I want you here to enjoy every second. Get your ass to your rooms."

Joel ran into the grand room in time to see her lifting her chin into the air. "No," she said coolly. She stood there, calmly, confidently, her eyes clear, not darkened by the fear that was so often in her eyes. She wore gym clothes, and in her hand she held a gym bag.

Tracy had never looked lovelier to him in that instant, as she faced down her abusive husband.

Pride burst through him, but it died as he saw the bruise on her cheek. "Vincent, you're a dead man."

Vincent jumped at the sound of his voice, and Joel had the pleasure of seeing one of the most feared men in the United States pale. But then he sneered. "She has something that belongs to me, and until I get it, our deal is off."

Joel smiled, a chilling smile. Without looking at Tracy, he held out his hand as he stared at Vincent. "The deal is off. She's leaving...with me. And you can go fuck yourself, Grainger."

As Tracy's hand folded around his, they both watched Vincent's face go ruddy with rage. "She's my fucking wife, even if she is your whore!"

Joel didn't remember letting go of Tracy's hand, or flying across the room. As he knocked Vincent to the floor, he growled, "Don't you call her that. Not ever. She never sold herself—she did what she had to in order to keep you from hurting her. That's not a whore. That's a survivor." Kneeling, he drew the gun from his back and placed the muzzle of the Browning at Vincent's chin. "Which is more than I can say for you."

Vincent's eyes widened, darting away, before meeting Joel's eyes again. "You won't," he rasped.

Dropping his voice to a gentle whisper, Joel said, "Believe me—there's nothing I want more. Nothing I mean more. You don't leave here alive...is that understood?"

"Get away from him, Mr. Lockhart."

He cut his eyes to the side, keeping the muzzle of the gun right at Vincent's chin, pressing until it pushed against flesh and met bone. When he saw Simmonds standing just behind Tracy, holding a gun to her head, fury arced through him. "You hurt her, old man, you die."

"Get away from Mr. Grainger, sir, and she won't be hurt."

"Not yet," Vincent rasped. Joel wanted to knock his teeth down his throat, but Tracy...she was more important.

Slowly, Joel rose, stepping over Vincent's body toward Tracy. "Come here, Tracy," he said quietly.

"No," Simmonds said, shaking his head. "Put the gun down."

Joel laid it on the étagère shelf at his right, taking one small step away, still focusing on Simmonds. "Let her go now, Simmonds. You don't want me angry."

Simmonds gave a stiff smile. "I can't do that just yet, sir."

"No!" Tracy screamed, shoving backwards toward the older man standing behind her. Simmonds fell back, swearing, and Joel heard the thick, wet thud of bone hitting something solid. His eyes cut to Grainger to see the man on his feet, drawing his gun.

Fuck...she had blinded Joel to the necessary things. His worry for her had made him forget, and now...

But before Vincent could level the gun, there was a cracking sound. Vincent's hand fell to his side, the gun falling from his fingers. Blood started to pour down the side of his face as he went to his knees, his eyes moving to Tracy.

"You...bitch..." and then he hit the floor.

There were shouts coming from all over the house as Joel turned to stare at Tracy. In her hand, she held a gun. The gym bag was open at her feet, but it wasn't clothes in there.

It was money—a lot of it. The money her mother had left her, Joel guessed, but he didn't have that much time to dwell on it.

Two of Grainger's men burst in behind her and Joel dove for her, grabbing her and shoving her to the side. He slid behind the men and grabbed the closest, jerking his head. When he heard the snap of his neck, he let him go and turned to face the other one.

Mick Forster wasn't one of Grainger's brighter men, but he fought like a machine. And he was brutal. Without looking at Tracy, Joel said quietly, "Get out of here, Tracy. Now."

As the bright blonde cap of her hair left his line of sight, he launched himself at Mick, ducking under the big ham-sized fist that came flying at him and driving a stiff hand into Mick's neck.

In the distance, he heard the powerful purr of Tracy's little Jaguar and he smiled coldly. She would get away.

That was what mattered…

* * * * *

Tracy waited.

Joel had taken her to the cabin three times, and each time had left one hot, sweet memory for her to look back on when she was alone.

But a day passed, and then two.

And she knew she couldn't wait any longer.

So she left. Maybe he just wanted to get her away from Grainger…maybe he wanted her forever.

Licking her lips, she reached up, touching the string of pearls around her bruised neck. At first, she started to take it off, but then she stopped.

Memories were all she was really taking with her.

What did it hurt to take these as well?

* * * * *

She abandoned the pricey Jaguar at a strip mall in Shreveport, parking it on the side, right under a camera. If she had done it right, the only thing visible would be the back end of the Jag, with the front end of the car out of sight of the cameras that monitored most of the area. Slinging the black bag she had traded out for the gym bag over her shoulder, she moved the strap between her breasts before climbing out. Drawing a small penknife from her pocket, she sliced a thin line in her forearm, wincing a little at the burning pain.

Bright red blood flowed and she turned her arm, letting the drops trickle down to splatter on the seat.

Then she covered the cut on her arm, wrapped a strip of cloth around it, made sure the sleeve of her light jacket covered it, and no more blood dripped down.

Disappear…make it look like you were taken…leave everything behind…

Joel had been coaching her on what to do—as though he had been preparing her for when he wasn't there.

Maybe he had been…Tracy shoved that thought out of her mind. Part of her worried that something had happened to him.

But she knew what she had to do.

She'd shot her husband.

She didn't know if he was dead or not.

It didn't strike her as a good idea to be seen watching the news. There weren't many pictures of her to be found, but if they tracked one down, it was going to be flashed across the TV for the next few days or weeks.

All it would take was one person to see her, just one. Too many of Vincent's friends would want her dead. She didn't know much about his businesses, hardly anything. But they wouldn't take that chance.

If one of his friends saw her, she was as good as dead.

She did one last look-through of the car as she blinked away tears. She had everything she needed tucked inside the bag on her shoulder.

Everything but Joel...damn it, where was he?

Heaven above, she wanted Joel.

But he hadn't caught up with her by now and if he was able to, wanted to, he would have.

She couldn't keep waiting.

Couldn't risk it.

No. She wasn't taking chances. She was going to do as she'd planned—disappear.

So she tossed the keys to the floorboard and walked away.

Walked away from her life.

Chapter Four

ಐ

He'd signed a plea bargain.

What was the harm in doing that?

Joel stood staring grimly out over the landscape surrounding the prison in Maine. He was guilty as hell.

It had been a year since he'd walked into this place. He knew it was entirely too likely that he'd never leave.

He'd gotten a reduced sentence since he'd turned over all the information he had on Vincent Grainger and all the other bastards. But Joel now had several very angry, unhappy enemies.

He'd testified against several of them. Received a few death threats in jail. Had to fight a few of them off. He even had a new scar.

The thin scar that ran down his left cheekbone could have blinded him—could have killed him. Joel wasn't really sure which it had been intended to do. But he hadn't spent the past twenty years of his life knitting.

The guy who had come after him with the knife was paralyzed.

After that, the attacks had stopped for a while.

Today, he was going before the parole board. Not that he'd get out. He was going to die in prison. Just as he deserved. Closing his eyes, he pulled up Tracy's image.

She was safe.

That was all that mattered.

You really don't want to spend the rest of your life in jail, do you?

Joel sighed as he felt Carly's presence settle around him. It was always just a little colder when she was there. Unless she was mad. When a ghost was mad, it wasn't a little colder. It was a lot colder.

Right now, though, it was just chilly. Carly wasn't happy with him, but she wasn't pissed. Just out of the corner of his eye, he saw the faint white glow of her body. She wouldn't materialize all the way, not here. Some of the men here were likely sensitives and she wouldn't chance it.

But that wouldn't keep her from talking to him.

The men out in the prison's exercise yard gave him a very wide berth and none were close enough to hear him as he said softly, "I deserve to spend the rest of my life in prison, Carly. But my sentence is only fifteen years."

She laughed. A ghost's laugh was like a cold breeze—it danced along his skin and made him shiver. *That's long enough. And you know they are going to keep coming after you. I don't want to keep trusting myself or your skill to save your cute butt.*

He winced.

Carly laughed again. *Baby, I changed your diapers. I know firsthand just how cute your butt is—even if it has changed quite a bit. You don't want to stay here. You can be a nice guy. Show some of that charm today. Don't antagonize them.*

Joel closed his eyes. "I really don't see why it matters," he said quietly. "She's safe. You told me she was safe."

She was, Marc.

The temperature dropped—very abruptly. His eyes opened and he turned his head, trying to see her better. "I'm not Marc. Not anymore," he said flatly.

You'll always be Marc to me, honey. And it's time for you to get out of here. He's waking up.

Everything inside him went cold.

* * * * *

172

The hospital floor was quiet.

It was a fairly quiet night at Salle Memorial. The lady with the hip replacement had developed pneumonia and had to be moved to ICU because of complications.

Everybody on the unit was sleeping. One of the patients hadn't done anything but sleep. The cop who had been stationed at his door for months had finally been reassigned a few weeks ago.

The patient in 502B had been in a coma for more than a year. He had taken a bullet in his brain, and it was a damn miracle that he was alive. Since he'd pulled through the surgery they'd thought maybe he'd wake up, but it had never happened.

The more time that passed, the less the chance that he'd come out of the coma intact, if he came out of it at all.

His name was Vincent Grainger—he'd been a pretty important man, married to a pretty lady who used to model in New York City.

She hadn't shown up in the news much after the marriage, but Vincent Grainger frequently had. He was a big-time businessman in New York, had a fancy mansion just a few miles up the Maine coast, rich as Midas. Yeah, he seemed like an important man, but an apparently dangerous man as well.

But nobody had come.

There'd been a report a few days after he had come in. Two young men had been pulled over while driving the wife's car. Later blood had been found in it, but the two men had sworn they'd found it at a mall.

No sign of her—foul play was expected. The hospital staff had been very comfortable having the cops there for a while. But slowly, people had forgotten.

The nurse glanced toward room 502B, then back to her chart. The pale strip of flesh on her ring finger caught her eye.

Just a few days ago, there'd been a pretty little diamond engagement ring there. Then she'd found out the truth.

The bastard was cheating on her.

Sighing, she tried to focus on something other than her pathetic love life. It was damn hard, though.

It was too quiet tonight. All the patients were sleeping and —

Her ears detected a harsh change in breathing in the room just across from her. Room 502B.

That couldn't be right. She sure as hell hoped not. That was the one who'd had an armed man standing at the door for weeks and weeks and weeks —

That guy was bad news — an image of his picture flashed through her mind. Cold eyes — shark eyes. Dead, flat, emotionless.

Lani blew out a breath as she stood up, irritated with herself.

The guy had been in a coma for a damned year. He wasn't waking up.

And even if he was, the calm, logical nurse inside her head said, *he's harmless, weak as a baby.*

The squeak of her rubber shoes sounded terribly loud on the floor as she walked across the hall. Jamming her hands into the pockets of her top, she closed one hand around a couple of pens, the other around the ring of keys.

Damn it, she felt like an idiot.

Cold chills ran down her spine as she drew closer to the door and for a second, she was tempted to run back to the desk and call security. Hell, idiot or not, this guy was dangerous — or had been, at one point. Why else would they have a cop on him?

Then she jerked her hands back out of her pockets and ran them through her hair. "He's a patient. That's what he is, Lani." Reaching out, she pushed the door open."

And found herself staring into his wide-open eyes—502B was awake all right.

Lying propped up in bed, as he had been when she'd made her rounds, but his eyes were now open and he lay there desperately sucking in air. His cadaverously thin face was covered with a sheen of sweat and he stared at her with those dead eyes.

Lani swallowed as she stared back at him.

Oh, yeah. She was calling security. It would only take Mike two minutes to get up there.

Chapter Five

❧

She had run.

For two years, she had done nothing but move around the country. After abandoning her car, she had managed to buy a black Taurus. It was boring, especially after the Jag, but it didn't draw attention, and she'd been able to pay cash for it.

That mattered. Because she hadn't had to provide any ID or any personal information to get a loan. Just cash, to get a key and the title.

It was ten years old, and it took forever to warm up, but the motor ran smoothly, and it got her from point A to point B.

That was all that mattered.

One of the first things she had done after she'd slowed down from that first headlong rush was get a lawyer. Aleisha Williams had helped her get a new identity. She'd gotten her a social security card, established a believable history, and given Tracy all sorts of advice.

The only contact Tracy had with that terrifying life was a monthly phone call made to Aleisha on a prepaid cell phone that she replaced every few months.

Officially Tracy Grainger no longer existed.

When she looked in the mirror, she saw a woman who only barely resembled the person she had once been.

And she *liked* it.

Her hair had grown out and instead of the short, tousled cap of curls she'd had, it was now long, and thick with barely a wave in it. She'd stopped dying it as well, and all the blonde locks were gone, leaving the deep, mink brown hair that Vincent had hated.

And weight. That was the best part. She had put on thirty pounds. She no longer looked like the razor-thin model Vincent had wined and dined and fooled.

Any time she'd put on more than three pounds, she had been barred from the kitchen. He'd put locks on the door, and the servants had known better than to allow her in. The few times it had happened, the servant had been thrown out on his ass.

And one had gotten a busted jaw for it. Of course, Vincent had the sick little fantasy in his head that she had been flirting with the poor kid.

But over the past two years, she'd gorged on burgers and French fries. She barely even looked the same anymore. Her angular face had softened and her mouth looked lush in the curves of her face, instead of the wide, mobile mouth that the fashion world claimed was unique.

No, she didn't look the same, didn't feel the same.

She was happy, completely happy.

Well, almost.

There was just one flaw.

For a while, part of her had waited for Joel to show up. Logically, she had understood he wasn't going to come.

She didn't know where he was. She could have asked. Aleisha would have found out, tracked him down. But she hadn't.

Joel was the kind, that if he wanted to find her, he would. He would have tracked her down and no fake ID, or new social security number could have stopped him.

But he'd never come—and she wasn't going to live her life according to how a man wanted her to look, or how she might think he'd want her to look. And she liked how she looked.

Tracy felt like a woman again, instead of a punching bag, or a rag doll. But she still looked behind her everywhere she went.

Part of her looked for Vincent. No amount of reassurance from Aleisha could still that voice inside her head.

Vincent was lying in a coma in Salle Memorial. The minute he stirred, Aleisha would call her.

"I'm safe," she murmured, wondering if she'd ever believe that.

And there was a part of her, she knew, that still waited for Joel.

As of now…that was going to stop. She pulled into the small town with a smile on her face. The little town by the Ohio River was as far away from her old life as she could get. Pretty, quaint, friendly.

The mansion in Shreveport, Maine hadn't been home for Vincent. It had been a place for private business, it had been Tracy's prison, but it hadn't been home. Vincent liked big, expensive cities — not pretty little small towns like this.

And it sure as hell hadn't been quaint and friendly. Or home.

This was home. It was already home. She felt it in her bones before she even climbed out of the car.

She breathed in the crisp fall air as it drifted over the river. Man, it was lovely here. It almost hurt her eyes just to stare at the sun setting over the river, the sky painted a million shades of gold, pink and red. Small wisps of clouds dotted the western horizon and as the sun hit them, they gleamed like they'd been dipped in gold.

Behind her, the small house she had finally dared to buy waited. She'd been scared to death to buy anything larger than a pair of shoes or a new shirt.

God, how long had it been since she'd been able buy even *that* — clothes, shoes — without worrying?

And now she had a house.

She had a career. Not a job. A career.

Although she had always loved to write, it had been something she'd been forced to give up a long time ago. Vincent hadn't tolerated it. The few times she had tried, he'd deleted files — and once he had beaten her bloody. Then he had calmly picked up her computer and thrown it out the window.

When she'd tried to buy another one, he'd beaten her with a belt and locked her in her rooms for a week.

Clenching her hand into a fist, she shoved those dark memories from her mind.

That wasn't part of her life now.

Her life now was as a writer. One whose name was gaining popularity...and a contract in New York.

The online publisher who had released her books for the past seventeen months had moved into print and was on its way to the big-time. A publisher from a major press in New York had read one of her books and offered her a contract.

While she still had a decent amount of her mother's money, the nest egg in the bank was growing pretty fat just from her new income alone. It wasn't as much as she'd made when she'd been modeling, but it was more than she'd had to call her own in a long time.

She played the reclusive author entirely too well. Partly out of a need for privacy, but more...she was still too afraid of Vincent to risk so much as putting her face on the internet.

Besides, the people wanted her books. They didn't need to see what she looked like.

Suddenly depressed, she turned away from the glorious glow of the sunrise and walked back into her small house, shoulders slumped, head low.

And totally unaware of the eyes that watched her.

* * * * *

Her dreams were restless.

Tormented.

The pain that she hadn't had to deal with for two years came back to haunt her, the metal of a belt buckle biting into her skin, the hard slap of a fist pounding into her flesh, the hot, salty splash of blood on her tongue as he busted her mouth again.

When she woke to the muffled sound of her own screams at three a.m., she lay there, curled up in a tight ball, afraid to move until the sun started to creep over the horizon some three and half hours later. Crawling from bed, she stumbled into the shower, grabbing one of the towels from a box as she went.

Turning the spray up as hot as she could stand it, she climbed into the stall and stood under it, feeling that hot needles pounding into her skin. Bracing her hands against the wall, she leaned her head forward, water sluicing over her skull to drip down her face and off her chin.

She was shaking.

Fuck, she could actually see her body quivering. She was cold to the bone, so cold she ached with it, even though her flesh was pink from the heat of the water pouring over it.

"You're not going to keep haunting me like this," she muttered grimly. "You're not."

She grabbed the shampoo and dumped some of the pale pearlescent liquid into her palm, scrubbing it into her hair, soaping the long brunette tresses. It hung halfway down her back now. Slowly a smile spread across her face as she smoothed her hair down over her breasts.

Long, *dark* hair, and round curves instead of the near anorexic body she'd sported since she was eighteen and had been discovered by a modeling agency. She rinsed the shampoo from her hair and then turned her back to the spray, staring down at her body.

Her breasts were just a little fuller now, thanks to the weight she'd put on. Fuller, just a little less perky than they had once been—damn, she was glad she'd refused that damn breast implant surgery Vincent had demanded she have. She'd gotten his fist in her gut over that.

"Stop it, Tracy... *Emery*. Stop it. It doesn't matter anymore. It's over."

Slicking her hands over her flesh, she rubbed in the simple, vanilla scented soap. Brushing her fingers over her nipples, she shivered at the small sensation that went through her.

Closing her eyes, she pushed Vincent Grainger's face out of her mind, summoning Joel's image as she circled her fingers over the hard little bud of her clit, shivering as pleasure streaked through her.

She liked touching herself—it wasn't as sweet as Joel's hands on her, but at least she knew how to feel pleasure, not just pain. Sliding her fingers over her breasts, she cupped them, tugging on her nipples until the aching spread down to her belly, and lower.

The slick folds of her sex were getting wetter and it had nothing to do with the shower. Pumping two fingers in and out of her pussy, she moaned as the tightening increased, until she could hardly breathe from the sensations coursing through her.

But her hands on her body just weren't enough.

Joel...where are you!

With a groan of frustration, she reached for the massaging shower head and tugged it down. Aiming the hot spray to her sensitive folds, she screamed, short and hard, as the hot, rapacious feelings spread.

She screamed as she climaxed under the spray of water and her knees gave out. Slumping to the floor of the shower stall, she leaned her head back against the wall, a wobbly smile on her mouth.

"Hmmm…oh, yeah, that was nice," she murmured.

A few minutes later, knees still a little wobbly, she climbed from the shower and dried a circle on the moisture fogged mirror, staring at her reflection with somber eyes.

"Tracy died," she whispered to herself. "She just now died. Tracy didn't know how to have pleasure, how to do anything but hate, and hide, and hurt. She's dead now. *You* are Emery."

Slowly, her mouth curled into a smile and she closed her eyes, tipping her face back. "Emery…"

And Emery wanted Joel.

* * * * *

The apartment was almost a mirror image of the one he'd grown up in. A little newer. It didn't stink of Mom's cigarette smoke or her alcohol.

But it had the same bland beige walls, the same threadbare carpet.

Walking through the door, Joel glanced at the two feds outside the door.

"Any idea how long I'm going to be stuck here?" he asked. He had been given a reprieve. He didn't feel he deserved it, but he had taken the deal. The feds would grant early, conditional parole if he helped them put away the crime lords. His parole required that he cooperate with the federal government and he had to testify. He had. Grainger was the only one left, and he was still a damned vegetable from what he had heard. Now he was itching to go after Tracy.

He wasn't staying. But he had to make them think he was.

The DA moved in behind him, smiling a polite, professional smile. "That depends on Grainger's recovery. Relax. It's almost over now. Once he's considered fit to indict and stand trial, you'll be home free."

A cynical smile edged up the corners of his mouth.

Home free.

He had sent three crime bosses to prison. They needed his cooperation to get a fourth one in there. He was now a convicted felon and although his debt to society was considered paid, that rap would follow him the rest of his life. And he'd deal with his own guilt for as long as he lived.

Home free.

Sighing, he shoved that aside. Tracy—he had to concentrate on Tracy.

The skin on the back of his neck prickled as the DA moved into his line of sight. "I'm a little curious—one of the people we'd love to question, we've never been able to find. I heard you had a relationship with her. Tracy Grainger, Vincent's wife?"

Joel cut his eyes to the DA. Lifting one brow, he said flatly, "Ms. Grainger is one thing I will not discuss. Period."

Mike Chaumers' face went cold. "It doesn't work that way. I have to know the details. Because if I've heard rumors, the defense will have heard them, too. I need to know what was between you two. So I can figure out a way around it. I also want to know where she is. We need her on the stand."

Joel smiled coolly. "I don't know where she is. And I don't know what rumors you're talking about."

Chaumers narrowed his eyes. "Don't dick around with me, Lockhart. I know what Grainger did with her—practically handed her to you on a silver platter."

Arching a black brow, Joel asked softly, "Have proof? Are there pictures? A movie? Eyewitnesses?"

The DA said nothing, just glared at Joel angrily. Lifting one shoulder in a shrug, Joel turned his attention back to the window and stared out at the gray vista of the parking lot. "Then, like I said, I don't know what rumors."

A hand came down on Joel's shoulder, and Chaumers swung him around. "You're supposed to be cooperating with us, buddy. You want me to throw you back in jail? I can do that—for a very long time."

Joel dropped his eyes to the hand lying on his shoulder and then slowly looked back at the attorney.

Chaumers paled and slowly backed away until he bumped into the two feds who had stepped into the room.

"Is there a problem here?" A new voice spoke up, but Joel never took his eyes away from Chaumers to look at third fed, Agent Casey Dowling.

It was Mike who slowly turned to look at the petite black lady. Only then did Joel look at her. She was having a stare-down with Mike though. Turning away from them, Joel went back to staring out the window.

He was a little sorry that he'd have to leave Dowling empty-handed. He liked her.

She had a serious grudge against Grainger.

But she had enough to put that fuck in jail without him.

"What's the problem here, Mike?"

"No problem."

"Then why did it sound like you were telling Mr. Lockhart he was going back to prison? He kept his end of the bargain. We've got three big, nasty fish off the streets, thanks to him. And one left to go—what's the problem?"

Mike hesitated a little. "We need the wife. Lockhart knows where she is. He's been holding back information."

"We don't need the wife. And she disappeared. Nobody has been able to find her."

Joel closed his eyes, tuning Dowling's voice out. He couldn't listen to that again. Tracy had done what he'd told her to do. That's all—nothing had happened to her.

Damn it, Carly said she was safe—

She is safe, baby…

The cold settled in but this time it came almost like a comforting hug as Carly wrapped her presence around him. *She's safe, honey.*

Where is she? he wanted to demand. He wanted to leave right now. Hell, he could get out of there. Three federal agents and one DA. Dowling was the weak link. Grab her, get her gun—but she was also the soft spot for him, because he couldn't hurt her.

He looked into her eyes and saw pain. Grainger had hurt somebody in her life as well. He couldn't add to it. Damn it.

Their voices murmured in the background, making no sense even when he tried to focus. He needed to get to Tracy.

Grainger wasn't a threat now, not while he was still out of it. But the minute he started recalling things, Tracy could be in danger.

Joel needed to get to her before that happened.

You will, baby...

"We need the wife, damn it! And the hell he doesn't know where she is. Half of Maine knows he was fucking her—"

Joel moved. Grabbing Chaumers by the neck, he slammed him into the wall, pressing against the DA's windpipe and watching as his face went red and then purple. "You don't want to talk about her again, Mike. You understand me?" Joel said, his voice casual, an easy smile on his face.

Footsteps moved up behind him, but then they stopped. "Back off guys. He's not hurting him."

Chaumers' eyes wheeled around, staring at somebody behind Joel and he heard Dowling laugh. "I told you, we don't need the wife. *You* can't find the wife. How is he supposed to know where she is? He's been in lockup for the past two years."

Joel smiled at Chaumers as he let go. The DA clutched at his throat, gasping for air and staring at Joel with wide, terrified eyes.

"Yeah, how am I supposed to know?"

Casey gestured to the two agents. "Why don't you all take Mike down to the café and get him a coffee or something? I need to talk to Joel for a bit here."

One of them paused only long enough to study her with a lifted brow. The other was already assisting the attorney to his feet.

By the time they were out the door, Joel was back to staring out the window.

"There's really nothing to see. It's a parking lot, Joel. Boring, gray. We don't have the budget to get you anything worth looking at."

Glancing at her, Joel shrugged. "I've seen worse."

"Hmmm."

Hearing that tone in her voice, he finally turned around and leaned back against the wall, staring at her with an expectant look on his face. "What?"

"There was something between you two. What was it?"

Joel studied her closely. "If I tell you, will you answer a question for me? Honestly, no lies? No FBI evasions?"

Casey arched a brow. "Well, I guess that will depend on the question. But I am very nosy. Sure—but I want the answer first. I don't trust you entirely."

"I love her," he said quietly, simply.

Casey's lashes lowered briefly. "I thought so. You have an excellent poker face, Joel. I've only seen it crack on rare occasions. And usually when it involves her. What would you do for her? What would you give up?"

Scowling, Joel shrugged, spinning away to pace the tight confines of the apartment. "Hell, what kind of question is that? I'd give up anything for her—everything."

"And you did—didn't you?"

Driving a hand through his hair, he turned and glared at her. "Hell, what are you, a fed or a shrink?"

She smiled, revealing dimples on either side of her mouth. "Both. I'm not wrong, though, am I? What aren't you telling us, Joel?"

He stared at her blankly.

Casey finally sighed, shifting on the couch. She propped her arm on the back and stared at him, her eyes dark and brooding.

"You have secrets in those eyes, Joel. I see them. I don't need evidence to know that."

He laughed bitterly. "You're a fed. Evidence is all you know."

An odd, secret little smile curved her lips upward and she shifted her gaze, staring past him into the corner. Joel's skin started to prickle and he felt that odd chill in the air again. "Oh, I wouldn't bet on that, Joel. I know a little bit more than just evidence...now, what was it you wanted to ask me?"

Narrowing his eyes, he stared at her. His skin felt tight and it was cold in the room. Very cold. Carly was there, hovering just beyond where he couldn't see her and although she wasn't afraid, she was—*something*. Worried, intrigued, curious.

Something.

Damn it, he needed to get Dowling out of here before she started wanting to check the air conditioner or something.

"Why do you want Grainger so much? He's your hot spot. You wanted the others, but him..." Joel shook his head. "You wanted him the most. Why?"

Casey's smile faded. "You sure you aren't a shrink?" Her eyes closed. "He's a criminal. That alone should be enough. But there is more. You are right."

Her eyes closed, her arm straightening out. She laid her head along it, looking vulnerable, and much younger. "I met him in high school—we were so alike. Two kids out to save the world. His name was Joshua. My dad almost had a heart attack—I think his did, too. I was a black girl, he was a white boy. Not what either of our parents wanted. But we loved each other. That was it for us—all that mattered. They came to accept that, even as young as we were. We got into college together, both wanted to become lawyers. It was our senior year. We both had gotten accepted into Harvard. We were going to get married that summer."

Her voice got softer and Joel watched as a tear slid out from her closed eyes. "One night, he never came home. We'd been living together since our sophomore year. I called the cops. You know the drill—forty-eight hours for a missing person. Then I get a phone call. There's a body." Her voice cracked and she fell silent for a minute.

Slowly, she lifted her head and opened her eyes, staring sightlessly into the distance. When she spoke again, her voice was steady, but the silent rain of tears continued. "He saw a drug deal—they shot him. There were witnesses but none of them would testify. I begged them to—and they wouldn't."

She started to speak again, but a sob choked her.

Joel walked away, leaving her alone for a few minutes while he went into the bathroom, getting a washcloth and wetting it.

By the time he reached the living room again, she was a little more composed. He held out the cloth and she accepted it silently. He turned away, waiting until she spoke again.

"I couldn't become a lawyer. They can't make you speak, Joel. No matter what—they can put you on the stand, but they can't make you talk. And if we can't make the people who see things talk, we can't put the bad guys away."

Guilt churned inside of him. One arm propped against the wall, he closed his hand into a fist, hiding his face from her. She'd lost just as much as he had. And instead of turning into a vigilante and going after Grainger like Joel had, she'd used the law.

There was silence behind him and then a hand brushed his shoulder. "I know bad guys, Joel." He stiffened under her hand, then slowly edged away, turning to face her.

She smiled at him, a sad smile that only added to the delicate beauty of her face. "I do. I've seen too many of them not to recognize them. You're no knight, but you're not the bad guy, either."

She stepped away, pausing to look down at the coffee table. He looked down.

There was a plain manila file there. It hadn't been there five minutes ago.

Her eyes lifted and met his.

"We all have our ghosts, don't we, Joel?"

She walked out, leaving him alone in the room.

Well, not alone. Joel was rarely alone. Carly's misty white form shimmered into view and she said in a puzzled tone, *What an odd woman.*

Joel ignored Carly as he bent down and took the folder, flipped through it.

His breath froze in his chest as he saw a photograph. She didn't look the same. Not at all. But it was her. The soft dove gray eyes didn't look quite so haunted, and that wide, mobile mouth looked softer in her face.

She had changed — but it was Tracy.

"She knows where she is."

* * * * *

Casey looked over the rim of her coffee cup at Bryson. "Yes, I know he'll take off. We don't need him. Not anymore. There's enough evidence, more than enough to convict him." Then she paused and lifted one shoulder, smirking a little. "That's if Grainger ever wakes up."

"You really want to let our star witness just walk away?"

Casey sighed. "He's not our star witness. What he is, is an ex-con. He's served a prison term and worked for us, I know that. But every time we put him on the stand, the deal we made with him was thrown back at us. We don't need him — not with the evidence he gave us, not with the witnesses we've unearthed from that evidence."

A knot formed in her gut and she sat back, rubbing at her belly. "Besides, you saw Grainger the other day. It's like looking at a blank slate. There's nothing there."

* * * * *

For the longest while, there was nothing.

No memory, no thoughts, no faces.

Just an empty fog.

But out of that fog came something ugly and black, a festering anger that ate away at him. Beyond that, it took longer for anything clear to emerge.

He'd waited though. There were people around him. He didn't trust them — too many people, coming at him, probing, asking questions. He stayed quiet, stayed silent, waiting for the fog and anger to clear.

When it did — he saw their faces. Not the people around him.

But *them*.

A man.

A woman.

They had to die.

He didn't know where they were. The man would be harder to find — in his gut, he knew that. The man was dangerous. Find the woman. She was the weak link. Find her and he'd get the man.

He had to get strong though.

First he had to get strong.

Chapter Six

ಬಿ

Yes, Agent Dowling sure as hell knew where Tracy was, but all she'd left Joel were breadcrumbs.

He could follow them, but it was eating away time he didn't have.

Frustration ate at him the weeks he'd wasted tracking Tracy to the small town in southern Indiana. By the time he approached realtors, hoping for clues to lead him to her, he knew he had wasted *too* much time.

Becky Cramer took one look at the picture and tapped her cheek, studying him thoughtfully. Tension knotted his gut but he just smiled and waited patiently.

Finally. She knew something.

It didn't matter whether she told him or not. She knew something and he'd find out what it was.

"Mind if I ask why you're looking for her?"

"That's between us, but I've reason to believe she's in danger."

Becky's eyes didn't even flicker. She wasn't going to tell him jack. But she knew something. And she'd seen Tracy. "Then perhaps you should consider approaching the authorities and not a real estate agent," she advised coolly, handing the photograph back to him.

Joel inclined his head. "Sorry to have bothered you."

He left, making note of the cars in the parking lot as he strolled away. Getting into her office would be child's play.

All he had to do was find out to whom she had sold houses recently. His gut told him that Tracy hadn't settled down until recently. She would have kept moving for a very long time.

How many young, single females would have bought houses in this area in the past few years? Small as it was, it couldn't be that hard to narrow it down.

* * * * *

Becky watched as he walked away—wasn't a hardship. The man had one fine ass. But he also had very, very hard eyes.

There was something dangerous about him.

And Becky had seen something fragile about Emery Hughes the minute she'd seen the younger woman.

Was this an ex? A private investigator? Becky didn't know, but she'd be damned if she'd lead the man right to her. Waiting until he disappeared from sight, she turned to her computer and clicked on the file. She reached for the phone. Couldn't hurt to call, right?

A chill danced along her spine and she shivered a little as she cradled the phone on her shoulder. She started to punch in the number, but the line went dead.

Frowning, she hung up briefly and tried again. Still just dead air.

Damn it.

Hanging up the phone, she reached for the cell lying on her desk. But it read "Out of service". "What the hell?" she muttered.

Scowling, she grabbed a piece of paper and a pen. From memory, she jotted down the first three numbers and then glanced at her computer screen. Her pen fell from numb fingers.

The computer screen had gone black. Her breath came out in frozen little puffs as she found herself staring at the misty face of a woman.

It was a young woman—her features vaguely familiar. Becky cringed and stood, backing as far away from the thing hovering in front of her as she could, a whimper rising in her chest.

He won't hurt her.

The words had no sound, just an echo that seemed to circle through Becky's mind as she stared at...whatever it was. Logically, Becky *knew* what she was staring at. But she couldn't, wouldn't admit it.

"Huh...huh...who?" Becky squeaked out.

There was a laugh that seemed to ripple through the air, unlike the voice that didn't really have a sound. The air warmed just a little. *You know who I'm talking about. She's safe — safer with him than she's been in her whole life.*

"She's fine here." Nothing ever happened here, not in Bethlehem.

She won't be. Not for long. And I'm sorry. I wouldn't do this if I wasn't trying to take care of her.

The cold came back, wrapping her in its icy grip. A wave of black rose up, crashing over her, pulling her down in its grip. Her breath lodged in her throat and Becky fell helplessly into oblivion.

* * * * *

Her back ached. Becky sat up slowly, rubbing at her neck and wincing. The office was dark. Confused, she looked around.

The hands on her watch glowed slightly and she blinked as she realized it was close to ten. "Damn it."

All the lights were off. It was quiet. Too damned quiet. It finally dawned on her why—her computer was off, too. The ever-present hum was missing.

Shaking her head, she reached over and clicked on the little table lamp.

Her head ached. Must have come from falling asleep. Too much work, not enough sleep. She started to try and sift through the files she hadn't taken care of but finally just stacked them up neatly on her desk.

"Later," she mumbled. "I'll do them later."

Reaching into the desk drawer by her right side, she pulled out her purse. With a sigh, she rose. Halfway to the door, she paused.

Glancing back to the desk, she frowned. Had she talked to somebody? Seen somebody?

Putting her hand to her temple, she scowled.

"I really need a vacation."

* * * * *

Vincent moved through the cool, quiet splendor of the silent mansion.

Where was Tracy?

He couldn't think.

Couldn't focus.

He remembered Joel coming in, remembered the flare of pain as Joel punched him. And Simmonds, holding a gun on Tracy while Joel put his down. Vincent had had a gun…hadn't he?

Now he was staring down at a pool of blood, at Simmonds' unmoving body.

They'd killed Simmonds… Fuckers. They'd pay for that.

But wasn't there something he needed to do first?

A gray cloud rose up and took his mind and for a while, he just drifted. Lost in the fog.

It was almost peaceful there. Drifting was easy. But it was getting harder.

People kept intruding.

There were new voices. New faces.

"Mr. Grainger, we need to talk to you...answer some questions...know you can hear..."

"...insane...he's in a catatonic state..."

"His eyes are open...he moves..."

The voices rattled on and on, sometimes making sense, but more often than not, they were just nonsense.

He couldn't keep blocking them out.

Tracy...

* * * * *

The alarm went off and Emery woke up, rolled over and smacked it with the palm of her hand. The cell phone on the bedside caught her eye and she sighed, pushing up onto her elbow. Long hair fell into her face and she shoved it back.

It was phone call day. Every month she called Aleisha. Reaching for the phone, she punched in the number. As it started to ring, she flopped over on her back.

Three rings, four...five.

She lowered the phone before the voice mail could pick up and hit the disconnect button.

That wasn't right.

It was early. Eight o'clock. Aleisha wouldn't be in court yet—just barely in the office. She always kept the cell phone with her. Always.

*Just call later...*rolling out of bed, she got up, leaving the cell phone on the bedside table.

* * * * *

Damned construction zones. The roads around St. Louis pretty much sucked all the time anyway, but with the road work going on I-64, it was worse.

Aleisha heard the phone ring and knew who it was. She started to reach for her purse but somebody cut her off and she had to slam on her brakes to keep from rear-ending the bastard.

Her purse went flying into the floor and she groaned. "Sorry, babe. I'm going to have to call you later." She had an early meeting anyway that she had to get to.

She'd call Emery from there.

"I hate early meetings," she muttered. Only reason she had agreed to this one was because this asshole had finally agreed to give her client a divorce.

Slowing down, she hit her blinker and started to try to move over.

Just as she did, the car in front of her slammed the brakes. Aleisha tried to slow down.

When the hit came from the back, she didn't have any place else left to go.

* * * * *

Emery tossed the phone down.

Two days had passed.

Damn it. Her gut churned with worry. There was a limit to how long she was supposed to wait before she gave up getting hold of Aleisha and started running again.

She was so tired of running, even though part of her had been terrified of slowing down. But after three years of doing nothing but moving town to town, talking to nobody but her lawyer in hurried conversations, settling down had been heaven.

Aleisha would tell her if something was wrong. If there was something to worry about.

And there was nothing to worry about.

It hadn't been easy.

Even being around anybody was enough to make her break out into a sweat. So many times before, she'd made friends only to realize they were people who were on her husband's payroll.

People he used to try and trip her up, catch her in nonexistent lies, and spy on her. After a while, she'd just stopped trying to make friends. After so many years of self-imposed solitude, coming out of her shell was almost painful.

Joel had been her only true friend. And she'd lost him...losing people *hurt*. She knew that. She'd lost her dad when she was eight. Her mama had been everything to her, then she'd met Vincent. Mama had gotten sick, and weak, but Vincent had assured her that he'd take care of her.

Yeah, he had. So he could use the dear woman against her.

And then Joel...but thinking of him hurt.

But friends. She needed friends...places to hide if she needed to. The woman who lived a couple hundred yards away from her was a young, unbelievably perky blonde by the name of Shelley. Shelley was married to a doctor who worked in the ER of the hospital in one of the nearby towns. Madison, Emery was pretty sure.

When Shelley had invited her to go shopping in Madison, it had taken everything she had in her not to refuse.

But now that she was out, she was having fun, giggling and talking with Shelley as if they'd been friends for years. As Shelley leaned over to whisper something about two of the Sheriff's deputies who had just left the Pepper Café, Emery felt a tightening in her chest.

She'd missed this.

Lunch dates with friends, laughing over a weird haircut, or eyeing some guy and pretending not to.

Something caught her eye.

As Shelley chattered on about the deputies, Emery felt a cold chill race down her spine.

There had never been any sign that anybody followed her. No sign that anybody thought she was other than who she claimed to be.

But fear settled in her throat as she sat there staring at the nondescript green Ford Taurus parked just across the street from the Pepper Café. Through the tinted windows, she could just barely make out the outline of a man—broad-shouldered, tall.

Just sitting there.

"Hey…hey, you okay, Emery?"

Jerking her eyes to Shelley's face, she forced a smile. "I don't know. My…my head just suddenly started hurting."

A sympathetic smile crossed Shelley's face. "Migraines? Man, I used to get the worst…c'mon. Let's get you home."

By the time they paid their bill and got outside, the green Taurus was gone.

"Imagining things," she muttered to herself as she walked through the house one more time, checking all the locks, checking the windows.

She even got her gun out. Emery hated the cold, lifeless feel of it, but she'd be damned if she didn't feel a little better as she checked the chamber.

Passing by the hall mirror, she paused and studied her pale reflection. She looked like a ghost.

A scared ghost.

How in the hell could just seeing a car do this?

Shaking her head, she started up the stairs, leaving the lights on behind her as she went.

Moving into her room, she closed the door and started toward the bed. She needed to get some sleep. Tomorrow…

"Hello, Tracy."

That voice...swallowing, she turned slowly, lifting the gun and leveling it at the man who had been hiding behind the door.

Joel! For one split second, she almost flung herself at him. She stopped just in time...it had been three years. *Three damned years.*

"What are you doing here, Joel?"

A slow smile creased his face. "Watching you. But you already know that. You saw me earlier, didn't you?"

"Is Vincent here?"

His dark blue eyes flashed at her as he snarled, "If he was, do you think I'd just be standing here?"

Emery swallowed and shook her head. "I don't know. Joel, it's been a long time..."

"Three years," he murmured. "I've been trying to find you for a year now. You hid well."

A year... "You've been looking for me?" she asked, her voice tight and rusty.

A slow smile spread across his face. She knew that smile. Knew it well...seconds later, he pulled her into his arms and she moaned as he slanted his mouth across hers, pushing his tongue deep inside, kissing her deeply, his tongue rubbing across hers, sweeping over the roof of her mouth, across the surface of her teeth.

Tasting her—like he had been starving for her.

Whimpering she pressed against him. Heaven knew, she had been starving for him. That worry, the gut-deep fear slowly faded away as he touched her. When he touched her...it didn't feel as though even a minute had passed since he had last kissed her.

He paused just long enough to mutter, "Fuck, I've missed you."

His hands stripped her clothes away as she rose onto her toes, burying her fingers in his hair. Cool air bit her flesh and then his hands were on her hips as he spun around. She felt the wall against her back, and then...oh, please. She whimpered as he let go of her for a second, but then she heard the rasp of his zipper.

Then he was pressing against her, and Emery sobbed. "Joel!"

"I've been dreaming of you...the entire time. Fuck, I thought I'd never find you," he rasped against her mouth as he pushed inside her, his cock hot, thick, and naked against the wet folds of her pussy. "Mine. I'm keeping you, Tracy..."

The name...it was wrong, but she didn't care. He wanted *her* — did the name really matter? She had been Tracy, once...his tongue stole into her mouth again and she closed her teeth around it, biting him gently. He growled against her lips as he circled his hips into the cradle of her thighs. The head of his cock rubbed against some hidden place inside her, and she felt as though her entire body lit up at that touch.

"Missed you," he rasped as he tore his mouth away, kissing a line down her throat, down her neck, raking the sensitive skin with his teeth before plumping one breast in his hand, pushing it up as he dipped his head and caught the nipple in his mouth.

"Fuck, this body is amazing...you've always been so perfect, how can you be even more perfect than before?" he whispered, lifting his head to stare down at her as he pulled out, working his cock back in as she struggled to catch her breath.

"Joel, please," she whispered, clutching at his shoulder desperately. "Stop talking...I need you."

"Shhh..." he crooned against her lips, his hands gliding down her sides, over her hips, cupping her ass for a moment and then he gripped her thighs, taking her weight in his hands, so that she was pinned between his body and the wall.

He pumped inside and she screamed as she started to come, clenching around him, exploding from the white hot streaks of sensation that filled her.

"Come for me," he whispered.

She forced her eyes to open, staring up at him. His blue eyes, those midnight dark eyes, stared down at her, hungrily, greedily, the same way she imagined her eyes looked. Under the layers of clothing that kept his body from her, she could feel him, that long, powerful body that had brought her so much pleasure.

She wanted to see him as she came—wanted to know this was real, not a dream.

His deep blue eyes stared into hers, his face stark with hunger. Her hands pressed against his shoulders, jerking at the coat that still covered him, wanting to feel his flesh against her.

But she couldn't focus—not long enough to jerk at the buttons, not long enough to push back the climax building in her.

As he lowered his lips to kiss her, a soft, gentle kiss, so at odds with the harsh, hungry motions of his body, Emery felt her heart tremble, just a little. He had really missed her...

"You aren't ever leaving my sight again," he muttered, nuzzling her neck. She shivered as he gently squeezed the flesh of her buttocks, slowing the greedy movement of his body against hers, his hands gentling just a little. "You don't know what it did to me."

Emery whimpered, trying to hook her legs around his hips, trying to ride the thick stalk of flesh impaling her, but using his grip on her hips, he wouldn't let her. She threw her head back as he continued to stroke slowly within her, his lips brushing against her neck.

Joel shifted and she arched against him as he hooked one arm under her left knee, opening her more fully. She clenched her inner muscles around him and he laughed shakily. "Slow down, baby. We have all night," he crooned.

201

Damn it, I don't want all night — I want now! She tried to scream it, but her breath was locked in her lungs.

Pushing away from the wall, he carried her over to the bed, lowering himself onto it, with her still astride him. Greedily, she tried to pump her hips, but he clamped his hands around her again, slowing her frenzied pace. "All night...forever," he whispered.

Her eyes widened as he arched up against her, rocking just ever so slightly within the embrace of her pussy. "Joel..."

His hand trailed up her thigh and she sank her teeth into her lip as he brushed his fingers against her clit.

The sensation of his touch darted through her and she clenched around him, arching her back. He did it again, and a third time, before she hissed and leaned forward, planting her hands on his chest and rocking against him.

That seemed to be what he wanted, her riding him, for the second time she started to move more determinedly against him, and the hand clutching her hip gentled, sliding down to cup over her thigh as he rocked up to meet her every move.

Sweat stung her eyes, rolled down her face while her breath sawed raggedly in and out of her lungs. Mesmerized, she stared down at him, the way the tendons in his neck stood out as he arched his head back, the way he gritted his teeth, the soft sexy growl that slid from him as she moved.

"Yeah," he muttered as she convulsed around. "Just like that."

His spine bowed, lifting his hips off the bed, driving the throbbing length of his sex so deep inside her. As he pulsed within her, she sobbed out his name and then he made a slight, circling movement, the head of his cock brushing over the notch buried by the mouth of her womb and she exploded, flying blindly into orgasm and screaming.

Through the convulsions and tremors that racked her body, Emery vaguely felt his cock jerk inside her pussy, and the hot splash of his seed spill deep inside her.

"Damn it, Tracy…"

She stiffened at that name, pulling away from him and retreating to sit at the edge of the bed.

"I'm not Tracy. Not anymore. She's gone," she whispered softly.

He pulled back and as he pulled out of her, she winced a little. "Sorry, baby…Emery."

At the sound of her new name on his lips, she looked up at him.

He crooked a smile at her. "Been following Emery Hughes for about six months now…I'm awful damned glad to know it's really you. You're you…doesn't matter what your name is. I'd know that taste anywhere…"

He pressed his mouth back to hers and she moaned, opening for him, feeling hunger stir in her belly again…even though she was still trembling from the climax.

Joel pulled back and lifted her against him, carrying her over to the bed. As he lay down behind her, she caught a glimpse of the smile curling his lips. "Changing your name, the way you look, you did good, Emery—very good."

She pouted a little. "Not too good. You found me."

There was an odd note in his voice. "Did you not want me to?"

Wriggling around, she turned in his arms, staring up at him with a sad little smile on her face. "Joel, I almost gave up waiting for you…"

His face spasmed and she watched something move in his eyes. "What is it?" she asked, arching up to him, pressing her lips to his chin while her fingers moved down to slip the buttons loose on his shirt. His hand caught hers before she could free them though.

Slowly, he lifted his eyes to look at her. "You've been keeping track of what's going on with Grainger," he said quietly.

Her lashes flickered. "How do you know?"

Joel smiled. "You're a smart woman, Tracy. You wouldn't have taken off without keeping track of him. You'd know that he'd come after you if he lived. You set up a new identity—you had a contact. Somebody who watched him."

Slowly, she nodded. "A lawyer. It was the lady who helped me become Emery. Tracy's gone, Joel. I don't even think I know Tracy anymore. She calls me…" her voice faded away and a frown darkened her face.

"What?" Joel asked quietly.

Emery turned away, reaching for the small blue cell phone on the bedside table. "She didn't call me back. She'd recognize my number. Aleisha would call…damn it, I called yesterday morning and this morning. I was going to call her house when I got home. That's always the last measure, but…"

Joel reached up and closed his hand over hers before she could punch in the number. "I'll have somebody look into it. Just give me her name. Don't call her house. That's too dangerous, you know that."

Dark gray eyes lifted and stared into his. "Aleisha would have called by now. I…I think I was trying not to think about it." She licked her lips, looking around her. "I bought a house, Joel. This is *mine*. The first thing that's been mine in forever. I can't lose it."

Reaching up, Joel wrapped his arms around her, pulling her down. She cuddled against him as he threaded a hand through the thick weight of her hair. "I'll take care of you, Emery. I will."

She lay there. "I know you will." Long moments of silence passed and then she pulled away. Joel released her reluctantly, feeling the silken strands of her hair sliding away as she sat up, staring down at him, her eyes wide and dark.

"Where have you been for the past three years?" she asked quietly.

Joel closed his eyes. "In prison." He heard her harsh intake of breath and looked back at her. "I'd never hurt you — and I'd kill anybody who did. But in a lot of ways, I'm not that different from Grainger. I've broken laws, I've stolen money, and I've killed people. My past caught up with me."

Her eyes narrowed as she stared down at him. Slowly, Emery knelt, putting her face level with his. "You can really be a dumb-ass idiot…" she whispered, shaking her head slowly.

Sitting back up, she arched a brow as she studied his face. "Vincent's pleasure in life is taking from others, causing them pain. The making of money is a hobby. He's good at it — but that's just a plus. He really gets off on the pain."

She looked away from him, her lashes lowering to hide her eyes. "And I know more about you than you think, Joel. A nice white-collar man isn't going to willingly do business with Vincent. Not if he knows the man. He might do it unwillingly — or blindly. But you weren't blind or unwilling. That means you were willing to break the law. I knew that. From the beginning, I knew you weren't a knight in shining armor."

Then she looked back at him, shrugging a little. "I don't need a knight, Joel. Maybe I needed one a little…then. Now I just need you."

Chapter Seven

ჹ

He heard footsteps. Squeaky, rubber-soled shoes, a sound he hated. Damned nurses.

He was surrounded by them.

His mind was slowly getting back into gear and he was figuring out what in the hell was going on, but it was slow. Thinking was slow.

It had taken a few days to even get past the thick gray fog that had obscured most of his thoughts. A few more days to figure out where in the hell he was.

Was he at the office? The high-rise in New York?

No. He wasn't at the office. If he had fallen asleep there, hell…he wouldn't have.

The high-rise, then…but no. That was his own space. Only his men were allowed inside those elegantly appointed rooms, and none of them would wear anything as annoying as squeaking shoes.

Somebody passed in front of him. White…she wore white. Another nurse, a safe person. It was the people who didn't wear white that he had to worry about.

He processed the information even as she dabbed at the drool he'd let dribble out of his mouth.

Disgusting, but there was a wariness about the way these people treated him that made him even more careful. Even the nurses.

Those who didn't wear white bothered Vincent the most. Feds. They came in wearing dark clothes—his eyes still bothered him too much to see but he knew they'd be wearing poorly made suits and they'd ask too many damned questions.

When the people in the suits showed up, he drooled as much as he could and acted even more disgusting.

It helped that he could finally figure out *why* he was here, and why the feds were watching him like hawks.

It seemed like forever had passed since he had been able to think clearly—but in the past week or so, things had been getting clearer.

His memory of that last day was incredibly clear now, not that he had let on. Even as the damned therapy people worked with him, he lay there like some slack-jawed yokel.

It was paying off though. Every day, his body got stronger and the muscle cramps that plagued him faded little by little.

For the past twenty minutes, he had lain with his eyes closed while the nurse checked his vitals and a doctor argued with some damn feds that he was completely incompetent.

Good doctor...he smirked inwardly, even as he wondered where in the hell the man had gotten his medical degree. Was it really that easy to mimic a catatonic state? Just sit there, stare straight ahead and drool a little?

Disgusting, yes, but he sure as hell wasn't going to jail and he was too damned weak yet to try and run.

"There has to be a test, something you can do to check for coherency."

"We've *done* them. There's brain activity, but he's spent years in a coma—he has to learn everything over again. Give him some time!"

He'd been wondering how damn long he'd been there. Three years. Damn.

Now, as everybody left, his mind whirled and danced. Memories spun through his mind. Watching from a rocky cliff as a woman fucked a man...a man he wanted.

They'd been so vague at first, but now they were crystal clear. Too clear.

207

That woman…*Tracy*…his hands closed into fists as he said her name silently to himself. Her face flickered in his memory, that exotic face and sleek body so many men had wanted. That was why *he* had wanted her. Because others looked and wanted and knew they'd never have. But he could.

He could have any damned thing he wanted…*almost*.

The memory of Tracy with that man…Joel. Joel Lockhart.

Vincent could remember one thing, clear as crystal. Joel, sitting across from him, wearing a black suit that fit that perfect body damned well. Vincent had been entertaining a fantasy where he moved to Joel, unbuckled that expensive Italian leather belt, slid the zipper down, and took Joel's cock in his mouth…

But then Joel had said words that had shocked the hell out of Vincent. He wasn't shocked easily.

"I want your wife." The man had stared at Vincent with emotionless, dark blue eyes, set in a face that was too harsh for true male beauty, but so damned sexy, so *male*.

"I beg your pardon?"

Joel's voice was cool, flat, almost disinterested as he had responded. "You heard me. You understand, too. You asked what it would take to get me in on some of your *business* ventures. Well, I have the answer for you now. I want your wife. Otherwise, I'll take my business elsewhere."

Vincent had forced out a laugh, lacing his fingers loosely across his belly as he'd leaned back in his chair, shaking his head. "No piece of ass is worth gambling a fortune on, Joel."

"Well, since you like dick more anyway, you probably wouldn't know. It's not like she's exactly your type. She can still be your little trophy wife — but I want her in my bed."

Those words had infuriated Vincent. Infuriated him and frightened him. Homosexuality was not something that was welcomed in his world. Too many of the sharks he swam with would see it as a weakness. *Weakness* wasn't welcomed in his world.

Joel Lockhart knew his secrets. Vincent didn't know how — but he knew.

Yet while Joel's words had infuriated him, scared him, they had made him hot, too...made him wonder if he could show Joel the pleasure to be found in...*liking dick,* as Joel had put it.

Not that it would ever happen. He'd learned to recognize those who could be tempted, bribed, or forced into his lifestyle.

Joel wasn't one of them.

And the fuck had wanted Tracy. *Tracy.*

Gnashing his teeth, he fought the images that flooded his mind. Too powerful, too strong, and he still felt weak. But he couldn't fight them off, so he fed off the anger they instilled in him.

How many times had he watched Joel fuck his wife?

Enough so that whenever he started to look at her, it was with jealousy. Then that day...yes. *That* day.

He'd fucked her, good and hard, and he could still remember how sweet that had been. Fuck, he could feel his cock jerking even now, and getting a hard-on wasn't good when a man had a fucking catheter in his dick.

The humiliation, the indignity of it made him seethe.

They had put him in here. He was suffering this indignity because of them. And they were going to pay for that.

As soon as he could get the hell out.

* * * * *

Joel came out of sleep with a vicious, sudden start. Staring up at the ceiling, he held his breath as memory swam back up through the dark fog of sleep.

Against his side, there was a soft, warm weight, and a scent he hadn't ever forgotten, sweet vanilla and woman.

Tracy...no...Emery. She called herself Emery now. Damn, she had changed. She'd always been fey, like a slender pixie, exotic, with that short chopped hair and that wide mouth in her heart-shaped face.

Now, though, she looked ethereal, like something too damned beautiful to be real.

He'd known that pale hair on her head wasn't her natural color, although it had looked amazing on her. The slender strip of curls that rested just atop her slit was a soft, warm brown. She still waxed the lips of her pussy—soft, silken flesh. He hadn't even taken the time to feel that soft flesh against his mouth—he had been too damned hungry to get inside her snug little sheath.

The shiny, soft brown hair suited her. It framed the softened curves of her face, falling into gentle waves to her breasts. And damn it, those breasts. Hell, she'd always had nice tits—he had loved cupping them in his hands, plumping them and sucking on her pretty little nipples.

But now...damn it, she was so soft and ripe. As he remembered how it had felt to take her, resting his hips in the soft cradle of her thighs, again and again throughout the night, his cock started to throb.

It went deeper than the surface though—there was strength inside her, confidence. He didn't know if it had always been there, although he suspected it had. The hell she had lived in had required strength—a weaker woman would have taken the easier way out. God knew, plenty of people walking a road not so difficult had done just that.

But that inner core of strength that had kept her going wasn't a quiet, hidden strength now. It shone in her eyes, in the way she walked, the way she talked.

Joel would be damned if that strength wasn't every bit as appealing as the frailty he still glimpsed in her eyes.

He still wanted to cuddle her, promise her that she'd never know another instant of pain or fear. But he also wanted to fuck her brains out—ride her hard, rough—the way he hadn't dared touch her.

His lids drooped as that image burned itself into his mind. That edgy hunger was one he had kept under control before. It had been easier. Tracy Grainger had been fragile. Most men didn't want to bruise somebody already so delicate—and Tracy had been just that.

But Emery—the woman she had made herself into—was a different story.

That hunger burned just under the surface of his skin, sizzling through his veins.

Clouding his mind.

Damn it. He had to focus.

Had to remember what was going on, because the last time he had lost himself in thoughts of her, that bastard Simmonds had dared to pull a gun on her.

Simmonds...he'd died that day, massive cerebral hemorrhage. The official story—the old man had pulled a gun on him and in the fight that followed, Simmonds had fallen back.

He'd never mentioned Tracy, although they had asked about her in the days that followed. His story was that he hadn't seen her since before he had left on his business trip days earlier.

They hadn't bought it—and more, Dowling had even been tracking the elusive Mrs. Grainger, maybe even from the beginning.

If he hadn't had that dossier, it would have taken a very long time to find her. Well, unless Carly had decided to shed some light on the subject.

He smirked a little at the thought. It wasn't impossible. There had been other odd things.

Emery sighed and he turned his gaze back to her, stroking one hand up and down her arm. Pressing his lips to her shoulder, he whispered, "I love you…"

The soft murmur that escaped her had him stiffening. He wasn't ready to tell her that just yet. Not when she was awake.

She arched and pushed back against him, stretching as she started to wake up. The ripe feel of her ass against him had him groaning. He rocked against her, pushing against her until the soft cheeks of her ass cuddled around his dick. She hummed, a soft little purring sound of pleasure as he stroked his hand up her side, cupping her breast and pinching the nipple gently as he lowered his head, scraping his teeth along the soft pad of flesh on her shoulder.

"Mornin'…" she murmured sleepily.

"So, Tracy's gone," he whispered. "And Emery…is Emery afraid of anything?"

She slid a look at him over her shoulder, her lids still heavy with sleep. "Depends on what you have in mind."

"I want to take you…like this…" he rasped, rising to his knees, tugging her onto hers. He pushed inside, watching as her spine stiffened. If she told him to stop…*I can stop. For her…I can…*

But fuck, she was tight. Staring down, he watched as he pumped back inside her, slowly, fighting the tight, resistant grip of her flesh. "I want to fuck you…I don't want to have to worry about looking in your eyes and seeing fear. I want to make you scream, and I don't want to be gentle."

"Joel," she whimpered, and she shivered as he pushed back inside her. The tissues of her pussy were slicker, the scent of her sexual cream rising to flood his head.

Splaying his hands wide across the dip in her spine, he jerked her back against him, forgetting the gentleness, the care he had always used with her. Plunging his cock inside the snug, wet well of her pussy, he groaned as she clenched around him.

She sobbed as he pounded against her, hearing the slap his hips against the round curve of her ass. Using his thumbs, he spread the cheeks of her ass apart, eying the dark rose of her anus greedily. He'd never touched her there, not even the softest caress—that wasn't a gentle way to take a woman, and she had needed gentle care.

But the hungry cries exploding from her mouth made him hot, made him careless and he licked his finger, probing the tight pucker, watching as he slowly breached the tight muscles.

She stilled, her head dropping low to the mattress as her arms collapsed. "Joel...?" she whimpered.

"Shh. This doesn't hurt...fuck me, you're so damn hot and tight..." the muscles of her sheath clutched at him as he screwed his finger slowly inside her ass.

"Joel..." her voice was still soft and nervous, but her body was pushing back against him, eagerly, hungrily.

He added a second finger and she yelped, her body going still as she stretched around the added penetration. "I want to fuck this ass of yours, baby...fuck it until you beg me to stop, until you beg me not to."

As he spoke, he rotated his fingers and that was when she climaxed, a hot rush of fluid soaked his cock so that as he pulled out, there was a wet sucking sound.

He thrust to the hilt, and flooded the wet depths of her pussy with his semen, holding her hips tightly to him as he rolled his pelvis against her ass. "Sweet..." he purred. The energy drained out of his body and he sank to the mattress, rolling to the side so she wouldn't be pinned beneath him.

Wrapping an arm around her waist, he pulled her back against him and nuzzled her neck, breathing in the warm, soft scent of her skin. "Damn it, I've missed you," he whispered.

Emery's body trembled, and her breath was coming hard and ragged. A little knot of worry started to form inside his gut as she remained silent. He hadn't hurt her—but had he scared her?

Then her hand slid up, covering the one resting on her midriff. Their fingers laced as a soft sigh escaped her. The tension inside him slowly dissolved as she cuddled back against him.

"Missed you, too, Joel. I've felt empty since the last time I saw you." She made another one of those soft little humming sighs, as she cuddled deeper into the pillow.

Within moments, she was asleep and Joel was left holding her against him, his mind working busily. In the silence of the room, he pressed his face against her hair and grimaced.

He still had to tell her about her husband.

* * * * *

Shoving a hand through her hair, Emery watched with sleepy eyes as Joel walked back down the drive.

Her body ached—the muscles in her thighs pulled with every damn move, and her pussy felt raw and sore. It was the best she could remember feeling in a very, very long time. As he slid into the car, he flashed her that slow smile that was uniquely his own, his dark eyes holding a promise.

When he drove away, she slowly closed the door, resting her back against it as she leaned her head back, closing her eyes. Hot tears rolled from beneath her eyelids—the emotions she'd fought to keep under control while Joel was there were breaking free, and before she knew it, a sob ripped from her throat.

It was relief. It was joy…and fear.

There was something Joel wasn't telling her.

From the beginning, he had coddled her, protected her, done his damnedest to keep anything from hurting her. Hiding her from the reality that had been her life for so long. And he was still hiding her from reality.

She could see it in his eyes. There was something he wasn't telling her — something that had him worried.

Emery knew Joel. If he was worried, then damn it, she ought to be terrified.

* * * * *

His steps were heavy as he stumbled into the small efficiency apartment where he'd been staying for the past few weeks.

Joel hadn't had a sound sleep since beginning his search, and for a while, he'd run on pure energy and fear, while Tracy — no, she was Emery now — had seemed to slip farther and farther away from him. Even as his body had begged for sleep, he had resisted, doing little more than catching a few hours a night. Fear had kept him moving — once he found her, once he caught up with her and knew she was safe, *then* he could sleep.

Last night, the thrill of having her close had been too new, and his emotions too raw for him to sleep. Joel hadn't slept even for ten minutes as he lay cuddled around her in the bed.

Hadn't slept, although his body had ached with exhaustion. Couldn't think clearly, although there was nothing more he needed to do.

That was why he had kissed her softly after she woke up and told her he had to get some stuff done.

Not stuff. He needed sleep. He needed the distance to think. To make phone calls…couldn't think around her.

Now he was exhausted. Collapsing onto the bed face first, he fell into a deep, heavy sleep, unaware of the soft, hazy white form that watched him.

Joel fell into a dream, the same dream that had haunted him for months. Ever since he'd come out of prison and wondered where in the hell his woman had gone.

Tracy Grainger had just fallen off the face of the earth—he'd damned near gone insane searching for her.

He'd exhausted his leads and gone through hundreds of thousands of dollars trying to track her down. She had slipped from town to town, always using cash, never leaving any sign of herself behind.

He had focused the car she'd bought as his only lead.

Emery Hughes had a birth certificate, a work history that seemed solid, but she hadn't existed until that day eighteen months ago when she left the office of an attorney who specialized in helping abused women escape from a dangerous past.

The dream was the same, always the same. He walked into the posh apartment where he'd found his sister all those years ago, but instead of Carly lying on the floor, naked, beaten, the evidence of a rape still on her thighs, it was Tracy...*Emery*.

And not as he was so used to seeing her, with that short, sophisticated coif of pale blonde hair and a thin exotic face. No.

It was her as he'd seen her earlier, with thick waves of mink brown, her mouth lush and full in the soft curves of her face.

Closing his eyes, he flopped back on the bed, pressing his palms against them. He had to keep her safe.

You will...

His hands fell away and he sat up, scowling at the pale misty form hovering on the chair by his bed. Carly's ghost had come to him that very first day after she'd died.

Grainger's men had been watching her apartment and when he had gone in there, they'd seen him. They'd called Grainger, apparently, because as Carly had whispered in his ear *Run*, Grainger had been driving to the apartment. Joel, called Marc then, had slid out the window to the balcony and monkeyed down to the balcony below, working his way down ten stories, sweating and scared to death. As he'd hit the street, he had heard the voice shouting overhead and he'd looked up, seeing one of the men he'd seen with Grainger before.

He'd taken off running. At the intersection ahead, he'd seen Grainger's black Porsche as it came flying around the corner and Joel had ducked down the alley to his left, running for his life.

And Carly had continued to whisper to him.

He didn't actually see her form for a long time, but her ghost was with him almost constantly as he grew up. She'd been taking care of him for so long—even after she'd moved away from home. Mama had been too busy getting laid or getting high…

They'd killed Mama, too.

Joel knew that, even though it had been made to look like an accident. When he'd tried to go home after running away from Grainger, Carly had whispered to him again. He'd gone home anyway…or tried to. And found ambulances and police cars surrounding the small, ratty apartment.

He'd disappeared after that.

Nobody was likely to notice another twelve-year-old punk on the streets of New York, and he'd done okay. When he was eighteen, he'd taken his the test for his GED and passed with flying colors, then joined the Army with one goal in mind.

To become a tough enough bastard to handle Vincent Grainger.

It had all been so simple. He could handle Grainger. Could kill him. Happily.

What wasn't simple was Emery. How did he tell her that Grainger was awake?

How did he handle letting her know what he had done? Killing Grainger was one thing—and he would kill him.

But the things he had done to move closer to Grainger, that was different. He'd turned into a fucking criminal, barely a step above Grainger.

That was the part that wasn't so simple.

Jerking his mind out of the past, he stared at Carly's surreal form, hovering on the edge of the seat as though she was just sitting down for a break. "What's wrong, Carly?" he asked tiredly.

She laughed. The sound was hollow, as though it came from some distant tunnel and it echoed. "Wrong? Why does something have to be wrong, Marc?"

"My name is Joel," he said wearily. "Marc Baker is long gone, Sis."

She sighed, and the sound was desolate. The room seemed to chill and Joel rubbed his arms. "Gone...just like me," she said forlornly.

"Carly..."

"No. No. I'm fine. Hell, for the most part, I'm more than fine. I don't have any bills, I don't have to worry about gaining weight...granted, I can't eat anything, but it's not a bad trade-off." She laughed softly. "I'm better off dead than I ever was alive. Too bad I had to leave you alone."

Silence fell and Joel tried to figure out what in the hell to say, if there even was anything to say. Staring down at the sheet that covered his legs, he closed his hand around it, wishing that somebody had killed Grainger long, long ago.

"Are you going to tell her? You can't just think she'll blindly leave. She's not the same woman she used to be."

"I know that."

"Then maybe you also know what you're planning isn't fair—it's not right. Tell her. Tell her about Grainger. Tell her what you've done."

No. "I can't do that. She doesn't need to know." Hell—if she ever found out, he could lose her. And she *wouldn't* find out. She wouldn't want to be in the same state as Grainger, so when she found out he was awake, and Joel offered her a safe place, she'd leap on it.

"Don't count on it."

Joel snarled at her, "Damn it, will you stay out of my head?"

Carly sighed. "You're setting her up as bait, baby. It's not fair. And you haven't even told her yet. When are you going to tell her—she's in danger, damn it."

"She's safe," Joel said flatly. "I'll keep her safe."

Starkly, Carly said, "She's not safe. He thinks about her constantly, her and you. Even while he was in that damn coma, it ate at him. He wants you both dead. That hatred consumes him, just like your hatred of him consumes you. Don't let it make you foolish, baby."

* * * * *

Emery knew who was at the door even before she opened it. She'd been restless all day, haunted by thoughts of Joel, plagued by memories of times best forgotten, the years she'd spent in fear and humiliation, awaiting another blow from Vincent Grainger.

And...the day she had all but been given to Joel.

Given, as if she was just a belonging.

A possession. She had just been a toy for Vincent, some pretty little piece for him to show off to others. When she'd tried to run, he had always found her, always brought her back. The whispers, *You're mine*...had left her shuddering and shaking in terror. How could those same words, coming from Joel, make her shake with need and blush with pleasure?

She was torn, though. Torn with the need to wrap herself around him...and the need to show herself she could stand on her own two feet. The first few months, when he hadn't come after her, she had been shattered, and learning how to stand on her own had been damned near impossible. It had been his voice, a voice from the past, whispering to her from her memories that had given her the strength.

That strength was her own now.

If she relied on Joel now, was she giving up on herself?

With a spinning head, she opened the door and stood there, staring at the craggy lines of his face, those impossibly deep blue eyes. "Hey," she said quietly.

A slow smile creased his face as he moved up closer, until his toes nudged hers, his breath warm on her face as he murmured, "Hey."

His lips brushed across hers and she sighed into his mouth, whimpering as his tongue pushed inside her mouth to tangle briefly with hers. His arms came around her and she gasped as her feet left the ground. Dimly, she heard him kick the door shut and then he was leaning back against it, hiking her thighs up around his hips so he could cup her bottom.

She arched up against him as those hard, hot hands kneaded restlessly at her ass. With her knees clutching his hips, the folds between her thighs were exposed and she whimpered as the covered length of his cock pressed against her.

A savage groan fell from his lips—the room whirled around her and then she was cold. Cold and sitting alone on the couch, while Joel stalked away from her. Arching a brow at him, she mused, "Well, nice to see you, too." Crossing her arms over her chest, she hugged herself as a chill raced down her spine and her body ached.

He sent her a narrow look over his shoulder, eyes slitted, mouth grim. "I can't think around you. I've never been able to think clearly around you," he muttered. He shoved his hand through his hair as he dropped to sit on the chair across from her. "And right now, I need to think. We need to talk."

Licking her lips, she stared into his serious face. She really didn't like the sound of that, or the grim look in his eyes.

"Okay," she finally said, her voice soft and hesitant. "What about?"

His face was cold, implacable as stone—his lips barely moved as he said flatly, "About your husband. And about your lawyer."

"What about Aleisha?" she asked, her voice worried even as her face went rigid. "And that bastard is *not* my husband."

His lids drooped and he murmured, "That's not how he will see it."

Emery swallowed, then forced the fear back under control. Restless energy filled her and she stood, unable to sit down any longer.

As she paced, she said, "He's in a coma, Joel. He has been ever since that day. It's not very likely he'll ever come out of it."

Joel's eyes closed.

A cold chill raced through her. She stared at him as his eyes slowly opened and he stared at her, those dark unreadable eyes holding so many secrets. She'd known he wasn't telling her something.

Emery stood still as he rose from the chair and moved toward her, closing the distance between them. His hands came up, cupping her face. She swallowed, the knot in her throat damn near choking her as she looked up at him.

"What is it?" she asked quietly, tears blurring her vision. One fell, and it seemed to burn a path down her cheek.

"He's awake."

The strength drained out of her. As though somebody had simply opened something inside of her and just let it all flow away. Emery started to crumple to the ground and Joel's arms caught her, pulling her against him.

"No." Struggling, she tried to pull away, but he just held her against him and carried her to the couch. "Damn it, let me go! You're lying—Aleisha would have called me. The nurses, the doctors, they know to call her…"

"Emery."

She saw it in his eyes. Shaking her head, she whispered, "No. Damn it, *no*! She was safe! She told me she was safe—he couldn't have hurt her."

"He didn't." Emery jerked away, but she couldn't break free from him, and deep inside she knew she didn't want to. She needed his comfort too badly. "She was in a car wreck a few days ago. An accident, baby. Accidents happen."

"No," she whimpered, shaking her head as a sob rose in her throat. Giving in to the need to cry, she crumpled against him. Harsh, bitter cries tore from her throat and she clung to him.

For the longest time, she could do nothing more than cry. The grief inside her had left her dumb, blind and deaf to everything around. For three years, Aleisha had been her one contact to real life. Her one contact to sanity—when she was running and hiding, she worried she'd forget *who* she was.

Aleisha had been her anchor.

And now her one friend was dead.

"W-was it fast?" she finally asked, her voice hoarse.

"Yes. She wouldn't have felt anything," Joel murmured, reaching up and brushing her hair back.

"Thank God for that," she muttered, closing her eyes again. There was an odd niggling doubt in her head and she sat back, looking up at him narrowly. "How did you know about her?"

"The FBI."

Emery's heart froze. "They know where I am."

Joel sighed, his head falling back to rest against the couch. "One agent does. I don't know about them as a whole. And I don't know why she hasn't tried to talk to you."

She felt his gaze on her as he studied her under the fringe of his lashes. "Don't you want to know more about Grainger?"

Emery saw something in his eyes that she had only glimpsed before. He hated Vincent Grainger. It was a gut-deep hatred, and somehow…old, she sensed. She had glimpsed it before, all the times she had run into him when he had come to the house on business, but he'd always hid it so quickly, and he never showed it around Vincent.

Why… Hatred was a personal emotion. Hate, like love, was generally earned. What had Vincent done?

Swallowing, she pushed insistently against his arms until he let her go. Wiping the tears from her cheeks, she rose and walked away.

I'll have to grieve later…think about why Joel hates Grainger so much later.

Right now, she needed to think. Moving to the window, she brushed aside the curtains and stood there, staring outside.

When Joel moved up behind her in silence, she never even heard him.

* * * * *

Emery whirled when Joel touched her shoulder. "What are you planning on doing about Vincent?" he asked quietly.

She licked her lips, staring at him with haunted eyes. She just shook her head. "I don't know. I need to think."

He watched, his hands curled into useless fists as she walked away, her head bent low.

Moments later, he heard the back door close quietly.

Dropping into a chair, he muttered, "Damn it."

He started to stand up. His arms itched to wrap around her, hold her. That scared look was one he'd promised he'd never see in her eyes again.

Let her have some time.

Narrowing his eyes, he said flatly, "Isn't that some strange advice coming from you, Sis?"

Carly laughed. *Maybe. She's not going to do what you want.*

Pulling the cell phone from his pocket, he tapped it idly on his leg, glancing around the room. He couldn't see Carly anywhere so he resigned himself to talking to thin air for the hundredth time. "She will. I'm not giving her a choice."

She's not as weak-willed as she used to be. She'll fight you. And you shouldn't try to make her, sweetie. She's got a right to stand and fight on her own terms.

"She's got a right to live without being afraid of him," Joel growled.

Then don't bully her — let her stand on her own two feet. If she chooses to leave, so be it. But let her choose.

He shook his head. "She stays safe. And safe is away from him."

With that, he lifted the phone and started to punch in numbers. They were running out of time anyway.

Ten minutes later, he verified that Grainger was still *allegedly* catatonic.

It didn't appear to be a line the feds were buying. Joel hadn't spent the past twenty years just burying landmines under Grainger's feet. He'd also been building a network of information and informants, all of them people who had hated Grainger as much as Joel did.

Once he'd made sure that Grainger was still in Maine, he headed outside.

Emery was out there, sitting in a swing, staring up at the sky. "I told you I wanted to be alone," she said in a level tone.

Joel arched a brow. *Damn.* She'd gone and grown some teeth. "I know," he replied neutrally. "I want to let you know I had to make some calls. Do some stuff. I'll be back tonight."

"No."

Narrowing his eyes, he said, "Excuse me?"

She turned her head and met his gaze. "No," she repeated coolly. "I need some time to think."

"It's not safe."

She snorted. "My ass. I know you. If it wasn't safe, you wouldn't be leaving. You apparently know everything that's going on with him, so I assume he's still in the hospital...or someplace where's he's being watched. Although I'm kind of curious as to why they haven't locked his ass up. But that's not the point. I need some time to think, Joel. Come back in the morning."

"Are you going to be here?" he asked, his voice low and gritty. He had this gut-deep fear that she'd panic and take off.

A smile curled her lips upward. "This is my home, Joel. It's the first thing that's been mine in forever. I'm not leaving."

Closing the distance between them, he lowered his head to hers and covered her mouth with his. "I'll hold you to that."

Turning away, he said silently, *You will have to leave for a while, baby. But you'll come back, I promise.*

* * * * *

Vincent stared at the man in front of him with narrowed eyes, watching as he closed the door gently behind him.

"Hey, boss," Carter said, a smug little smile on his face.

Vincent just stared slackly at him.

Carter smiled. "It's okay. You can talk to me. Your babysitters are taking a nap. Permanently."

Narrowing his eyes, Vincent straightened up just a little in the hospital bed.

With a grin, Carter moved closer. "That's more like it. Don't worry. I've got a cousin working the desk here. And I know the feds aren't due in for a while yet, but we got to get you out of here."

Finally, Vincent asked in a soft voice, "We?"

225

Carter beamed at Vincent, "Yeah, *we*. I knew you weren't in no *vegetative* state. Smart move, though. Real smart. Come on, we don't have much time. How much can you move?"

Suspicious, Vincent stared at Carter. "What are you doing here?"

Carter grinned. "Been waiting for you. I told you…my cousin Rachel."

Vincent was too fucking tired to argue, or debate, or worry about the good fortune that had landed one of his men right where he needed him. Normally, he would have been a little more suspicious, but right now…right now, he needed to get out of there.

As Carter came around, he said, "How many people are available? I need to find an old friend."

Carter paused, smiling. He lifted a yellow legal-sized envelope. "If it's Lockhart, that's already done."

Chapter Eight

ഇ

Kneeling in the dirt, she felt the summer sun shining warm on her face, and smiled as she ran her hands over the blooming bushes of flowers, stripping away some of the branches.

A shadow fell across her hands and a rose appeared in her line of vision.

Instinctively, she breathed in the sweet scent and then she lifted her head, squinting up at Joel. He squatted down in front of her, twirling the rose between his fingers. "You grow nice flowers."

Emery tried to force herself to scowl, even though all she wanted to do was throw herself at him.

She'd dreamed of him last night. Ached for him until she finally felt asleep, hours past midnight. Then the dreams had come, black, ugly ones, full of pain and torment. They'd had her struggling, shivering and shaking, tossing in her sheets, until they finally woke her, screaming.

Joel could have kept those ugly dreams away. Just one touch of his hand made her feel cleaner, stronger.

But right now, she wanted to lash out at him. There was a fury in her gut and it was centered on him.

Damn it, why in the hell was she so mad at him?

Slowly, she reached out, closing her fingers around the fragile stem, twirling it as she slid him a look from under her lashes. "Gee, thanks. I couldn't have grown a prettier one myself."

He just shrugged. His eyes ran over the backyard and she had the oddest feeling that he was aware of every little thing around them, from the way the breeze drifted across, to the new bushes she had planted. There was an odd, tense set to his shoulders, and his mouth was rather grim.

"You look pretty serious for a man stealing flowers," she mused.

A slow smile creased his face. "Sorry." His lids drooped, and he suddenly looked sleepy. Sleepy and hungry. "I missed you last night."

Emery licked her lips, sniffing the rose before glancing up at him. "I missed you, too." Lifting one shoulder in a shrug, she murmured, "I didn't sleep well...bad dreams, half the night. The other half of the night, I couldn't sleep for wanting you too much."

Joel groaned. Then his hands were on her and Emery gasped, then started to giggle as her dirty hands left damp stains on the white button-down shirt he wore. "I'm getting you dirty," she whispered.

His arms closed around her, snuggling her against him. "Don't care. Damn it, I don't feel complete without you against me."

His gruff voice sent a shiver down her spine. One hand slid up to cup her nape, his mouth brushing against her earlobe.

He sighed, and his body seemed to shudder with it, then he pulled back. Narrowing her eyes, she demanded, "Now what?"

His hand cupped her cheek, his thumb rubbing over the curve of her lower lip. "I need to talk to you..."

Her brows lowered over her eyes and she poked out her lip. "Damn it, don't you think we had enough serious talks yesterday?"

Joel sighed softly, dropping his forehead until it pressed against hers. "No, sweetie. There's not as much time as I thought."

That sent a frisson a fear racing through her. Slipping away from him, she wrapped her arms around herself, staring out at the lush green lawn, the bright bursts of flowers planted here and there. "What is it, Joel?"

"Grainger's missing."

Her hands fell limply to her lap and all the strength left her body. Her breath escaped her in a rush and she tried to breathe around the knot that had suddenly formed in her chest. "Missing?"

His eyes went flat and grim. "Since early this morning. Last seen about six hours ago. The two guards stationed outside his room are dead, shot in the head. He had outside help. I'm taking you away—"

"Like hell."

Terror swarmed up, threatening to close her throat, but damn it, that bastard wasn't doing this to her again.

He'd already ruined her life once.

Joel caught her face in his hand, lifting her chin and leaning down until the tip of his nose touched hers. "I am taking you away. I've got safe places all over this damn country and I'll put you in one of them—hell, I'll hand you over to the feds if I have to. You'll keep that fine ass of yours safe."

She swallowed and it was close to painful. Blood rushed in her ears as she jerked away.

"I am *not* leaving my home! How in the hell can he find me, anyway?"

"I did, smartass. Why couldn't he?" Joel demanded.

Hands clenched into fists at her sides, she glared at him. Fury and fear danced an ugly tango inside her, turning her insides into a mess. Lowering her voice, she repeated harshly, "I am not leaving."

His hand closed around her arm and she turned around swinging. Her hand just barely clipped him on the chin. He caught that hand — but she swung at him again with the other.

Joel caught it, too, and before she realized it, he had swung her around, and braced her back against an oak. Sunlight fell across his face in dappled slices, highlighting his eyes, the curve of his mouth, the line of his jaw. Struggling against him, she demanded, "Let me go! Don't you understand? He's already controlled too much of my life. I won't let him do it again!"

"I won't risk you, Tracy. Damn it, I have to keep you safe."

"Emery!" she screamed at him. Struggling harder, she again screamed, "It's Emery!"

He dropped her hands, but before she could go back to shoving at him, he jerked her against him, his hands closing around her upper arms. "Stop. Emery, listen to me. Damn it, I can't stand the thought of you being near him."

"Do you think I *want* to?" Unaware of the tears that filled her eyes, she shoved against him but he wouldn't let her go. "The thought makes me sick. But I promised myself I'd never let anybody make me that afraid again. And I *won't*. Damn it, I won't. You can't make me."

"Tra…" his voice trailed off as he stared down at her. Closing his eyes, he said, "You don't understand what you're asking.

Her hair fell over her shoulder as she stared up at him. Slowly, she reached up and cupped his face in her hands. "Maybe you don't either. I found something, Joel. Something I didn't have before. Self-respect. And if you try to make me leave, I lose that."

"He's lost most of his power base — they are in jail, some of them are dead. And a lot of the money is frozen by the government. Aleisha did tell me some of that. He's lost a lot of his power — including the power he held over me. I won't let him take that back just because he used to terrorize me. I can't."

Joel stared down at her, his face as hard as stone. "What kind of man would it make me, letting you so close to the bastard who beat and raped you?"

She smiled then. "You act like I don't have a clue what you're planning."

He arched a brow.

"You want him here. If he doesn't know where I am...or where you are...you're going to let him know. You want him here — because you want him dead. You plan on killing him."

Leaning forward, she rose on her toes and pressed her lips to his. "I know you, Joel. Better than you think. Now tell me...am I wrong?"

Chapter Nine

ജ

Stupid…

Joel told himself that for the hundredth time as he watched Tracy settle down at her computer.

Then he told himself, *Emery*. Hell, even after he had loaded that son of a bitch full of lead, she wouldn't go back to Tracy.

Tracy was dead. She wanted Tracy dead.

Maybe it was easier for her. Made it easier to handle what had happened to her.

"You writing?" he asked neutrally.

She cast him a look over her shoulder. "Is there anything you don't know about my life?" she asked, her tone amused.

Damn it, why didn't she look more worried. Joel was terrified. He'd called two people. He didn't trust anybody, but there were two guys who had reason to hate Vincent and he wanted more eyes on this house.

But it would take them a few hours to get here.

And she was sitting there, working, as though there was nothing wrong.

"Carter Manning is missing."

He watched her spine stiffen. Manning was one of Grainger's favorite bastards—Joel had no doubt that Manning had witnessed some of the humiliations Grainger had dealt his wife.

As Emery slowly spun in her chair to face him, he saw nothing but blankness in her eyes. "Is that supposed to make me want to run away screaming in terror?"

Guilt riddled him but he shoved it down. Harshly, he snapped, "If you're smart, it would."

"Carter is a puppet, Joel. Nothing more. Cut his strings and he's useless."

"His puppet master has been lying comatose the past three years."

An amused smile curved her lips. With a shrug, she just said, "Somebody was filling Vincent's shoes. Not of all his companies collapsed. I've kept an eye on the business world. Somebody who knows those businesses has been running them. That's who has been pulling Carter's strings."

Narrowing his eyes, Joel said, "You always let on like you didn't know a damned thing about his business life."

She shrugged. "His business *life*—I didn't. Him, I knew plenty. I know the companies he owned. I don't know what kind of laws he broke, although I can probably imagine." With a smirk, she added, "Every one imaginable."

"And then some." Joel rubbed a hand over his eyes. "You aren't going to leave, are you?"

"Nope." With that, she spun around and faced her keyboard.

Staring at the long, mink brown hair cascading down her back, he blew out a tired breath.

They were coming here. Joel knew that as well as he knew his own reflection. They were coming here, coming after Tracy—but the plan had been for her to *leave*.

And now because he hadn't planned on this streak of courageousness, she was going to be here.

I'll keep her safe, he promised himself, unconsciously echoing his promise to Carly. Closing his eyes, he muttered, "It will be over soon. No matter what."

It didn't matter what it took. His life, his death. His everything, so long as Grainger died, and Emery was safe.

That sounds so final…

Jerking his head up, he saw the faint white outline of his sister's form, hovering in the air near Emery. Clenching his jaw, he stalked out of the room, onto the porch where he braced his hands on the railing. "Damn it, don't do that."

Carly laughed. *What...don't talk to you when your girlfriend is around?*

He glared at her, glanced through the window to see Emery's head lowered over a book. Jerking his head back to Carly, he just stood there with a brow lifted, waiting to hear what she had to say.

My...you usually aren't so patient, baby brother.

Joel sneered automatically. Damn it, he'd been after a killer for more than twenty years, if that wasn't patience, what was?

There was a soft sighing sound, one that drifted through the air and seemed to chill everything around them. Joel felt the goose bumps break out over his skin, and when he breathed out, his breath formed a foggy little cloud. *You aren't going to die, Joel.*

Joel shrugged. The thought had occurred to him, more than once, that one day, Vincent Grainger would kill him. He'd never really cared before, so long as he took the bastard with him, but Tracy had changed things. Emery had changed them even more. It was as though there were two women living inside that skin — soft, sweet Tracy who he had fought to protect, and Emery, the woman who'd been strong enough to run, strong enough to build a life of her own. He loved them both. And so long as his woman was fine, he could handle what came.

Don't think like that. You want a life with her...reach for it.

Joel turned away, sighing. "She deserves better, Carly. Damn it, I've got almost as much blood on my hands as Grainger."

The air around him chilled even more and Joel winced as Carly's angry voice seemed to cut right through him, like a frigid wind. *Don't! The blood of murderers. Damn you, your soul isn't as stained as you think. I know how many lives you took. I've been with you since the beginning. You killed the ones who killed me. And you've killed bastards who put drugs in the hands of babies, men who rape children. The lives you've taken saved the lives of countless others. Stop blaming yourself for that. Let it go.*

Live for yourself. For once...you deserve to have something in life that you want...not just revenge.

"Revenge is all I ever needed."

Until her...look at her, Marc...Joel, look at her and tell me that you don't want to be with her as you both turn old and gray. That you don't want to see her belly get big with a baby...that you don't want lie beside her every night for the next hundred years. Can you tell me that?

Slowly, he turned and stared through the window at Emery, watching as she reached up and pressed a hand against her eyes, watching the way her shoulders rose and fell as she took a deep breath. "A hundred years isn't enough," he said thickly, feeling the foreign sting of tears in his eyes.

Then stop preparing yourself to die. You've been mentally doing just that for years... stop it. Prepare yourself to live...and you will.

Turning away from the woman he loved, he stared out into the night.

"It's not that simple."

In a soft husky voice, Carly murmured, *It is. Just reach for what you want...stop searching for what you've always searched for. Revenge isn't the most important thing anymore. Taking care of her is. Isn't now more important than the past?*

And with those obscure words, she faded away. The temperature returned to normal and Joel's breath no longer came in foggy clouds. Slumping against the porch railing, he scrubbed a hand over his face and tried to figure out what in the hell Carly had been getting at.

* * * * *

Emery jumped at every sound.

Every shadow in her house had turned ominous and she felt cold, no matter how many blankets she piled on top of her, no matter how thick her sweater, or how high she turned up the heat.

Cold and terrified.

No matter how brave her words were, she was still scared. And part of her *did* want to run. There was a voice murmuring to her in the back of her mind like a mantra. She couldn't tell Joel that.

If he knew she was afraid, he'd never let her stay.

She couldn't focus on her work though, and none of the books she'd tried to read made sense. After a couple hours of pacing, she settled on the couch and tried to watch TV.

Nothing there held her interest.

Desperate for a distraction, she finally decided to ask Joel the one question that had plagued her for ages.

"Why did you get involved with Grainger?"

She'd surprised him. She saw it in the widening of his eyes, the subtle tightening of that carved, sensual mouth, the way his hands flexed on the paper he was reading.

"He had what I wanted."

Emery snorted. "Not good enough. He didn't have a damned thing you couldn't have gotten on your own."

A slow smile edged his lips up. "He had you. There wasn't another you in the whole world."

She flushed slightly, but she shook her head. "There's more than that. You hate him. You always did—I've seen it in your eyes before. What did he do to you?"

Joel met her eyes, and she almost shivered at the flat black look in his. He seemed colder, somehow. A lot colder. Distant. When he shook his head and murmured, "It doesn't matter,"

Emery knew he was lying. Even though there had really been no change in his expression, the lie was so heavy in the air, it almost choked her.

"I want the truth."

One straight black brow rose and he said quietly, "He abused you...hurt you...you're terrified of him. Isn't that reason enough?"

Shaking her head, she said, "No. It's older than that. You hated him before you ever saw me."

His lids drooped, shielding his eyes from hers.

Jerkily, she rose from her chair, and stalked past him. "Fine. Don't tell me." Under her breath, she muttered, *"Trust me,* he says."

Just as she reached the foot of the stairs, he came up behind her, and laid a hand on her shoulder. Freezing under his touch, she continued to stare straight ahead as he lowered his head to murmur in her ear, "Don't... Don't walk away from me. This doesn't have anything to do with trust."

"Then why in the hell don't you tell me?" she asked stiffly, refusing to relax back against his body, the way she wanted to.

He sighed. His breath brushed against her neck, exposed by the thick braid she'd woven her hair into. Her skin tingled, tightened, a chill raced down her spine. Her nipples tightened and she could feel the heat of his body reaching out to her. When he remained silent, she tried to tug away, but his hands shifted, clamping around her waist as he dragged her back against him.

"You don't want to know this, Emery. Not really. There are things about me that you don't want to know, things you don't need to know. You *think* you know me. You claim you don't need a knight in shining armor. But you deserve one. And I'm so far from a knight, it's pathetic."

As he turned her around, taking her chin, lifting her face until her eyes met his, Emery wondered if it was too late to

237

say, "I take it back." Staring into the bottomless depths of his tormented eyes, she decided he was right. She didn't want to know. But then his hands tightened around her waist, lifting her against him. Automatically, she wrapped her legs around his waist. Staring into his eyes, helplessly, she found she couldn't speak as he lowered them to the couch, keeping her astride him. His hands started to roam over her back, down her hips, over her legs, in constant, restless motion as he stared over her shoulder.

"I was twelve years old when she met him. She was nineteen...beautiful, smart. She wanted more than we could have. Carly liked money, liked pretty things. She was going to school, but at night, she stripped. She was pretty enough, exotic enough, that she landed a job at a very high-end gentlemen's club. That was where she met Grainger."

His lids lowered and when he looked back at her, for one brief second, the blank mask he always showed the world was gone.

Emery wanted to cry at the pain she saw exposed on his face.

Then once more, his eyes became shuttered and he hid himself from her again. "I told her he was bad news. I was there the day he came to pick her up at the house. He had bought her a condo. I told her, 'that guy ain't right'. I told her...but she went anyway. By the time she understood I was right, it was too late for her to just walk away. She'd seen too much, heard too much..."

His voice trailed off. For a long time, he didn't say anything. His hands moved to knead restlessly along her back, moving down her hips, then along her thighs, then circling back again—his hands couldn't seem to stop moving. "Who was she?" Emery asked quietly.

His hands stilled, for just a second, and he opened his eyes, meeting hers. In a hoarse whisper, he said, "My sister. She was my sister...and he killed her."

"Oh, God." Tears flooded her eyes and she reached out, cupping his cheek gently. "No. Joel, I'm so sorry."

"My name was Marc." His mouth twitched as he tried to smile. "I left that name behind. He'd find me. I knew he would. Couldn't take the chance that Carly had said anything at all to me. Not even the smallest thing...our house burned down. Mom was still inside. I don't think about her much. From the time I was just a baby, Carly took care of me more than Mom anyway. But he killed her. I know he did. The autopsy said she died of a broken neck. She was found at the foot of the steps—they basically decided that she tripped trying to get out of the house. Said the house fire was an electrical malfunction. But he started it—or one of his men. It's weird though. I'm not as mad about that. Mom was dead inside long before he killed her—hell, she died the minute my father left her. Grainger just finished the job. But Carly—"

Joel's voice broke off and his hands tightened almost painfully on her hips. Leaning against him, she wrapped her arms around his neck, one hand stroking the thick black hair that curled at his nape. "I'm sorry."

A harsh sigh shuddered through him. She felt the heat of his breath on her neck, felt the tears that stung her eyes, and her heart broke for the boy he'd been. "I'm sorry, Joel...Marc."

He laughed. A harsh, bitter sound. "Marc's dead. He died when he saw what that bastard did to his sister."

Emery went stiff. "You saw?"

"He tore her apart, Emery. And Marc died when he saw it."

She lifted her head to see one lone tear trickling down his cheek. Her throat knotted and she lowered her head, gently catching that salty drop with her lips. "You've been after him all this time," she murmured gently.

"Yes. Everything I've ever done...I did to get close to him, to find out everything I could about that night. He wasn't alone, you see. I had to find out who was with him, who helped him."

Her chest ached, and she realized she was holding her breath. Slowly, she released that pent-up breath and drew in another, releasing it, waiting for the aching in her chest to ease. But it didn't—the ache only grew as she stared at him and tried to understand the pain he had gone through.

"That's why you got into this life—to get close to him? That's why you didn't just kill him?"

Joel nodded, a bitter smile on his face. "Keep your friends close...your enemies closer. A man who trusts you will tell you much more than he would ever tell another."

"And what about me?" she asked, cocking her head, sinking her teeth into her lips. "What did I have to do with it?"

He moved one hand up, running the tips of his fingers up the center of her body, trailing them along her neck, her jaw, then he brushed his fingers over her temple and murmured, "I still remember every mark I saw on your flesh—every bruise, every black eye. Looking at you made me feel something other than hatred. Looking at you made me think of something other than revenge. I had to have you...and I had to see you safe. Even if it did totally fuck up everything I'd been planning for years."

"How could it fuck it up?"

His mouth tightened and his head dropped back, his eyes staring up at the ceiling. "I made him a bargain...if he gave you to me, I'd be one of his partners, bring money and everything else I'd gotten good at. But it was a gamble— people in his world don't usually want anything enough to risk everything. And I was afraid he'd see right through me, see how badly I wanted you, how much I'd risk to have you."

Blood rushed to her face and she looked down, staring at her hands on his shoulders, trying to breathe through the heat that suddenly flooded her. "Everything you'd done, up until you met me, was to get to him. You're thirty-two" she glanced at him and he nodded. He hadn't lied about his age—just damned near everything else.

His eyes met hers and she felt a cold chill rush through her. "Yes. And I've been after him since I was a kid, using whatever means I had. I did things that no sane man would have done, things that would have you run screaming into the night if you knew."

Meeting his eyes, she cupped his cheek in her hand as she shook her head. "Joel, nothing you ever did could make me run screaming."

A muscle jerked in his cheek and in a harsh voice, he said, "Don't count on that."

Smiling at him, she leaned forward, pressing her mouth to his. "No, Joel. You can't make me run, not from you."

His eyes stared into hers, and began to smolder. He rose from the couch, shifting her in his arms until he had one arm looped under her knees, the other at her shoulders. "Prove it."

Her breath froze in her lungs as he carried her through the house, into her darkened room. "I want things from you—things nice gentlemen shouldn't want from a woman."

"That sounds like a dare," she murmured as he tossed her down to bounce on the sheets. Before she could sit up, before she could say another word, he had covered her body, his mouth slanting against hers, kissing her with bruising force. She arched against him, hot licks of pleasure blazing through her, even as some deeper part of her froze with nerves, and the first whispers of fear.

"It's not a dare," he muttered against her lips. "It's just a fact."

Arching her head back, she stared at him through her lashes. "I don't need a gentleman. I don't need a knight. At this point in my life, I don't think I'd know how to handle one."

Leaning forward, she kissed him, catching his lower lip between her teeth and tugging it lightly. "I just want you. I want you to want me."

His mouth left hers and she hissed as Joel raked his teeth over her neck. "And if I want you in ways you aren't so sure of?" he whispered in her ear. "What then?"

"Try me, Joel. I'm not going to break."

"Hell, I hope not," he muttered against her skin.

His low, raspy voice sent shivers down her spine. Her nipples drew into tight, hard little buds and she felt something knot low in her belly. He drew back, staring at her with deep, unreadable eyes. She stared back at him, half terrified, half nervous, completely aroused. Slowly she nodded, sliding her tongue along her lips.

His eyes dropped to her mouth, following that movement with greed. "You deserve soft, whispered promises, gentle hands...I've given you that, but I want more." Then his eyes slid up to hers and he whispered, "I want to touch you, take your sweet body in ways you never dreamed could bring you pleasure. I won't be soft. I won't be gentle. Be sure. Very sure. Because once I start...I won't stop.

"I can make you scream in pleasure even if you're terrified and wanting me to stop." He cupped her crotch, grinding the heel of his hand against her clit—she could feel the heat of his palm burning her through her clothes and she whimpered. "So if you think you're going to get too scared, tell me now."

Emery was surprised that she had the voice to speak as she said, "I'm not going anywhere."

He tore her clothes off. She cried out as he grasped the edges of her shirt and jerked, the buttons popping off and flying everywhere. He pulled her up, half off the bed, jerking the shirt halfway down her arms. The cloth pinned her arms to her sides, and she wheeled wide, panicked eyes to his face, but he never even looked at her as he dipped his head and caught one nipple in his mouth, sucking at it through the lace of her bra, sinking his teeth into the soft flesh surrounding her nipple. He bit down until it was just shy of pain and Emery was shocked at the lightning-hot streak of pleasure that arrowed down to her pussy and throbbed through her sex.

He jerked her jeans away with quick, rough hands, growling as he crouched between her legs, cupping her hips in his hands, staring at the apex of her thighs. The hungry look on his face had a hot rush of blood rushing to her cheeks, and she squirmed, but then all embarrassment fled, replaced by startled pleasure as he dove down and sucked her clit into his mouth. His fingers circled around her opening, edging closer and closer.

The teasing strokes quickly pushed her into a mindless frenzy as she rocked her hips against his face. The moment he pushed his fingers inside her, she orgasmed, screaming as her hands gripped the sheet under her.

His hands left her, but she barely noticed as she sucked air, trying to breathe through the hot, syrupy satisfaction that had overtaken her.

When he came back, he drew her up against him, his hands still touching her with hard, greedy force. Joel's hands and mouth burned over her body with excruciating thoroughness, his teeth raking her neck, his hands pulling the shirt completely off her—freeing her hands. Her bra followed but before she could shrug it off, he caught her hands, pulling her against him, molding her body to his as he pinned her hands behind her back.

"You've got marks on you...and I love seeing them, love knowing I put them there," he muttered against her mouth.

As he pulled away, she looked down, startled to see the red marks all over her torso. Pink love bites peppered the pale flesh of her breasts. He traced his finger over one, then moved lower, circling it around her nipple, watching as she shivered. Lowering his head, he whispered against her ear, "Your eyes are dark...you know that, Emery? You don't know whether you're aroused or scared. Maybe you're both...maybe you can't figure out if you want me to stop or not."

His tongue traced around the outer rim of her ear and then he sank his teeth into the fleshy lobe. "I'm not going to. I'm going to make you scream, make you squirm, make you beg…make you come like you've never come before, and even after I do all that, I won't stop. Not until I'm done. You had your chance to run."

Swallowing, she met his eyes as he shifted away. "I don't want to run."

A slow smile edged his lips up. "You ought to." The hard, hot strength of his hands gripped her waist and he spilled her back onto the bed, flipping her onto her belly. He tossed something down on the bed beside her head and as she pushed herself onto her hands and knees, she saw the bottle of apricot baby oil there. Frowning, she stared at it but then she felt his hands on her ass, spreading her cheeks. The heat of his gaze was as palpable as a touch and she felt a hot flush spreading up from her chest, staining her cheeks.

What is he…?

She licked her lips nervously as he reached for the oil. Was he going to…? *Oh, hell.* Hot, slick fingers started to probe the tight, virgin entrance of her ass. Cream flooded her pussy as she remembered the pleasure from his touch just a few days ago. But she knew, with a gut-deep instinct, that he was planning on putting more than a finger inside her ass.

"I'm fucking this ass," he murmured, as though confirming her thoughts. "Are you ready to run away yet?"

As he pushed first one, then a second finger inside, a burning slice of pain arced through her and she arched back with a scream. But as he pulled out and pushed back in, the pain was equaled by hot pleasure, the two mingling until she couldn't separate them. Run…*run?*

She might. If she could work up the energy to move, the energy to focus, to force her body to move. But she couldn't. Everything inside her was focused on his touch, the probing caress of his fingers in her ass. When she heard the rough rasp of his zipper, she tensed, but a moan escaped her and she pushed back against his touch yet again.

"You don't want to run, do you?" Joel murmured, stroking a hand over the curve of her rump. "Do you want this?"

He nudged his cock against her backside and Emery whimpered.

"Answer me!" he barked, and he gently slapped her ass.

A blow from a man...something she'd learned the hard way brought nothing but pain. But she yelped, shocked at the startled pleasure that shot through her. "I don't know," she wailed.

His hand fell away, his fingers pulling out of the clinging embrace of her ass, and she whimpered as he moved closer, his hips cupping her ass, his cock, now slicked with oil, cuddling between the cheeks. Joel bent low over her body, purring into her ear, "Good..."

When he pressed the fat head of his cock against her, Emery keened low in her throat, her elbows giving out. Collapsing against the bed, she clutched the sheets as he slowly pushed inside. It hurt...it burned...tears stung her eyes and she sobbed. Too big, too much, she whimpered and tried to pull away but his hands gripped her hips unyieldingly.

"Push down, Emery," he demanded.

It was gut instinct that made her obey—the painfully acquired knowledge that she had to obey a man when he spoke like that. But it wasn't followed by a rush of terror...just some inexplicable urge to do everything he asked.

Taking a breath, she pushed down and then she gasped as he slid a little deeper. Pulling out, then rocking back inside her. She bore down on him again and he pushed deeper inside. They continued like that until he was completely buried in the tight grip of her ass.

"You're hot," he grunted, rolling his hips against her ass as he slid one hand around her hip, his fingers seeking out the hard bud of her clit. "Are you ready to scream, Emery?"

He pinched her clit, a sharp, insistent touch and she wailed out his name as he pulled out, and then slammed back inside her.

The pain and the pleasure…they mingled, became one until she could not tell one sensation from the other. Screaming out his name, she climaxed, feeling the hot rush of fluid as it flowed from her, soaking her thighs and his hand as he started to fuck his fingers in and out of her pussy.

Drained, Emery felt her body trying to collapse to the bed but Joel continued to grip one hip with a hard hand, his hips pumping, his cock digging into her ass with hard, short thrusts.

"I'm not done with you yet," he grunted, pulling his fingers from her pussy, trailing the damp pads along her torso before he gripped her waist and jerked her body upright. "You haven't screamed enough…"

Scream…damn it, she couldn't scream anymore. Her throat was hoarse, her mind going dark with exhaustion and pleasure and confusion, her entire body quivering from his touch. "Joel," she whimpered, clutching at the arm banded around her waist.

He rolled his hips against her ass and she shuddered as the movement pushed his cock deeper inside her bottom. His teeth raked along her neck, his chin pushing her hair out of his way so he could whisper in her ear, "I told you…I don't dream of making love to you until you sigh. I dream of fucking you so hard, so deep, you don't know where you end and I begin. You're mine, Emery. You'll scream that out when I'm done with you."

His arm released her waist and she sagged back against the bed, her breasts pressing flat against the sheets, while his hands gripped her waist, holding her ass up for the plundering thrusts of his cock. His hands gripped her cheeks, pulling them apart just a little as he pulled out, a slow, torturous stroke, then surged back in, his movements slow and thorough, designed to tease her back into mindless arousal without allowing her to come.

"You're mine, aren't you?" he purred gruffly, and she shivered at the rough sound.

Sucking in air, she whimpered out, "Hell, yes."

"Scream it..." he started plunging harder, his cock penetrating the tender tissues of her ass, harder, faster, his fingers biting into the soft skin of her hips.

"Yours," she moaned.

He stilled, reaching up to brush her hair aside, and she could feel his eyes on her face. Rolling her eyes just a little, she met the dark, turbulent blue of his gaze, watching as his lips moved, shaking at his words.

"You're not screaming it...scream it, Emery. Tell me that you're mine and you'll do any damned thing I want."

The words locked in her throat. Her fingers closed convulsively around the sheets and she mewled, rocking her hips back against him.

He snarled and shoved forward, using his weight to crush her into the bed, surrounding her. His hands came up, catching hers and pinning them to the bed. Instinctive fear rose, and he rasped against her ear, "No. You're mine, don't think of him...don't think of anything but what I'm doing to you. I'm fucking you, fucking your tight little ass, making you scream..." His tongue trailed a slow line along her shoulder, up her neck. Then he sank his teeth into the fleshy pad of muscle on her shoulder. "Marking you."

The hot, burning pain of his teeth tore through her and she screamed, startled by the hot wash of pleasure it sent through her.

His hips kept hers pinned as she tried to rock against him, kept her from moving more than a scant inch one way or the other. Emery screamed out in frustration as she tried to ride the thick pillar of flesh impaling her, swearing hoarsely.

"What do you want, Emery?" he rasped against her damp flesh.

Her nipples ached and swelled, almost as if that voice was a caress. Her pussy burned, ached, so empty… And she could feel each hard pulse that echoed through her womb, tightening her clit. She needed to come, couldn't breathe…

"Damn it, Joel, fuck me!" she pleaded, screaming it out as she tried to shove back against him. "Fuck me, please!"

Slowly, his hips retreated and her breath lodged in her lungs as she prepared for a hard, heavy thrust. "You know what I want to hear," he purred, sinking slowly back inside, the tight tissues of her anal sheath resisting his entry.

"I'm yours," she sobbed out, the words tearing from her throat painfully. Tears burned in her eyes and rolled down her cheeks and her entire body went limp under his. "I'm yours, Joel. I'll do anything, everything you want…just fuck me."

His hips withdrew and he slammed into her once, then he lodged back inside her, laying his cheek along hers. "Tell me you love me."

Her heart slammed against her ribs and she jerked against him. *Love*…had she ever thought about the word connected to Joel? She knew she needed him, had relied on him, then she'd learned to live without him. But she hadn't really been alive until she felt his hands on her again. If that wasn't love…it was damned close.

The truth rushed through her with blinding intensity and her lashes drifted closed, a small, replete smile on her lips, even though her body ached for fulfillment. Softly, she whispered, "I love you, Joel."

He shifted again, rising to his knees, bringing her with him, his hands on her hips so that once more, her ass was lifted for him. He throbbed and jerked inside her ass and she whimpered, shivering around him. Without saying a single word, he started shafting her, pumping his cock in and out of her ass, his thrusts deep and hard and strong.

Keening in her throat, she exploded around him, bucking against him, thrashing against the sheets as she came. The orgasm didn't roll through her this time, it clawed its way through her with a biting intensity that was damn close to painful.

As she slumped against the sheets once more, she felt him come, the hot wash of his seed flooding her depths. A hoarse moan fell from him and then he, too, sagged against her, rolling to the side so that he didn't pin her underneath him.

That had been the most exquisite sexual encounter he'd ever had.

And guilt damn near choked him.

Emery lay on her side, curled into a ball, the slim line of her back shuddering and shaking.

Hesitantly he reached out and touched her shoulder. "Are you okay?" he whispered gruffly, tugging her onto her back, afraid to look into her eyes, but refusing to take the coward's way out.

The soft, smooth flesh of her body was marred here and there by faint red marks from his mouth. As he pushed up onto his elbow, staring down at her, he saw faint purplish marks on her hips from where he had gripped her soft skin as he fucked her.

He'd marked her.

Nausea roiled inside his gut, but he still had to look into her face. Had to see what he had broken...

The soft smile on her face startled him. Her eyes were hazy, clouded with satisfaction. "Okay? Ummm...I don't know if I'll ever be okay again..." she stretched her arms over her head, and then she giggled. "Damn, how can I handle going back to feeling okay, after feeling like this?"

Joel licked his lips. Confused, uncertain…but he knew what that look on a woman's face meant. "I didn't hurt you?"

Her eyes cleared just a little, as she shrugged. "I don't know. Haven't taken stock yet…but if you did, it was worth it."

Her arms came around his neck and he sank against her, cuddling his head between her breasts. "I shouldn't treat you like that," he muttered. "You don't deserve…"

Her fingers came up to lie across his mouth. "I deserve to be treated like a woman. To know that you want me, that you want to make me feel a pleasure so damned intense it hurts."

Wrapping his arms around her waist, he burrowed against her. "I want you like that…so much it hurts. But that doesn't—"

She stiffened in his arms, shoving at him until he finally let her go. As she sat up, she winced in pain, shifting so that her weight was on her hip, not her butt. Shame rolled through him once more and he looked away.

But her hands came up to cup his face, bringing his eyes back to hers. "Don't." She cuddled against him, lying down beside him and wrapping her arms around his neck. "Don't. I'm not broken inside—not anymore. I was, until you came into my life. But I'm not broken now—you make me whole and I love the way you make me feel inside."

She kissed his neck. "I love you, Joel. More than anything."

The knot in his chest finally loosened and he sucked air, wrapping his arms around her tightly, crushing her against him. "I love you."

She sighed against him as he lay back on the bed, keeping her tight against his chest. "Don't ever stop, okay?"

Chapter Ten

Emery narrowed her eyes until just a thin rim of gray showed around the black of her pupils. Propping her hands on her hips, she glared at Joel with an outraged look on her face.

"You want me to *what*?"

Joel mildly replied, "I want you to leave. I'll handle this. And I'll deal better knowing you are far away from him."

Sputtering, she demanded, "And where in the hell am I supposed to go that he can't find me?"

Joel levelly returned her furious glare as he coolly said, "Within ten seconds of him stepping onto your property, he's dead, so it won't matter."

"If it's *that* easy, then why in the world do I have to go?"

Joel crossed to her, that slight smile on his handsome face, his eyes meeting hers, the dark blue gaze impossibly warm, impossibly gentle. "So I don't have to worry, Emery. He won't come alone. I know I can handle him, and most of his lackeys, but I'm too realistic to risk taking the chance of something going wrong."

Poking out her lip, she sulked. Damn it, she *should* be overjoyed at the thought of running...she would have been, a day ago. What had changed?

Everything...

The knot of fear that had lived inside her for so long was gone. Joel would take care of her. He wouldn't let anything happen to her...and she felt compelled to do the same with him. She didn't like the thought of driving away from him, leaving him to face that monster she'd foolishly married.

Vincent Grainger was a monster, a monster in a silk suit. He had played the part of the dashing, enchanting older man very well, suckering her in. She hadn't been the only one, but that hadn't made the sting any less. She felt as if she needed to be here when it ended.

But gazing into Joel's eyes, she knew she wouldn't.

If he was worried about her, that meant he'd take less care of himself.

"Where do I go?" she asked thickly, swallowing around the knot that had formed in her throat.

For one second, his eyes closed and the subtle tension in his body relaxed. "To the cabin…remember our cabin?"

Emery nodded slowly. "When do I go?"

"Now. He could be here any time. And don't drive straight out…go up Highway 3, head toward Indianapolis, then head east from there. Take your phone…if you need me, call me. But he's going to be expecting you to be here." He brushed his lips across hers, and Emery felt a bittersweet pain fill her heart. "I'll come for you when it's done."

Stepping back, he squeezed her arms reassuringly then jerked his head toward the bedroom. "Grab a few things…and get out of here. Don't tell *anybody*."

She rolled her eyes, turning away with a huff. "Who in the hell am I going to tell? Been here for all of a month," she muttered, heading for the door at the end of the hallway.

Joel asked softly, "Where are you going?"

She pointed at the door at the end of the hall. "That's the attic. That's where my bags are stored. You don't mind if I take a bag with me, do you?" She batted her lashes at him, and when he scowled at her, she just snorted. "You've lost your sense of humor."

Joel laughed quietly. "I never really had much of one to begin with…"

Whatever else he said was too faint for her to hear as she quickly climbed the steps. Get out...*now*, before she changed her mind.

It was better this way, anyway. Safer.

She crossed the dust covered floor of the attic to the pile of luggage under the window that faced the front of the house. As she bent to grab her duffel bag, something caught her eye.

Slowly, she straightened, her heart banging against her ribs as the black Benz pulled into the driveway.

The bag fell from her limp fingers and she inched back one tiny step at a time as she watched the driver's door open. *Carter...* She swallowed. Her throat was so tight, it hurt.

She heard Joel's furious growl filtering through the vent right at her feet. "Joel?" she called out softly.

"I see him," he said softly, his voice carried through the vents and old ductwork.

Wrapping her arms around herself, she watched as Carter moved to the back door and opened it.

Carter...one of Vincent's most trusted goons.

He *was* a goon, a big, baldheaded man who looked as if he belonged in a wrestling ring. His eyes were small and mean, too close together, and his mouth was too big for his head, his lips thin to the point of being nonexistent. Feet pounded on the steps and she turned slowly and stared into Joel's eyes. He crossed to her and grabbed her arms, shaking her slightly. "Stay up here, Emery. You hear me? If there's someplace to hide, then do it, but *stay here*."

He pressed a hard, fast kiss to her brow and was moving down the stairs by the time a firm knock sounded on the door.

That knock seemed so out of place.

Vincent was here to kill Joel. She knew it in her gut. But he was knocking...

A hysterical laugh rose in her throat and desperately, she muffled it, her eyes wheeling around the large, empty expanse of the attic. *Hide?* Where in the hell was there to hide?

There was a pile of boxes in one corner and that was the best she could do. Grimly, she started to cross the attic, stepping lightly, scared of making a single sound.

Cold chills broke over her and she wrapped her arms around her body, rubbing at her flesh, feeling the goose bumps break out. Cold. Nerves, that was all…right?

As she rounded the edge of the stack of boxes, she breathed out shakily.

That was when she noticed her breath was forming puffs of fog in the air. In an attic that had no air conditioning…on a day that was nearly seventy. Slowly, she turned around.

A faint white haze met her eyes and then darkness rushed up, taking her mind and pulling her into unconsciousness.

Joel felt the chill in the air and he wanted to swear.

Damn it, he couldn't deal with Carly right now.

He'd moved in a circle through the house, not wanting them to see his shadow as he approached the door. Drawing his gun, he took the safety off, holding it in a loose grip, breathing in slow, shallow breaths.

Through the thin glass panes of the door, he could hear their voices as they murmured, and then there was another loud knock. A final one. Carter bellowed out, "Open the door, Tracy. Don't make your husband wait any longer."

The temperature continued to plunge as Carter broke out one beveled pane of glass in the door with the butt of his gun. He stepped through slowly, swinging his head to the left, then to the right and that was when Joel pulled the trigger.

Carter was dead before he hit the ground and Joel dove across the hall, keeping the planter wall that divided the dining room from the living room between him and Vincent.

"That wasn't very smart, Joel," Vincent said, his voice cold and flat with anger.

Keeping his back pressed against the wall, he stared into the hall, watching for the shadows on the floor to shift. "Maybe not, but it sure as hell felt good. I've wanted that bastard dead for ten years now."

"You killed one of my best men, Joel. You know I can't let that pass. One thing to kill some useless punks I hire off the street, another to kill an important member of my organization."

His voice was getting fainter and Joel circled around the wall just in time to see Vincent heading down the other hall, the one that would lead to the kitchen, and then into the dining room. The stairwell leading to the bedrooms was at the end of the hall, and Joel had to keep him downstairs.

"Well, seeing as how you die today, I don't think what happens in your business much matters anymore." He stepped around the wall, facing Vincent just as the man spun around and met his eyes.

Vincent laughed. The sound was cold and lifeless, echoing through the quiet house. His eyes seemed darker in the pale circle of his face, larger, and even crueler than before. "You sound so sure. Joel, a lot of people have tried to kill me. None of have succeeded." He held a gun in his hand, a small Beretta that was aimed directly at Joel's gut.

Joel smiled, a slight flex of his lips, as he replied, "None wanted you dead as much as I do."

Vincent opened his mouth to respond. A fog of condensation formed at his mouth as he breathed out, and Joel had to fight not to shiver as the room's temperature plummeted. Damn it, it hadn't ever gotten this cold...

Vincent's eyes narrowed and he gritted his teeth trying to keep his gun hand from shaking. Joel saw the confusion in his eyes, and he let the smile on his face spread. "I was wrong…there is one other person who wants you dead as much as I do. Guess she came to see me finish it off…"

From the head of the stairs, Joel heard the soft creak of wood floors. Then he heard a voice, a solid voice that he hadn't heard in twenty years. This wasn't the insubstantial echo he had always heard before, but a real, solid voice. Carly's voice.

"Marc, honey…I'm not here to see you finish it off…"

Vincent spun around, and Joel slowly lifted his gaze, terror streaking through him as he found himself staring into Emery's face.

But it wasn't Emery's eyes he was staring into.

The soft gray eyes he loved to gaze into were gone, replaced by dark, dark blue pools so like his own. And when her mouth opened, the words that came from her throat weren't the low, melodious tones of Emery's voice, but rather, a deep, raspy voice. "Hello, lover…" she purred, ignoring Joel as he gaped at her.

"*You*…" Vincent rasped out, lifting the gun and leveling it at her.

Joel tried to lunge for him, but something had frozen him. Battling against the invisible bonds, he struggled to get to Vincent before he could shoot Emery.

"Damn it, I killed you, you fucking whore!" Vincent screeched and his voice was high, wild.

She laughed, and it wasn't Emery's laugh, wasn't Tracy's laugh. Joel reached up, scrubbing at his eyes, relieved to find that he *could* move a little. As he tried to focus on Emery's face, the image seemed to shift, like a heat mirage, flickering from Emery one moment, to Carly the next.

"Yes…you did. And I've been waiting a long, long time to return the favor."

Her eyes moved over Vincent, unconcerned by the gun he held as she met Joel's gaze. "I tried, a few times, to do it this way with Marc, but I couldn't ever penetrate his head."

"Marc?"

Vincent wheeled around, shifting the gun from Carly to Joel, and back again. Then he stared at Joel as though seeing him for the first time and his face twisted into a mask of hatred. *"Marc...*you're the little fuck who got away from me. The slut's sister," he snarled.

Joel smiled. "Yes," he said simply.

Vincent howled and Joel watched as his finger tightened on the gun, dodging out of the way as Vincent pulled the trigger. The loud, booming thunder of a gun firing ripped through the air, but he never heard an impact. All he heard was Carly laughing. Glancing around the wall, he watched, in shock, as the bullet seemed to slow in midair and finally clatter to the floor.

"Vincent, sugar, you don't really think I'm going to let you hurt him, do you?" she whispered, shaking her head. The blue eyes, so foreign looking in her face, sparkled merrily and she wagged her finger at him.

"Bitch!" Vincent screamed out, wheeling around and aiming the gun at her face.

He squeezed the trigger, again, again, and again, and each bullet fell harmlessly to the floor. His eyes got larger and more terrified as he stared at Carly.

She laughed, a merry, happy sound in the cold, silent house. As she moved toward Vincent, Joel felt his heart stutter to a halt inside his chest.

She blinked, when her eyes opened, they were gray, but unseeing. As Emery fell unaware to the floor, a white mist seemed to launch itself out of her, and Vincent screamed as the incandescent streamer of air wrapped around him and started to squeeze.

Joel lunged for Emery, shouting her name. The strong, steady beat of her pulse under his fingers reassured him, and he dragged her away from Vincent as the force that was Carly slowly choked the life out of him.

Emery shuddered in his arms, a soft cry escaping her. Joel pressed his lips to her hair, but he continued to stare at Vincent. He was suspended in the air now, his face turning a dark, angry purple, his eyes bugging out of his face, lips moving in a soundless scream.

There was a violent, cracking sound, and then the lifeless corpse fell down to the ground, dead.

Joel sucked air, his body shaking from the cold.

There was a soft, sighing whisper in the air, and then the cold faded away, replaced by the warmth of the early spring day. Her voice, once more, was distant. *I never understood why you didn't kill him sooner…the others didn't matter. Just him.*

"They mattered to me," he said hoarsely, staring, stunned, at the broken, dead body in front of him. "He knew things I needed to know." His voice trailed off for a moment, and then he whispered, "Know your enemy…keep him close."

Carly laughed and it was the same carefree sound it had been in her youth, before she'd gotten entangled with Grainger. *I prefer 'Keep your enemies dead in the ground'.*

Let it go, Marc. The others don't matter. I can't say it hurts to know most of them are dead, but the others, they are useless without him to pull their strings. They'll meet their end…soon enough. Just let it go, Marc. Be happy.

"Happy," he muttered, thickly, staring down at the pale face of the woman he loved. "I don't think I deserve that."

I do…and so does she. Can you stop searching now?

Emery started to stir in his arms.

He stared down at her, and knew the answer to that. "Yeah," he murmured. "Yeah, I can let it go."

He heard Carly's voice…one final time…*bye, bye baby brother…take care of her.*

When he looked up to try and find her, to say something, she was already gone.

Joel knew in his gut she wouldn't come back.

258

A weak, shaking sigh escaped Emery and as he kissed her temple, the thick black fringe of her lashes started to flutter. Seconds later, he found himself staring into her eyes.

"What happened?" she asked weakly.

Joel just shook his head and held her tightly to him, hugging her as close as he could.

A soft gasp left her and he glanced down, found her staring at Vincent's lifeless body. "It's over now," he murmured. "All over."

Emery licked her lips. "Ummm, well shouldn't we do something about his body?"

That startled a laugh out of him and he hugged her tight. "Eh, might not be a bad idea."

A shuddering sigh escaped Emery and she whispered, "It's really over…"

Joel kissed her slowly, loosely cupping his hands over her neck, his thumbs resting in the notch of her collarbone, feeling the steady beat of her pulse. "Actually," he whispered, catching her lower lip between his teeth and tugging. "It's just beginning."

Why an electronic book?

We live in the Information Age — an exciting time in the history of human civilization, in which technology rules supreme and continues to progress in leaps and bounds every minute of every day. For a multitude of reasons, more and more avid literary fans are opting to purchase e-books instead of paper books. The question from those not yet initiated into the world of electronic reading is simply: *Why?*

1. *Price.* An electronic title at Ellora's Cave Publishing and Cerridwen Press runs anywhere from 40% to 75% less than the cover price of the exact same title in paperback format. Why? Basic mathematics and cost. It is less expensive to publish an e-book (no paper and printing, no warehousing and shipping) than it is to publish a paperback, so the savings are passed along to the consumer.

2. *Space.* Running out of room in your house for your books? That is one worry you will never have with electronic books. For a low one-time cost, you can purchase a handheld device specifically designed for e-reading. Many e-readers have large, convenient screens for viewing. Better yet, hundreds of titles can be stored within your new library — on a single microchip. There are a variety of e-readers from different manufacturers. You can also read e-books on your PC or laptop computer. (Please note that Ellora's Cave does not endorse any specific brands.

You can check our websites at www.ellorascave.com or www.cerridwenpress.com for information we make available to new consumers.)

3. *Mobility.*   Because your new e-library consists of only a microchip within a small, easily transportable e-reader, your entire cache of books can be taken with you wherever you go.

4. ***Personal Viewing Preferences.***   Are the words you are currently reading too small? Too large? Too… ANNOYING? Paperback books cannot be modified according to personal preferences, but e-books can.

5. ***Instant Gratification.***   Is it the middle of the night and all the bookstores near you are closed? Are you tired of waiting days, sometimes weeks, for bookstores to ship the novels you bought? Ellora's Cave Publishing sells instantaneous downloads twenty-four hours a day, seven days a week, every day of the year. Our webstore is never closed. Our e-book delivery system is 100% automated, meaning your order is filled as soon as you pay for it.

Those are a few of the top reasons why electronic books are replacing paperbacks for many avid readers.

As always, Ellora's Cave and Cerridwen Press welcome your questions and comments. We invite you to email us at Comments@ellorascave.com or write to us directly at Ellora's Cave Publishing Inc., 1056 Home Avenue, Akron, OH 44310-3502.

THE
⚱ ELLORA'S CAVE ⚱
LIBRARY

Stay up to date with Ellora's Cave Titles in
Print with our Quarterly Catalog.

To recieve a catalog,
send an email with your name
and mailing address to:

catalog@ellorascave.com
or send a letter or postcard
with your mailing address to:

Catalog Request
c/o Ellora's Cave Publishing, Inc.
1056 Home Avenue
Akron, Ohio 44310-3502

erridwen, the Celtic Goddess of wisdom, was the muse who brought inspiration to storytellers and those in the creative arts. Cerridwen Press encompasses the best and most innovative stories in all genres of today's fiction. Visit our site and discover the newest titles by talented authors who still get inspired - much like the ancient storytellers did, once upon a time.

13960169R00168

Made in the USA
Lexington, KY
02 March 2012